ZOMBIE BUFFET
AN UNDEAD ANTHOLOGY

EDITED BY
ANTHONY GIANGREGORIO

NOW AVAILABLE AND COMING SOON
FROM
OPEN CASKET PRESS

RATS
BIGFOOT TALES
CREATURE FEATURE
MONSTROPOCALYPSE
DEAD CHRISTMAS
HOLLOW POINT: A ZOMBIE NOVEL
WARRIORS OF THE APOCALYPSE: BOOK 1

ZOMBIE BUFFET
Copyright © 2011 Open Casket Press
ISBN Softcover ISBN 13: 978-1-61199-030-0
ISBN 10: 1-611990-30-0

Table of Contents

R.I.P
R.I.P.

HANG 'EM HIGH

ALAN SPENCER

The last thing Adam Logbeck expected eight months into a worldwide zombie outbreak happened today.

The police finally showed up.

The three-story house on Hill Drop was ripe for the picking: boarded up shutters, garage door closed and undamaged, windows iron-barred, and every entry and nook and cranny had been meticulously secured.

Reams of barbed wire snaked across the house like a gigantic bow wrapped around an expensive present. He expected a laser tripwire to be triggered once he edged up the steps to take a better look at the fortress. A shotgun rigged with a rope tied around the trigger could go off, but he didn't care. Whatever was inside was well protected; that meant something useful had to be within.

He hadn't eaten in nearly a week. He'd lived off of Gatorade and teriyaki beef jerky, and even that was running low. Hunger was plenty of motivation to brave certain danger, he believed. The well-secured house could be a picking frenzy, he kept reminding himself. Frozen foods. Canned goods. Guns. If there was electricity, there could be meat to cook. He could take a hot bath, maybe, if the water was running. Since the epidemic, he'd taken more sink baths than a baby.

Adam decided it was worth the risk of drawing attention to himself, so he used wire cutters to snip the barbed wire that was snaked across the front door. He then wedged his crowbar into the crack where the door met the frame and busted his way into the possible survival treasure trove.

The best part of everything: there were no zombies.

The house smelled stale. There was no moving air, the place was sealed tight. Another silver lining to his find: it didn't stink of death. Mold and mildew he could handle, but rotting flesh...

Forget about it.

Adam gave himself thirty minutes to pick a house. That was after checking to make sure no one else was inside. He called out to make sure. Explained he was only hungry. He meant no harm to anyone. Nobody replied. After minutes of searching the upstairs bedrooms and the other rooms, he found no one on the premises, living or dead.

This was now a search and recover mission for necessities. The kitchen was first, only the cupboards were bare. The refrigerator was empty except for condiments, moldy bread, and the greenest eggs he'd ever seen.

That left the basement. He prayed there were canned goods. He wouldn't last much longer burning the cheap food fumes he'd been running on.

Stepping down into the basement, the lights wouldn't turn on, so he used his flashlight. The batteries were new, so the beam was strong. The space was crammed with holiday decorations and old clothing; it all stank of a flooded basement: black mold, moth balls, rotting wood.

Adam had just about given up hope when he discovered the shelves of tools: hammers, saw blades, chains. Things he could use for self-defense.

The best part was the rickety wooden shelf to the right of the tools was heaped with canned goods: beef stew, Vienna Sausages, pork and beans, tuna, chili, mixed vegetables, tamales, and so much more.

He was drooling as he stuffed the cans by the armful into his backpack until it was bulging. Then he used his can opener and ate a can of apple pie filling with his fingers, and was about to start in on the barbeque pork 'sandwich in a can' when he heard the bend of a wooden floorboard from above.

The creak of a step.

Something was coming down to join him.

The whiff of a slaughterhouse came to him, like blood squeezed out of raw meat or an outhouse on fire, or maybe brine sauce mixed with ether. He'd made hundreds of comparisons to what the dead smelled like.

And there it was, a fucking zombie on the stairs.

Adam didn't mean to laugh. This zombie was a melting magpie, with tissue sloughing off the bones like that from overcooked ribs. Its flesh was the tone of gangrene, with skin gleaming with a burst pustule sheen. The teeth were bared back without lips, rheumy eyes flicking back and forth. The funniest thing was that the zombie was wearing a blue police uniform. The gold badge was crooked on his pocket. The fabric was soaked in blood and what looked like grease.

The hammer was cocked and the .38's muzzle was aimed at Adam.

"Fuuuuh," it moaned.

Did the walking dead cop just say *freeze*? he wondered.

He was laughing so hard that he dropped the 'sandwich in a can' on the floor. "You think you're a cop, do ya? So what? You gonna arrest me? A *zombie* arrest *me*?"

Maybe he'd been alone too long and hadn't had anything to laugh at in what seemed like forever, so he was making up for lost time. But there wasn't anything to laugh about when four more cops each armed with Mossberg shotguns shambled down the steps and cornered him. He raised his arms up as each of them wheezed, "Fuuuuh."

One maggot-faced female officer slapped a pair of handcuffs on him.

They weren't going to eat him.

They were arresting him.

A police van was crookedly parked against the curb outside. Another squad car was stopped in the middle of the street. They'd called the big guns in on this call, he thought. Adam guessed they were on patrol, and they'd noticed the front door was ajar.

He'd seen zombies act like their old selves before. Checkers counting down their drawers in supermarkets. Plumbers banging against sink pipes. Postmen delivering the mail. Bakers rolling out crust for pies and bankers stuffing pennies in coin rolls. And now policemen were on the clock and taking the trash off the streets.

Two undead officers with pot bellies the size of a pony keg lowered him into the back of a squad car. Flies kept buzzing off of them, and he could hear the maggots squirming under their skin.

"Quit touching me. I only wanted something to eat. I'm not guilty of anything. You hear me? You're the bad guys. You're the ones eating people!"

He could run for it. Even cuffed, he'd escape, but he feared that the guns they held were loaded. They could shoot him. No one would be around to help him. No doctors in these parts. He'd bleed to death, easy.

Without a plan, the car door was closed, and he was locked in.

The two zombies piled into the car, while the others behind them drove the van. The van backed up and made the slowest progress. Five minutes later, the van was making its way south of the house he'd tried to pick, burning rubber at five miles an hour.

He turned his attention back to the patrol car he was in.

"Are you even putting your foot on the pedal?" Adam shouted, banging his cuffed hands against the Plexiglas barrier. "Jesus, I could pogo faster!" He coughed on the stench coming off them. He nearly vomited when a centipede slithered out of the driver's right ear. "Hey bugs for brains." He couldn't believe he was asking them this. "Why the hell aren't you eating me? What kind of a zombie are you anyway?"

A set of deflated eyes glared back at him in the rearview mirror.

He gave up pleading his case. The zombie patrol wasn't hearing it.

Adam stayed quiet the rest of the tedious five mile an hour drive to the police station.

Inside the Hill Drop police station, the zombie at the check-in desk fingerprinted him, though the ink smudge was obscured by the wet hunk of potato peel skin flesh that slathered the paper. Another cop in the background guided him to a wall where he posed for a picture. The dead woman taking the picture had no hair except for one golden curl on top of her head. Her face was the color of a blue black bruise. The single eye she had left was floating in a plum sauce of blood and bile. With that eye, she glanced at him after the picture, then moved on, as if she really did have a job to do.

One officer guided him up the hallway and into a back area. The other kept the shotgun trained on him. The leading zombie's hand was squishy against his arm, and he could feel the bone articulations shift beneath the zombie's skin.

Again, Adam did his best not to throw up.

Once in back, he was uncuffed and placed in a jail cell. The cops went about their business, despite the questions he hurled at them. Why was he being held? What were they going to do with him? Why wasn't he in their stomachs? Frustrated, he decided the next best thing to do was to talk to the man sitting in the cell beside him, and finally get some answers.

The man sitting on the cot with his back against the wall wasn't much of a talker at first. The state of his overgrown beard and long hair went to show he'd either been in prison for a long time or had been in hiding for even longer. He was as pale as the institutional paint peeling off the walls.

"What are you in for?" Adam asked, breaking the silence between them.

His cell buddy didn't say a word. Wouldn't look his way. His eyes were locked right in front of him.

How long had the man been here? Was he insane? Brain dead?

Adam tried numerous times to get words out of him, and it wasn't until an hour later that the man spoke up on his own.

"You're not from around here I take it."

"I'm not sure what you mean," Adam said.

"If you haven't lived here before, you wouldn't understand. Before all this started, the police were hard-asses. They kept this town crime free. You couldn't litter without a pig in blue getting on your ass. These cops were the types that wanted the death penalty in every state. Maximum punishment. This is a tourist town. A rich white suburb, you get me? This was a safe white upper class town before this shit happened."

Adam shrugged. "So what are you getting at?"

"These zombies think they're cops. They see you breaking the law, they arrest you. Then they sentence you. And then," the man's face went slack, "they execute you."

The man introduced himself as Clifton Greene, then explained what he knew about the local police zombies. When the dead were escaping from their graves and spreading their disease, the local police arrested any and all law breakers. The fervor for citizen control spread into an outright lynching party.

Across from the police station was the Sharks high school football field. There, a nine foot high standing wooden gallows had been erected. People were hung public-spectacle style. Hungry for answers and payback for the death of their loved ones had caused people to change. Fear and reasoning had turned the town into an archaic killing machine.

Once everyone in town was infected, the dead carried on those hang 'em high ambitions. But the dead had their own version of justice. Clifton had witnessed it on and off while in hiding, even up to the point he was captured while sneaking water from the local creek.

He said he'd been put on trial.

Today was his execution day.

Whatever form of justice the undead believed in, Clifton warned, Adam would be experiencing it very soon.

Two hours passed, and they talked a little about how they'd lost their families, how they'd survived, and how the dead carried on with who they were once most of the living were eaten.

Then two cops shambled up to Adam's cell. A shotgun was aimed by one, and the other unlocked the door. Once again, he was being escorted out of the building, though this time he was directed up the street to Hill Drop's courthouse. Two armed zombies were standing with rifles in their gooey clutches at the entrance. The husk-skinned faces regarded him as another common criminal.

Walking beyond the oversized double doors, Adam entered the courtroom. He gasped in shock at the thick offal stench in the air. The overhead fans swished the smell of death, swirling it into a noxious cloud. The room thrummed with insects, as if they were trapped inside a giant glass jar. The carpet was stained in every shade of the death color wheel. To his right, animated corpse jurors were seated, their flesh suffering various stages of decay. They watched him approach the defendant's table. His lawyer, complete with suit and tie, stood and awaited his arrival. The 'lawyer' was nothing more than a well-dressed scarecrow, the skin tight and stretched to breaking over its bones. A stenographer sat at her station, her mother of pearl phalanges poised over the keys of her typing machine. The judge suddenly struck her gavel from behind the bench, the female judge's stomach actively popping with bodily gases.

The prosecutor, the zombie whose guts hung out of his belly all the way down to his ankles, stood in front of the jurors. With the speed of a terminal geriatric, it gestured with its hands. It wheezed and hissed and groaned, as if stating its case. The jurors' eyes were deadlocked on the prosecutor, riveted to every word.

Adam sat in silent fascination for twenty minutes as the prosecution stated its case. Then the defense lawyer stood up, and its spine cracked, as if three of its vertebrae had just shattered. Stooped, Adam's lawyer approached the bench. The two spoke in whispers like two lobotomized patients sharing anecdotes about fishing vacations and annoying husbands and wives.

The defense had no opening or closing comments.

Then one of the jurors stood up from her chair. It sounded like she was trying to say 'guilty.'

Clifton wasn't in jail when Adam returned to the station. On his way back to his cell, Adam caught a large group of the dead walking towards the football field Clifton had mentioned. What he assumed was to visit the gallows.

Clifton was being executed.

As the afternoon drew on, everything became silent. It was as if no one was out there, but Adam could smell them. He pictured zombies in uniform around a conference table planning out their day, their patrols, and how to deal with him: public enemy number one. Sitting on his cot, his stomach roiling with hunger, he didn't expect a meal, but that's what he got.

Three zombies stood in front of his cell, each armed with shotguns aimed to kill, and a fourth stumbled in carrying a plate of food. On the plate were severed hands cut crudely at the wrists. Half hands. Fingers connected to a row of meaty gristle. The hands were missing fingers, as if the zombies delivering them weren't able to resist eating a digit or two during the delivery. A few of the zombies had lips painted with fresh blood.

The zombie placed the plate onto the cell floor and limped out, finished with his job. The group left him alone with the meal, as if he needed privacy to eat the bleeding stack of body parts.

He stared at the plate. He counted seven crude hands in a pile. The dish was garnished with an eyeball and a piece of wilted lettuce. Had they gone to great lengths to procure the pieces? Adam pictured a zombie leaning over a dog pile of human refuse and severing the hands from various bodies with a cleaver. The hands looked fairly fresh. The walking dead had hunted high and low for the parts and had kept them refrigerated, he figured. How else would the hands stay fresh for so long? If he touched them on the plate, would they be colder than room temperature?

Then the harder question hit him. Was this just a meal, or his 'final' meal?

He wasn't sure how long it would be before his execution. How long would he have to stare at that disgusting plate of hands and question his lifespan?

An hour later, he couldn't take it anymore. The staring contest with the appendages had come to an end. He thought about shoving the hands through the cell bars, but the hands would still be on the floor in clear view. His problem wouldn't be solved.

He shot the idea down.

Then it occurred to him. The toilet didn't work, and there was no water in it, so he dumped the plate into the bowl and closed the lid.

Out of sight, out of mind.

Bored and tired of staring at the walls and thinking about life, death, and zombies, he fell asleep on the cot. His dreams were filled with horrors. People being eaten by zombies. Leftovers splattered and baking on the street like hot tar. Bodiless heads calling out his name, crying out for him to run, escape, that they were everywhere. There was no hope for survival but to run. His wife was among them. Angie had suffered a horrible death.

They had both been running from a horde of zombies when the outbreak first occurred. She jumped a fence through their neighborhood ahead of him and broke her ankle upon landing. There was no time to pick her up because the dead were closing in so fast, and she gave up, tired, exhausted, and hungry. She chose death over fighting. And now she was still being eaten in his dreams, holding out her hands to him, and screaming, "Run, don't stop—don't turn back! You can still make it."

But it was too late to 'still make it.' He snapped awake from his dream to see that the dead had surrounded him in his cell. They'd shackled his ankles and cuffed his hands. There was nowhere to run. When the guns were pointed at him, he had no choice but to obey. They led him out of the cell and escorted him outside. He was going down a long stretch of grass towards the high school football field.

The gallows.

Dead man walking.

The football field was covered in zombies. Throngs of them. They filled the stands as casual spectators or standing in groups around the wooden gallows, ready to watch a hanging. He should've let them shoot him. It could've been an easier death. He even dropped onto the ground and tried to escape, but they wouldn't do anything but wait him out. They watched him flail like an idiot until he was too tired to keep up the act. It didn't help that he hadn't eaten much food, and was weak with hunger. His attempt ultimately failed; even the dead could see right through it. He was a scared man in a helpless position, and their maggot-filled brains knew it.

They finally guided him up the steps and tied the noose around his neck. The fibers itched against his skin, and in the heat, he wished to God that he had the use of his hands so he could scratch.

The zombies left him standing there, up high on the platform, facing his accusers. A zombie dressed as a preacher read from the Holy Bible. He mumbled and moaned verses. Adam might have heard "God save your soul," at one point, but he didn't know for sure.

The preacher made his exit back into the crowd. Now Adam was alone again with the horrible stench of death. The helplessness. The sunken dead faces were watching him with disgust. Others ogled him in whetted fascination. *Kill the bastard,* their eyes announced. *Hang 'em high!*

His death could have been much worse, his inner voice said, in order to keep his heart from exploding in his chest in fear. He could have been devoured alive or left to starve to death in some basement. Dying by starvation was one of the worst ways to go—next to being burned alive.

The dead had it right; they feared hunger as much as the living. But it would be over soon for Adam. He wouldn't die by teeth dissection. He wouldn't pass through rotten guts or be left in unidentifiable pieces on the road. His death would be swift and somewhat painless, unlike the many masses of the living that had died before him.

He was lucky.

Thinking about death in a positive light, Adam knew he was hysterical, and he let it explode out his mouth. "Hang me high! I did it. I'm guilty—and fuck you all! Hang me, baby! You bastards won't eat me alive! Fuck you all very much!" He was laughing now, long and loud.

The trap door went out from underneath him and he fell, plummeting downwards. The rope went taut. His body jerked twice, bouncing. A *gaaack* escaped his throat, squeezing air from his diaphragm.

He swung back and forth, his legs thrashing as he waited to die. He was losing air, his head tightening, his eyes bulging out of their sockets. His heart pounded faster than ever as his vision grew blurry. His ears throbbed with each beat of his fading pulse. He felt his face change color; his sweat burn hotter.

The moment was dragging on forever.

You won't eat me alive, he kept thinking. *You won't eat me alive. I win! I WIN!*

What he didn't realize in his hyper state was that he was swinging below the gallows out in the open. Every living corpse in the football field came in at once to devour Adam while he was in the deepest throws of strangulation. The zombies had found that as a human dies, they tasted so much sweeter as they hovered on the verge of death.

He was very wrong about his previous death prediction.

Adam was alive for three and a half minutes before nature excused him of the agony of being eaten alive by every zombie in town.

TO EAT THE LITTLE THINGS

VINCENZO BILOF

I

I couldn't believe how much I was sweating. There was blood all over the leather seats, blood on the seatbelt, and blood all over my hands.

"We're lucky to be alive right now!" Sharon said from the passenger seat, but like always, she didn't know what she was talking about. Not a clue. This was right before we ran out of gas. The Mustang had taken us down one country road after another at ninety mph.

It wasn't fast enough, and it wasn't far enough, to get us away from those zombie bastards.

The sun. Glaring light poured through the windshield. My shirt was soaked. Sharon mumbled and complained, but her words were soundless, while Megan screamed in the back seat, bleeding on the leather.

I'd had enough. I figured I could give the girl a little morphine to shut her up, but it would have been a waste of good drugs: no one recovered from a bite. Something had to be done, so I stared into the rearview mirror where Jeff's eyes met mine.

"Fuck you!" Jeff shouted, because he knew what I was thinking. "It's not happening! You hear me? I know she ain't gonna turn!" He leaned down over Megan and caressed her cheek. "Right, baby? I know you ain't gonna be like them. I know you won't turn."

Jeff, you used to be the best tech guy to ever coordinate a damn good bank robbery, I thought. *You were once a professional, and oh, what a mess you are now.*

The needle on the gauge hovered over **E**. I hit the brake pedal, and rubber peeled along the sun-drenched concrete. Smoke temporarily obscured the bright light of the sun and I could see again. For one second, I thought Megan had stopped screaming. I wasn't that lucky.

Sharon kept prattling, and I still couldn't hear her. She wanted to argue with me, but I opened the door, helping Jeff peel his dying girlfriend off the back seat, her hot, blood-stained skin sticking to the leather. Jeff continued to apply pressure with his hands to her neck where she'd been bitten. Annoyed, I tried to wipe her blood off my hands, and a lot of it wouldn't come off. That's the thing with blood: it stains.

We were miles away from dead and dying Cincinnati and still not far enough.

There were shapes in the foliage. The bright sun beat down on us, while Sharon kept talking and Megan kept screaming. I carried a backpack full of drugs and money, and all I could think about was that damn sun—hot enough to cook my flesh, it seemed.

"You have a plan?" Sharon asked.

I ignored her. The air tasted like wet salt, and I realized that Megan's death would be a complete waste of a sexy body. As the leader of the pack, it had been my duty to allow Megan to perform oral sex on me multiple times, an obligation that I fulfilled willingly for my crew. Megan was also a hard-ass with a penchant for maiming people. She and I had been a bad combination—Sharon provided a sort of equilibrium between us, and she was hotter. Jeff was last to join our crew, and I pawned Megan off on him. Best lay the tech-geek ever had.

With all of the coke and opiates pumped into my body, I thought that the Motel 6 at the edge of the road was an illusion; a mirage in a desert of heat and pain, tears and drugs. The sun was getting to me and I was tired, very tired.

Jeff pointed down the road. "Hey, a motel!" He stroked Megan's hair. "See, baby, you'll be okay. Don't you worry."

I couldn't resist a good joke. "Watch out, she's a man-eater."

"Shut up, Max!" Jeff lashed out. "You don't know what you're saying! She's gonna live! You'll see!"

"She's dead weight," I said. "In more ways than one. We'll drop your girlfriend off at the motel."

"You ain't doin' shit, Max. She's part of our crew."

"Not anymore."

Jeff drew his gun. His face shone with sweat and the gun shook in his hand. He'd never used it on anyone before. I stopped and started laughing. Jeff shouted at me and dropped his girlfriend to the pavement. The scene became all the funnier when lovely Sharon stepped between us. All of us were so incredibly stoned.

I put my hand up. "All right, brother! We can stand here until we get munched on, or we can set up shop at the motel. You're responsible for your girlfriend."

Something moved around us. Maybe birds. Maybe the shapes that I thought I could see.

We all stood there for a very long time. Jeff finally lowered the gun.

In a husky voice, Sharon said, "Eventually, we'll run out of drugs."

The sun was shining, the birds were singing. Megan whimpered. I really wanted to shoot or leave her there.

I could feel my eyelids blinking when I said, "Yeah. We'll run out of drugs."

There was a red pickup truck and a sea-green sedan in the parking lot of the motel, and I knew that even if we didn't find the keys, Jeff and I could break in and hotwire them. But I wasn't looking for a car. I heard rustling and a group of birds took flight, and a moment of shade struck the pavement as a meager group of clouds hid the light. I turned around and there was a shape, like a man, stumbling through the overgrowth and clutching at the trees.

Inside the reception room, there was blood all over the desk and a spinner rack of potato chips. I grabbed a bag of barbecue and ripped them open, spilling some and watching them skitter in broken pieces on the threadbare carpet. The salty chips tasted good.

"We should have separate rooms," Sharon said with chips in her mouth, always the planner.

I nodded slowly. My head felt like it was going to pop off my neck. "Whatever you say. Any cash lying around?"

Sharon rummaged around. She was tall, blond, and athletic. Boy did she love to steal. She loved the thrill of it. She wasn't in to making a mess of people like Megan and I were, but she was a damn genius. College-educated, like Jeff. As a matter of fact, I met her accidentally—we'd bumped into each other while robbing the same bank.

"Nothing," Sharon said flatly.

"We'll stay here for the night," Jeff said. "There's gotta be an army convoy around here and they might have to come through these parts, so we could find more people out here, man. We gotta think about the army."

"What?" I had no idea what he said.

"The army. They ain't gonna let none of this fly. They'll save Megan, too. You watch."

"Are you kidding me? Shit, use your head. There's a ton of loot out there for us, waiting to be grabbed. And we don't need your weak-ass to help us take it."

Jeff and I started shouting at each other. Sharon put her hands up and Megan started screaming again. I pointed my gun at Megan's head. Jeff didn't take too kindly to it, so he slapped my hand away and dared me to shoot her, because he'd do me, next.

Yeah, right.

It was then that one of them damn things stumbled in. It'd been a good ol' boy with a mullet and black tobacco-stained teeth, but he was missing a left arm and there was a piece of bone sticking out the shoulder. We stopped for a split second and stared at it, until Sharon snapped its neck. She'd taught herself that trick.

"Always wanted to see if I could do that," Sharon said with a smile as the good ol' boy fell to the floor.

"This place isn't safe, either," Jeff said.

"It's as safe as any other place," I added, because at the moment I'd decided that Sharon and I were going to leave him there. She wouldn't let me shoot him, but she would let me leave him. I had no intention of robbing the place, either. Anything we grabbed would be useless, unless we took it to Mexico. But I figured the same thing was going down everywhere.

"Okay," I said to Jeff calmly. "Go hit the backup generator, all these places have one. We'll take a break for a couple hours and hit the road again. We can't do no worse or better right now, especially if we want Megan to get her second wind."

Megan was quiet.

"You got it," Jeff was happy to be doing something. He dropped poor Megan into a chair where she continued to bleed, and went looking for the generator.

Sharon grabbed room keys from the board behind the register for two rooms that were next to each other. She threw a set on Megan's lap and walked out the door. I followed her out. When we got to our room, I realized the real reason why I wanted to stop at the motel.

"I feel like we're in a very bad movie," Sharon complained as we entered our room.

"We are," I reminded her.

Our room had two beds; it looked like the entire place had been cleaned right after the last attendants left. I thought that we should have grabbed the keys to all of the rooms and checked for dead people, but then I sat down on the edge of a bed instead.

Our room was musty but was a little cooler than outside. I opened the window and Sharon went into the bathroom and turned on the light. Jeff worked fast, and had turned on the power.

I dropped my bag, opened it, got my tools together, and rolled up my sleeve. Sharon sat down on the other bed.

I wasn't surprised when I heard Megan's scream.

Sharon stood up. "That's Megan."

"I know."

"We should go and find out what's wrong."

"Go 'head."

"Aren't you coming with me?"

"No."

"What if she's in trouble?"

I didn't answer her. It wasn't worth it.

The sun was still out and light poured in through the window. Sharon took her clothes off, and the needle went into my arm.

II

My dream was a replay from two days ago. In my dream, the Mustang was still spilling exhaust, still running. Sharon was with me when I parked it in my mom's driveway. I looked at Sharon and told her what my plan was.

"I've got to get a few things," I told her, my hands still on the steering wheel. "You're going to wait for me."

Sharon wanted to protest, wanted to ask questions. "What if your mother...?"

"I'll deal with it," I said.

I didn't wait for more silly protestations. The sky had gone all gray, and even though the neighborhood was normally pretty quiet, I knew it was quiet because everyone was dead, or they'd been left to die somewhere else. Good for them.

I hadn't seen my mother in twelve years, after she kicked me out for all of those bitter disappointments I made her endure, all of those promises broken by a child who fails before their mother's eyes. She never stopped my bookie father from beating me bloody with a leather belt. She never stopped my gangster-wannabe father from calling me a 'little fag' because I wanted to play the guitar. She never stopped my coke-head father from dying of heart failure after selling the car and giving away my college fund to pay off his gambling debts.

The least I could do for her was pay her a visit while the world ended.

I walked into the old stale house, my eyes watering from the smell of damp clothes that had sat out for too long. The house was neat, just as it was both times I got out of the joint and came home.

She was in the kitchen, seemingly resting in a cheap dining chair. Her silhouette was sitting casually, arms hanging limply above something black that had stained the kitchen linoleum. I said her name softly, and slowly. She stood up from the chair, which skidded across the floor. She used to hate it when the chair made that noise.

I knew what had happened to her before I saw her pale, dead face emerge out of the awkward light. I retreated then. I was afraid and I hadn't expected to be. My father had been the only living person to make me afraid. I backed into my old bedroom where *The Texas Chainsaw Massacre* poster hung over my bed. I opened the closet and found my old acoustic guitar, the first one I'd ever owned. It was stolen. I sat down for a moment on the edge of my bed and plucked at the strings.

Holding it by the neck, I walked out of the room and smashed it over my undead mother's skull. She fell to her knees, and blood ran from her eyes like tears—eyes that looked at me, unblinking. I saw the long scars across her forearms where she'd opened her veins to die in the kitchen.

To the kneeling corpse, I said, "Every time I hurt a woman I think of you, Mom."

It was true. I'd got into fights because I liked it, and I especially loved hurting women. I believed myself to be transcendent, a superior being that preyed on the weaker.

I drew the 9mm from the waistband of my pants and ended my mother's second life. I walked into the kitchen where a composition notebook sat open. She'd been reading the songs I used to write in school during math class. Before my father croaked, he'd beat the shit out of me because he'd found the notebook and declared that 'little faggots like you write poetry.' Then, he gave me the greatest lesson of my life, words of wisdom that served as my life's creed.

He said, "There are little animals in this world, and they can eat the same things that you do." He held a mouse in the palm of his open hand, and then my father's hammer- fist closed in on it, darkening its life for all time. Blood flowed from between his fingers, and tiny bones crunched, as the quivering tail stretched outward from that justifying fist.

III

Eventually I woke up, and the first thing I thought about was the sun.

Sharon was lying next to me on her stomach and the blankets were wet. Drenched. Soaked in sweat. The small television was on and there were two men wearing cheap suits and eyeglasses bickering at each other. I don't remember who turned on the TV, but I was surprised by it, though the banter was nonsensical.

I wondered if Jeff and Megan were dead.

I wandered the corners of the room in a helpless fugue, the volume from the TV making my head pound. I wanted to watch a movie filled with gore and nudity, but the only program on was the debate, and it was on every station. I felt ripped off.

Sharon moaned in the bed sheets. I was in a bad mood, and I thought if I went over to Jeff and Megan's room, and the girl was still alive, that I would have my way with her in front of Jeff, then finish him off. I'd taken out a member of my own crew once because it had to be done.

The nightmare still lingered behind my eyes. My dead mother kneeling before me, blood running from her eyes, her flesh so pale. I remembered I'd said something to her. A confession. I should have thanked her, or maybe told her it was all her fault. I would have been right either way.

Usually after waking up in the middle of a drug haze I'd do more drugs, but the supply was precious, and I needed to see my friends. When I opened the door leading outside, the sun slapped me in the face with searing hotness. Blinded, I put my arm up in front of my eyes and walked barefoot on scalding hot concrete to the room next door.

The room was unlocked, and I really should have been thinking clearly enough to bring a weapon.

The door opened noiselessly and the room was empty. I hovered in the doorway for a long time before entering. Their drugs and guns were scattered all over the room. At the foot of the bed there was a large, glaring bloodstain.

The sudden urge to take a shower overpowered me. I thought it would be a shame to lose Megan—she'd been there with me in the early days, the back-alley days, the shivering days, the homeless days. Those were the days in which our innocence bled from our noses and no homeless man was safe. I could always find another tech guy, but there was a chance I didn't need him anymore.

I thought I might not need any of them anymore—for anything.

I returned to my room and took a shower. The water felt cool and refreshing against my skin. There wasn't any soap or towels. I put my shorts back on while I was still wet and walked into the room, where Jeff sat on the edge of the bed holding his gun.

I stopped, not walking all the way into the room. Jeff looked sad, withdrawn and distant. He knew I was there but he didn't look at me. I was a bit disappointed that he was still alive.

"Hey, Jeff, where's Megan?"

"Oh man," he shrugged, still staring at the carpet. "She'll be here in a minute. She moves a little slow these days."

I swallowed hard. Droplets of water slid off my body as heat once again stifled my breath. The door to the room was wide open and I saw Megan's shadow before she entered. I heard her shuffling feet, her painful moaning.

"Jeff," I said calmly. "What have you guys been doing? Why didn't you come to me if you needed help?"

"It's cool, dude," Jeff replied. "We were just hangin' out. Not a whole lot going on. I was tryin' to get the news on the TV because I want to know what's going on but it won't work."

"I know," I lied.

"That really sucks. I can't figure out what I've done to deserve this. I mean, all the stuff I did that people think is really bad is all I know how to do. I was working. You know what I mean? You understand. Identity theft is so easy, you know. Hacking is so easy."

"I understand."

"All of those banks were insured by the Federal Government," he said.

"You're right."

"It's like you always said, Max. You always used to say that we're not regular people. We don't punch in every day or collect a paycheck on Fridays. We don't answer to anyone but ourselves. I had to do it."

Megan finally made it into the room. Her head hung on her right shoulder and she didn't see us. A thin line of drool hung from her chin and stretched down to her knees. She'd been out in the sun for a long time—hours. The skin on her face was red and crispy.

Jeff turned around. "Hey, baby, I told you Max was straight. I told you all along he was cool. He's like Mad Max, like in the movies. That's what I always said, baby. Now you finally agree."

Megan moaned, as if in horrible pain.

"Sit down, honey," Jeff motioned over to the bed with his gun. "Sit down, baby. You look tired. I think I have something that can speed things up a little bit."

"You still have some coke?" I asked him.

He shrugged. "I think so. I'm not really sure. Hey, Max, that reminds me. You never told me what you think about Megan. I told you that Sharon's a pretty decent chick, but you never said anything about Megan."

"I respect you more than that," I said. "She's the girl you like. It shouldn't matter what anyone else thinks of her."

"You're right, man. You're always right. You know, my dad wanted me to play sports. Be an athlete. Be a man. I hate sports, especially football. You like football, Max?"

"Never robbed a football player before," I said.

Megan sat down on the bed next to him. The bed slowly sank beneath her weight, as if she weighed more now than she had in life. She moaned louder and her hands limply reached for Jeff's arm. He didn't resist as she brought his arm up to her mouth and tore away a huge chunk of his flesh with her teeth. Jeff didn't even flinch.

"See," he said, a smile on his face. "It's not all that bad. I can handle it. It even tickles a little."

I could have saved him, could have prevented it from happening. Even then, I could have offered him some final apology for being an asshole to him for so long. I could have thanked him for his services. I could have shot him in the head.

I watched Megan carefully and slowly chew the meat in her mouth, blood dripping down her chin to land in her lap. Jeff's arm was bleeding very badly from where she'd bitten into it. I walked up to Jeff and took the gun out of his hand. Megan took another bite out of his arm like one might chew and suck on a piece of steak that's smothered in barbecue sauce. That's what I was reminded of. I like barbecue.

"You're a standup guy, Max," Jeff said, his eyes following me as his fingers let go of the gun. "You know, if you ever need me to vouch for you, I'll do it. Anyone would be happy to have you as a partner because you get the job done. You're efficient and quick. You're so fast you fake me out, like I didn't think you moved but you really did move and I can't believe it, man."

"Thanks, Jeff."

"I promise I'll take care of Megan forever," he said.

"I know you will." Warm blood squirted onto my bare feet.

With his gun in my hand, I left them to their feast. The sun was out but the intensity of the light and the position of the sun told me that the sun was about to go down. Besides the shower, the sunset was the best thing to happen to me in a long time. It was a huge relief to see it finally lower behind the horizon, resting, while we try to go on with our lives.

IV

The television was on and there was an Asian man in a suit and tie, reading from the teleprompter in front of him. He looked perfectly calm and neat, as if he were reading the same kind of boring news he'd read last year.

Sharon smoked a cigarette and the window was open. A cloudless, starlight evening had descended upon us. She was completely naked after snorting OxyContin for about an hour.

I could hear the Asian man's words but they didn't make any sense. He said that the end of the world was an isolated incident in the U.S., while the U.N. and the E.U. were sending medical aid to us. Gasoline prices were reaching record highs. The economy was in the toilet.

"There are reports," he said, "that the…living dead are attacking and eating the flesh of American citizens."

I couldn't stop laughing for a good five minutes. I was in tears by the time I finally recovered. Sharon stared at the cigarette she held in front of her face. I missed everything else that the news reporter said.

The Asian man was soon replaced by a black priest, who stood in front of a blue background that might have represented the sky or Heaven, and he talked about God and how much we needed Him right now, in this time of crisis. He waved his hands around a lot.

Loud banging came from the door. A cool breeze blew in through the open window. Sharon looked up while cigarette ash collected on her perfectly-cut stomach.

"Go see who it is," I told her.

"No." She shook her head slowly.

"Do it."

"No. I don't want to." Each word seemed to echo.

I looked straight into her eyes. "You're gonna open that door. You're gonna get up and open that door because I'm really sick of you just lying around and doing my drugs."

"They're not just *your* drugs. I'm not getting up. I don't feel like getting up and besides, you're not gonna do anything if I don't. You always let me do what I want to do. I own you. I have you…whipped."

She may have been consciously resisting me. She may have been trying to oil me up for kinky sex, but the nightmarish world and all of its consequences dictated my thoughts and my movements. Maybe the world had always been my own personal nightmare. At that moment, I thought only about my father standing over me with bloody fists, two of my own teeth broken, and my mother watching from my bedroom doorway with her apron on, her arms folded across her chest.

There was another knock at the door.

"You know what I'm capable of. Do you think I need you? Do you think I need you slowing me down?" I said.

I called her by my mother's name, not aware I'd done it.

Another knock at the door.

"You're high," Sharon said.

"Maybe not," I replied. "Do you remember what happened in Cleveland? How I made you and Megan watch?"

That was the one member of our crew I'd personally taken care of. Her name was Donna. Back then, there were eight of us. Donna had stolen money from me, personally. In the middle of a dirt road, I rode Donna hard and made everyone watch. Then I killed and buried her, slit her throat. Megan had laughed as it went down, but Sharon had been afraid. She'd said I'd called Donna a different name.

Sharon's eyes widened. "You're evil…so evil. You're an animal. I stayed with you after that. I don't know why I stay with you, 'cause you're an animal."

"I enjoyed it, too. I'm thinking about how I want to do that to you right now. I think about how you want me to do horrible things to you. I'd like to show you how much I really love you."

"Stop it, Max. Let's forget about this. Let's forget this whole conversation. I don't want to argue right now and I've tried to forget about the things you used to do. I only stayed with you because of the money. The money was always good but there isn't any money any more."

"Answer the door!"

"Please, I love you Max. I love you so much. Forget what I said. You're not an animal. Please don't make me answer the door."

I got on top of her wearing only my boxer shorts, and I knocked the cigarette out of her hand. I held her by the throat. "I could do you a favor. Do you think I could trust you? Do you think I'd let you watch my back? You're just like me. It's gonna come down to this sooner or later."

I clutched her hair in my fist and yanked her off the bed. She whimpered like a puppy that's been kicked, and I found the sound of her tears to be inspiring. She knew what was waiting outside the door, and she knew I was far more dangerous.

Sharon struggled to get up. I gave her time, because I have until the end of the world.

There are animals that would eat what I eat.

When she stood up against the wall, her chest rising and falling rapidly, I was drawn to her big eyes. I stopped breathing for a minute as her eyelashes quivered. As she crossed the room and opened the door, I watched her with a smile on my face.

It was Jeff. Half of his left arm was gone and there was just a thin bone hanging from the shoulder socket with tattered remnants of cloth. He didn't look happy.

"What do you want?" Sharon asked, oblivious of the bloodied, hanging bone that used to be his arm thanks to her drug-induced high.

He took a step forward and reached out to her.

"Oh, Jeff," she said and shoved him back weakly. "What are you doing? Why do you have to be like this? You know I'm with Max." She sniffled and wiped at her nose.

"Maybe he heard a loud noise," I said, grinning. I could hear the priest shouting a prayer on the TV. "Maybe he just wants to make sure you're okay."

"Everything's fine, Jeff," she said. He reached for her again and she shoved him back. "You know that Max will get very upset if you keep staring at me like that. Go back to your room. Go back to Megan. Is she okay? Are you treating her right? What's wrong with you?"

I pushed her against the door and shoved Jeff outside. I landed on top of him and reached for a brick, one of a dozen lying on the ground. I brought it down on his head and watched his skull crack open until his hands stopped reaching for me.

"Oh my God," Sharon said from the doorway. "You killed Jeff!"

I ran my fingers through my hair. "No, I didn't."

"I just watched you kill Jeff!" she screamed at me. "Stay away from me!" She edged along the wall for a moment while I stood up slowly. She suddenly ran into the room.

There are things that eat what I eat, but I should eat them all.

I crouched down in the doorway to our room, Jeff lying at my feet. The night beasts chattered. The moon was full and there were no clouds.

I could hear the rustling of tree branches and the leaves that would one day fall gracefully from their branches, and I could hear all of the beasts salivating at the sight of the fresh meat that walked amongst them.

I slid along the lengths of darkness and shadow to avoid the light of the moon. I passed the room that my friends once stayed in for a day—or two, or three?—and I expected to see Megan with bloody meat in her clutches and pieces of Jeff's arm on the floor. Megan wasn't there.

When Sharon fled the room, I followed, but I allowed her some distance. I wanted to stalk her, to surprise her one last time, to afford her that moment where she might believe that she could win a satisfactory conclusion.

Slinking against the wall, I knew she was hiding in the reception office. There would still be barbecue chip crumbs scattered on the floor. There would still be blood from Megan on one of the chairs. There was a light on in the front office and I could hear snippets of conversation. The tone was that of relief, or temporary happiness.

"Oh, Megan, I knew you'd be okay." It was Sharon. "Max has gone insane. He killed Jeff and I'm afraid of what he'll do to us. I'm so afraid right now…oh my God, Megan…who are your friends? I didn't mean to interrupt anything…"

There was a group of four zombies sitting around at a table as if they were talking. They saw me standing outside and looked upon me with patient faces. One of them was an old bald man wearing a Hawaiian shirt, his mouth toothless. Another zombie was a fat Mexican woman wearing clothes that were too tight on her, and her skin looked like the color of old, yellow Swiss cheese. Another zombie might have been her teenage son, and the fourth zombie might have been her husband. He had tattoos on his neck and a large black moustache over his lip.

Megan was standing in front of Sharon silently. Sharon leaned in and hugged her old friend tightly. She sobbed on Megan's shoulder. The four zombies gathered at the table stared at me silently. Megan opened her mouth and took a huge bite out of Sharon's left shoulder.

"Oooh, Megan, I like being kissed there." Sharon closed her eyes to savor the pleasure of their embrace. She reached up and grabbed the back of Megan's hair. "I've wanted to do this with you for so long. But we need to hide right now from Max. Oh…but don't stop, please don't stop."

Blood ran down Sharon's naked back like tears awakened by an emotional fury. Megan looked up with a mouthful of Sharon's flesh in her mouth and a thin line of blood ran from her chin like the drool that I saw earlier when I was with Jeff. Sharon closed her eyes and her cheeks flushed red, her lips parting slightly. Megan looked like she might be smiling.

"Megan…" Sharon whispered with a gasp. Her nipples had hardened and her lips were stretched out in a wide 'O.' She tightened her arms around Megan and gasped.

I took two steps back while the other four struggled to get out of their chairs. I walked back to my room, disappointed that I wouldn't be the one to kill Sharon.

V

In my room the television was showing footage of people running out of a massive department store.

A tan anchorman with bright blue eyes and a white silk tie said, "The Wal-Mart store just outside of Memphis has announced it will be closed until further notice."

I started to gather up my things. I left all of the drugs out of my bag. I looked through Sharon's things and I took her box of Ritz crackers. I got dressed and immediately felt different in my clothes.

On the TV they were interviewing a reputable sociologist, and I listened intently.

"Dr. Fisher, what do you think is proving to be the most problematic issue that we face by this recent menace?"

"Well, Jim, I think it's more to do with the people than the menace. There's been so much looting and rioting that it makes it hard to truly gauge the threat this new problem poses. I feel right now we need to band together and help each other, but it isn't happening."

"Yes, I think you may be right about that. It's as if so many people are acting viciously and without any sense of who or what they were before this happened. As good Americans it should be important to help one another, to unite."

"Most importantly, this incident seems to be isolated to the United States," Dr. Fisher said.

"Do we have any idea how these American monsters were created?"

I paused and stared at the television.

"Do we have any idea how these American monsters were created?" It echoed in my head.

Out of the corner of my eye, I saw a zombie standing in the doorway. It was lingering there, as if waiting for me to hurry up and finish.

I left the TV on. I turned off the lights in the room and took a moment to light up one of Sharon's cigarettes while the zombie stood there. It was a younger man who must have cut his wrists to kill himself because the slash marks and black stains on his sleeves were the only indication he had died at all. His complexion was pale, and he wavered as if it was difficult for him to stand up.

I put the cigarette between the man's two fingers as his hand reached out for me. "Enjoy it, brother," I said. "You look like you might need it more than I do."

The zombie's eyes went wide and his mouth opened with a hiss. I shoved him and walked by, then I shoved the other one who'd been waiting outside for me.

I adjusted my backpack to be sure it was tight, and when I looked at Jeff's corpse lying on the ground, I considered going into his room and getting whatever supplies might be in there. I decided against it; I wanted to leave.

I went through the bushes, wanting to avoid the main road and whatever obvious dangers awaited me. I could have taken the pickup truck or the sedan, but I was more comfortable on my feet.

The next day was hotter. I always wondered what to do about the damn sun.

"Do we have any idea how these American monsters were created?"

A question for the ages.

JOHN DOE

SUZANNE ROBB

Paramedics John Hawkins and Carly King were working the late shift on a Saturday night in New York City. They both knew it meant they could count on being very busy.

"Hey, John, want to stop and get a coffee before things get nuts?" Carly asked.

John looked at the clock on the dashboard while he drove the ambulance and noticed it was 11:45 p.m.

"Good idea, the bars will be letting out in about an hour, and then we'll have the fun task of picking up drunk driver bits."

John steered the ambulance towards a local doughnut shop, known to paramedics and police. As he pulled in to park, the two-way radio crackled.

"Bus 543, get to Doorcrest and Lane. Male in his thirties described as acting strange, medical help requested."

Carly sighed. "Well, it was worth a shot."

John nodded his head in agreement and pulled out of the parking lot and hit the button for the lights and siren.

When they arrived on-scene, both grabbed their gear bags from the back of the ambulance, then ran to where all the commotion seemed to be centered.

They saw a man in his mid-thirties acting erratically, ranting about infections and government conspiracies. He didn't seem to be armed, but several bystanders were scared.

"Great, another cokehead. When will people smarten up and stop doing this stuff?" Carly sighed and bent down to open her bag.

"I have no idea, but as far as I'm concerned if you're stupid enough to do it in the first place, you're helping Darwin out, and cleaning up the gene pool."

Carly laughed as she filled a syringe with a sedative. "I love your pessimism, John. Now let's get to work."

Speaking in calm, soothing voices, the two paramedics approached the man. It didn't work, in fact, the closer they got to him, the more agitated he became.

"Stay away from me, someone has to kill me. Don't you see what they've done? Are you blind? I'm not the first one, this is just the beginning," he ranted, his eyes wide with fear.

"Hey, pal, we just want to help you, okay? You've got all these nice people worried about you." Carly tried to distract the man as John approached him from the side.

"You can't help me; it's too late for help. If you don't kill me, it'll be too late for all of us. I'm…"

John tackled the man and had him in a choke hold on the ground in seconds. Carly ran up and injected a sedative into the man's arm. He began to calm after a minute passed.

Carly ran to the ambulance and pulled out the gurney. She wheeled it over, hit the lever to lower the gurney, and she and John rolled the man onto it. When he was secure on the gurney, John made sure to strap him in.

"Let's get this guy loaded up and down to Mercy General," she said.

John simply nodded at Carly in agreement.

On the ride to the hospital, Carly sat in the back, evaluating the man. There were no signs of needle usage, no obvious signs of trauma, and his pupils weren't dilated. Whatever drug he'd taken, it didn't have the usual side effects.

Instead, the man had a fever, low blood pressure, an uneven pulse rate, and his eyes seemed to be clouding over. She'd never seen anything like it.

"This is bus 543, we have a Caucasian male, mid-thirties acting strange. Drug use of some kind is assumed, ETA is three minutes. He's currently sedated."

Moments later they were pulling into the emergency bay for ambulances at Mercy General. John got out of the front seat and went to the back to open the rear doors. Carly helped him get the gurney onto the ground, and together they rolled it into the ER

Dr. Monica Simmons had just worked a sixteen hour shift. Her feet were killing her, and she was dead tired. The seconds ticked by on the clock; as long as there were no emergencies within the next five minutes, she could go home.

Monica couldn't take her eyes off the clock, she wanted to go home so much. Any minute her replacement, Dr. Woodcomb, would walk through the door and take the emergencies coming in. Any second now, she would wave to Dr. Woodcomb and leave. She would head home to her husband Jim, and Bones, her dog. They would have a nice late meal to celebrate ten years of marriage.

"Dr. Simmons we got a bus pulling in with a Caucasian male, mid-thirties, drug overdose of some kind," Henry said, then ran off before she could reply.

"Of course there is, I have four minutes left on my shift." She stood up from the chair she was on, and headed towards ER 3. Scrubbed up and gloved in less than a minute, she turned around to greet the paramedics as they entered with the patient.

Monica studied the man on the gurney. "What are his vitals?" The room became a rush of movement as paramedics tried to give information, nurses tried to set-up IV lines, and Monica tried to size up the situation.

"His pulse is irregular, blood pressure is falling, fever is starting to spike, and breathing is shallow," Carly said. "When conscious he's violent and erratic. Sedation doesn't last long, he's metabolizing it at an incredible rate. Whatever he's on, I've never seen a reaction like this before. On scene he ranted about us being able to see what they had done to him. He wanted us to kill him; the usual crap we listen to when someone overdoses." Carly signed off the paperwork and handed it to Monica.

"Thanks, Carly." Monica absently placed the file on a small table, then approached the man for a closer inspection.

"See ya later, Doc," Carly said as she and John left the room, giving the hospital team more room to work.

Monica used her stethoscope to listen to the heartbeat. She looked at the monitor to watch his blood pressure, and pulse rate. They were constantly changing. She opened his eyes, and noticed they weren't dilated, but did have a cloudy covering on them. She wondered if it could be contacts. As Monica leaned in for a closer inspection, the man started choking, blood coming out of his mouth and nose.

As the man began to choke more, blood gushed everywhere. Then he sat straight up and looked at Monica with eyes void of color. He made a gurgling noise and Monica thought his lungs were full of fluid; he had to be drowning in his own blood. To her that had to be the explanation, it was the only one which made sense.

"Hold him down. I have to incubate him. And for God's sake, someone sedate him!" Monica yelled.

Jenny, the nurse, and George, an intern, held the man down as Monica incubated him. She'd had a hell of a time doing it, but after several minutes, and two sedatives later, the job was done.

"Draw some blood. I want you to run every known substance. We can't help him until we know what's in his system."

Monica looked at the patient. Something about it didn't add up. His vitals were weakening at a steady rate. He was slowly dying, and she had no idea how to stop it.

The man wore khakis and a button top. His brown hair was short, like a military cut. He had a muscular build, which indicated he took care of himself. None of this added up to the type of person who would use an experimental drug.

"What do we have on him, ID, wallet, anything?" One of the nurses went to the corner of the room where all his personal belongings had been put into a dish.

"We have a watch, one ring, and that's it. No ID."

"John Doe," Monica sighed. Those were the worst. The paperwork was a nightmare because the police had to be called, and it took hours of interviews and answering questions. Since the case had landed in her lap, she had to see it through.

She needed to call Jim to let him know she'd be missing dinner—again. Then she'd call the police, and let them know she had a John Doe and a possible new drug on the streets for them to worry about.

Pushing the door open to leave, she heard the alarms on the monitor go wild, then silent. John Doe had just crashed.

"Get some adrenaline now, and prep the paddles!" Monica took three strides to the side of John Doe in less than two seconds. She grabbed the paddles from the intern and held them at the ready. "Clear." She shocked the patient and waited. "Turn it up by fifty." She watched as Jenny did as told. "Clear." Monica shocked the patient again, and waited.

She put the paddles to the side where they wouldn't hurt anyone, and held her hand out for the adrenaline shot. She jabbed it into the heart of John Doe and began doing chest compressions, as George grabbed the breathing bag to do it manually.

Nothing, no reaction at all. She tried to resuscitate for fifteen minutes before she gave up and called T.O.D. (time of death).

"All right, T.O.D. is approximately 12:35 a.m. Let's call for a clean-up, then change our clothes and take showers to decontaminate. Someone call for an orderly to take John Doe down to the morgue."

Monica paused at the door. She removed her lab coat and rubber gloves, tossing them into the bio-hazard bin. The entire front of her shirt, and top portion of her pants were covered in blood.

She needed to change and take a shower, but two men in military uniforms stopped her.

"Excuse me, ma'am, have you seen this man?" His name tag read Harris.

The man on Harris' left held up a photo.

Monica nodded. "Yeah, he's dead. Look in ER 3, but be careful where you step." She pointed to the room behind her, and tried to move past them.

"Ma'am, does the blood on you belong to that man?" Mr. Harris asked.

"Yes, Mr. Harris, it is his blood, so if you don't mind I'd like to go and shower."

"Sorry, ma'am, that's not possible right now. Please wait here."

Monica watched as Mr. Harris took out a cell phone. The call lasted about three minutes. Flipping the phone shut, he returned with a serious look on his face.

"Ma'am, this wing has just gone into quarantine. No more ambulances will be allowed in, and everyone who has been in contact with Henry Williams, the dead man in ER 3, isn't going anywhere for now."

Monica shook her head. "You can't be serious. It's a Saturday night, the amount of car accidents and other medical emergencies is too high for you to shut us down. And why do we need to be quarantined? What aren't you telling me?"

She had hundreds of other questions, but got caught up short when two dozen men in fatigues entered through the emergency room doors. They set up a barricade, and a team carrying large cases went down the hallways over a hundred feet in both directions.

Monica watched Jenny and George get collected by the uniformed men and brought to stand next to her, then the orderlies who had gone into the room were collected as well. Down the hall, plastic tarps were put up, indicating the area as a bio-hazard. Two soldiers were sent to guard each hallway.

Monica looked at the men standing in front of her, and knew something bad was going on. The men were going over John Doe's file, now known as Henry Williams. One of the men came out and indicated something on the file.

"Ma'am..." Monica had had it.

"Don't call me that, my name is Dr. Monica Simmons. You can call me Dr. Simmons."

"Dr. Simmons, the two paramedics on this form, Hawkins and King, were they injured in any way by Mr. Williams? Did he perhaps bite them or did he bleed from a wound they might have had contact with?"

Monica didn't know how to answer. She didn't want to drag Carly and John into this, but figured it didn't matter. She had a feeling these men had already put a call in and the paramedics were on the way back.

Five minutes later, Carly and John were being man-handled through the doors by four soldiers. They had now collected everyone who had been in contact with the mysterious Henry Williams, right before he died.

A man walked in behind them. He wore a suit, and had a look about him which gave Monica the willies. He struck her as the type of man who had an answer for everything, without actually answering anything. They were about to get the mother of all snow jobs.

"Dr. Simmons, the rest of you, please follow me," the man said.

Monica followed behind Harris. He led them into the break room. There were some nurses and orderlies already there, sipping their coffee nervously. As the entire group assembled in the room, there were over a dozen hospital workers, three soldiers, and the man in the suit.

Monica looked around and found a seat in the back of the room. Her feet were still killing her, and she had a feeling the man in the suit would say something upsetting, and then the questions would begin.

"My name is Mr. Jones. I'm here on behalf of the U.S. military to explain why you're all under quarantine for the next few hours. Henry Williams was a security guard at a military facility. An accident occurred and he and a few others were exposed to a new bio-weapon we're working on."

Monica raised her hand. "Mr. Jones, are you telling us that we've been exposed to some sort of weapon, and might end up dead?"

The others in the room began to whisper among themselves.

"Let me clarify, I'm not here to answer your questions. I'm here to serve in the capacity of a liaison of sorts. Now, as I was saying, Mr. Williams was exposed to the virus a few hours ago. We didn't know at the time that he'd been exposed. He left after his shift presumably to go home. When the lab went into lockdown, technicians handled immediately, and those who were possibly at risk were contacted. Everyone has been tracked down, and the people they were in contact with put into quarantine, too."

Mr. Jones paused in his speech as one of the soldiers came up to him. Moments later, screaming could be heard outside. Monica positioned herself so she could see out the small window.

Private Willy Ferguson had no idea what the hell was going on. They told him to keep an eye on the dead man, and then next thing he knew, the dead man got up. He called out to tell his commanding officer, and then went back into the room to see what the dead man was doing.

Willy watched the man open his eyes. They were a milky white color, and he moaned. They didn't tell Willy's unit anything other than that they had to quarantine the hospital, and to shoot anything seen as a threat.

Rumor had it some sort of killer virus had gotten out of some lab, but looking at the dead man standing in front of him, Willy knew they were dealing with something much worse. The man began to move towards him, and Willy pulled out and raised his gun, aiming it at the man.

"Hey, man, back off or I'll shoot you. I mean it."

The man continued to move towards him.

Willy watched the man stop and sniff the air, then he zeroed in on Willy, and in a move faster than Willy thought possible, the man was on him. Willy raised his arm to defend himself and felt the man bite his forearm. With a grunt, he pushed his attacker off, then kicked him hard enough to cause the man to fly back through the door behind him.

Willy grabbed some gauze and wrapped his arm. He'd heard talk as to what they were doing to anyone who had come into contact with these people. He knew he couldn't let anyone know he was bit. Unrolling his uniform sleeve, he covered his wound and twisted the torn and bloody side of his sleeve so it was facing inward, then entered the hallway.

A second later, he heard a gunshot, and saw the dead man drop to the floor, this time really dead, he hoped. Unseen by all of them was the fine pink mist the impact of the bullet caused. The mist floated along the hallway, and up to a vent, via an air current. The vent was connected to the ICU and a waiting room one floor up. Over half of the soldiers present had breathed in the fine pink particles within a minute.

"Private, you okay? Did you have any contact with that man?"

Looking his commanding officer directly in the eye, Willy lied through his teeth. "No sir, no contact. I kicked him out the door into the hallway when he came at me."

His CO looked him over and seemed to buy the story. "Good, go tell the removal unit to pick up the body."

"Yes, sir." Willy left as fast as possible.

Monica had to be wrong, what she saw wasn't possible. Henry Williams was up and walking around. Then a single shot was fired and his head exploded, leaving bits of bone and brain matter spread across the wall.

Everyone in the room jerked in surprise. Those who saw what happened began to murmur to the others. Mr. Jones kept his cool the entire time, as if hearing gunfire was expected, which in this case Monica assumed it might have been.

"Would you mind telling me how the hell a dead man just got up and walked out of his room, and why your men shot him?"

Mr. Jones looked at Monica, his expression never changing. In the same monotone voice which made her crazy, he said, "I'm not here to answer your questions, I'm here to give you the necessary information for your situation."

The soldier was dismissed with a nod of the head from Mr. Jones. "Now, as I was saying. You'll be held under quarantine for the next few hours to make sure you haven't contracted the virus from Williams. We'll be taking blood samples, and keeping an eye on you for the time being. As a precaution, we've set up a special shower room where you'll be taken, scrubbed down, and provided with clean clothing. We'll meet back here later once you've all washed and changed."

Monica watched as Mr. Jones left the room. He didn't even pause at the blood and gore spread across the wall. He nodded to someone, and she watched as two men in hazardous material suits came into view and began to spray down the walls with something.

"All right, you heard the man, get up and make a line in front of me. I'll be taking blood samples, after which you'll be escorted to the shower room," Mr. Harris said.

Monica stood and got into line towards the end. She didn't like the situation at all, and had a very bad feeling building up in her gut. She watched as the man deftly found veins, and drew blood. At least he knew how to do his job.

The line moved along at a nice pace, but Monica found herself getting impatient. Her feet hurt, and now her head pounded. When she reached Mr. Harris, he motioned her to sit. As she did, he began tying the rubber hose around her arm. Seconds later, he had the needle in and a vial filling with her blood.

Monica sighed, and rubbed her temples.

"Ma'am, are you feeling all right? Is there anything we need to know, any prior conditions, or possible new symptoms?"

Monica shook her head no. "I've been working for almost seventeen hours. I'm just tired," she said.

He nodded, but she didn't miss the note he made when referring to her name.

"Thank you, *ma'am*, move out to the hallway. A private there will show you to the shower area."

Monica stood and went out the side door of the room. She'd wanted to use the other exit so she could see what had happened, but didn't push her luck. In the hallway, she met a nervous-looking private.

"Hey, is everything okay?" she asked.

The private looked at her suddenly, and she noticed his eyes were bloodshot. "Yes, ma'am, everything's fine. I'll show you to the decontamination showers."

Monica thought about how bad that sounded. Decontamination couldn't be good, but a shower had to be the worst. She knew what it involved, and began to drag her feet to try and delay the inevitable pain and embarrassment.

The *showers* were set up in one of the bathrooms. They consisted of two people in protective gear, holding a hose. Monica was ordered to strip down, her clothes tossed into a bio-hazard container.

After she stripped, they directed her to the center of the room where one individual sprayed her with a hose, while the other scrubbed her with an abrasive sponge on the end of a pole. She could smell chemicals in the water they were hosing her with, and she felt it burning her skin. By the time they finished, she had several bleeding spots from them rubbing to hard.

As soon as they were done with her, they handed her a towel and let her exit the 'shower.' Monica met the same private as before. He led her down the hall to the break room they had gathered in earlier. A pile of scrubs were laid out on a chair, and one set had her name in paper on top of them.

As she tried to get dressed, the others in the room politely turned their heads to give her some measure of privacy. As soon as she finished, she walked over to Jenny.

"Hey, Jenny, have there been any updates?"

Jenny shook her head. "No, and they still refuse to answer any questions." The last part Jenny raised her voice.

Monica thought about what the *supposedly* dead Henry Williams had done. It didn't make sense. Perhaps the *bio-weapon* was something that put people into some sort of coma-like state mimicking death. Though that didn't explain why they blew his head all over the wall.

Monica looked at the clock; it had been over two hours since Henry Williams had entered her emergency room. She'd pronounced his time of death over an hour and a half ago, and it had been an hour since she'd seen him walking in the hallway to then be shot.

She glanced at the other people in the room, assessing them. No one seemed sick, no one ranted or raved. Everyone seemed okay. She hoped that meant they were all fine, and she would be telling Jim all about this over pasta and garlic bread.

People in the ICU waiting rooms were starting to complain of headaches. Dr. Frank Jameson was the attending physician for the night. With the ER closed down, things were fairly quiet, or at least they were until recently. About thirty minutes ago patients in the ICU started developing fevers, and other complications he couldn't explain.

Frank sighed as yet another person approached him. He understood they wanted answers about what was going on with their loved ones, but he just didn't have the patience to deal with it tonight.

For the last hour he'd let his temper get the better of him on several occasions. The people kept asking him to help them, they weren't feeling well. He yelled at them to go home if they weren't well, as there were truly ill people he needed to look after in the ICU.

"Dr. Jameson, I know you talked to me, but I really need something for this headache. It getting worse and worse, and now I feel hot."

"Right, I'll have the nurse get you some aspirin for it." He moved past the person and entered into the waiting room. He looked around; there were at least twenty people sitting, watching TV, drinking coffee, reading a book, or doing nothing, all of them waiting for news on a loved one. He didn't know what to do anymore. Visiting hours were over, but the hospital tried to accommodate people who were in severe or acute situations when it came to the ICU.

He wanted to ask them all to go home because one of them must have gotten his patients sick. Right before he made his announcement, an argument broke out.

"I'm not going to share this with you so quit asking me to." An average sized man leaned over a bag of some sort, shielding it from a woman.

"Why are you such a jerk? You never treat me right." The woman stood up and began to pound on the man, obviously her husband.

Frank ran over to the woman and grabbed her from behind. "Hey, there's no reason to get violent. I'm sure we can find you something to eat."

"Let go of me, you bastard!" she screamed.

Frank maintained his hold.

The man that moments ago was being hit by the woman, now came to her rescue. He stood and said, "You best be letting her go."

Something about the demeanor of the guy made Frank obey. "Look, I didn't mean to upset anyone, I just want to keep people calm." Frank started backing away. He turned when the couple sat back down and returned to bickering. He sighed and rubbed his face with his hands.

He approached the in-take desk and the nurse on duty.

"Hey, Lois, can you do me a favor and call over to whomever had this damn lockdown put in place. Let him know the ICU's been exposed to something, and I need another doctor and a nurse to help with all the complications the patients are developing."

"No problem, Dr. Jameson," Lois replied with phone in hand.

Frank walked away, and headed towards the break room. If he could just get in a nap; ten minutes, that's all he wanted. Ten minutes of sleep. His head pounded and he felt like he had a fever. It would be just his luck to catch whatever his patients had contracted.

Mr. Jones entered the room and all conversation stopped. He looked around, then consulted a piece of paper in his hand. "The results of your blood work are back. It appears some of you might be affected. We're not sure how long the virus takes to manifest itself, so even if you aren't infected at the moment, we're still going to keep you here for monitoring purposes."

A murmur went around the room. "What are you going to do for those who are infected? What's the treatment regimen?" Monica wanted some answers; this had gone on long enough.

"Dr. Simmons, that will be addressed by the man who is in charge of the project. He'll be arriving shortly. In the meantime, everyone please stay here and remain calm."

"That's easy for you to say, buddy," one of the orderlies called out.

Mr. Jones motioned to the nervous-looking private from before to come over. Monica noticed the private had paled considerably since she last saw him and was now sweating profusely. Something was definitely wrong with him. She glanced around the room, and saw several people holding their heads, and fanning themselves with whatever they could find.

Mr. Jones dismissed the private, and Monica watched as he skittered out of the room. Seconds later a cell phone rang. Since hers, and every other person in the room had theirs taken away, it had to be Mr. Jones'.

Monica watched as he went into a corner to answer it. He listened for a few moments, furrowed his brow, then got a brief look of worry before yelling, "I don't care, lock it down now!"

Whatever had happened here, Mr. Jones hadn't been able to quarantine it in time. A moment later, an alarm went off, and Monica recognized it as the Code Red for the ICU. Mr. Jones looked around, and then got back on his phone. Monica had had enough, if the ICU was having an emergency, she needed to be there. She stood up and began walking to the door.

Mr. Jones stepped in front of her as he snapped his phone shut. "Where do you think you're going? I distinctly remember telling you to stay here."

"That alarm is the ICU Code Red. I'm a doctor, which means I can help. I'm a lot more useful there than I am in here."

Mr. Jones leaned in close to her and said in a low voice, "You're one of the people who might be infected. The virus seems to have mutated after being in Williams. You'd be more dangerous to your patients than helpful at the moment. Besides, the phone call I received informed me something happened in your ICU; everyone just died. Some sort of fever, so your talents aren't needed. Dr. Jameson is looking into it."

"You mean to tell me every single person in the ICU developed the same illness and died at the same time? Do you know what those odds are? About a billion to one," Monica said in a deathly calm voice.

"Well, then I guess it's a good thing you're not a gambler, because it just did," Mr. Jones said smugly.

She swallowed hard and stood back. She'd just been given a lot of information, the most pressing being she was one of the possibly infected. She'd no idea what she might be infected with; she just knew the end result—death.

"I want to talk to my husband."

Mr. Jones looked at her and shook his head.

"I have the right to talk to my husband if I might be dying, at least let me say goodbye."

"Dr. Simmons, I understand what you're going through, but I can't allow any of you to talk to people outside this room. Now please be quiet." He returned to the corner of the room and kept a silent watch over them. Monica wanted to scream.

Frank had no idea what had happened. One minute he was catching some sleep in the break room, and the next, all the alarms were going off. The lock down had left him short-handed. He ran out into the hall and saw the lights flashing for all the ICU rooms.

Nurses, and he was glad to see, one other doctor were running around like chickens with their heads cut off. He grabbed a nurse and went into the room closest to him. The patient was a seventy-year-old man who just had a triple by-pass the day before. Frank and the nurse worked to resuscitate him, but failed.

He called time of death, but as he did, he saw the man's eyes. They were a milky white color. He motioned to the nurse to follow him into the next room. The patient was a thirty-five-year old woman with severe head trauma due to an auto accident.

She was dead, flat lines across all the monitors, alarms sounding. Frank noticed the same milky white eyes; he ran into several other rooms. Every patient was dead, and every patient had the same eye ailment. He went to the nurse's desk and told her to call the people in charge of the lock-down.

As soon as the words were out of his mouth, three soldiers came in and began to place plastic doors up at the exits and entrances. Frank's heart sank. He knew they were now under quarantine. He leaned against the wall and slid down it, letting himself focus on the pounding in his head.

Monica was about to pick something up and throw it in anger when the private from earlier entered the room. He went straight to Mr. Jones, where he promptly began to throw up blood.

Mr. Jones panicked and cursed loudly. When Mr. Jones raised his hands to push the private away, the soldier bit one of his raised arms, then suddenly turned his attention towards Carly, the paramedic. He broke into a run right at her.

She put up her arm to protect herself, but the private reached her before anyone could react, and he bit her, too. A gunshot rang out. The private's leg gave out for a moment, but then he stood up abruptly, turning to look at Mr. Jones, who had shot him.

The private ran out of the room. Screams were heard, and then multiple gunshots seconds later. Mr. Jones looked down at the blood covering him, his face filled with fear. "Oh God, get it off, get it off of me."

No one in the room moved a muscle to help him, they were too busy getting the items needed to look after Carly. Moments after the incident with the private, a man in a lab coat entered the room, escorted by two soldiers holding M16s.

He surveyed the room, zeroing in on Mr. Jones, then Carly. "Take Jones to the shower room and then bring him back here," he said.

The soldiers walked over to the man in question.

"No, you can't do this to me. I'm not one of them. I'll tell them everything. I'll tell them the truth!" Mr. Jones yelled.

"On second thought, I think more drastic measures need to be taken."

The two large soldiers nodded and carried Mr. Jones kicking and screaming out of the room. A minute later, a single gunshot echoed down the hallway. Monica knew they had taken care of a security risk. The truth would not be getting out today. She wondered if she and the others would ever get to go home, but she already knew the answer.

"You there, with the bandage on your arm, what happened here?" the man asked Carly.

Monica wanted to tell the young paramedic not to answer, but she didn't have time. Carly was mad, and let her temper speak.

"That idiot just bit me. What the hell's going on around here? People are biting one another, we have to be quarantined. And you think guns are the answer?"

The two soldiers returned. As soon as they entered the room, the man said, "Take her out back with the others."

John, Carly's partner said, "Hey what are you doing? Where are you taking her? She didn't do anything. Put her down."

John tried to physically stop them, and got the butt of a rifle to the temple for his efforts. He went down like a rag doll, and Jenny the nurse went to help him. She sat on the floor, cradling his head in her lap as she held a rag to the oozing wound.

The two soldiers grabbed Carly once more, who like Mr. Jones had done, was kicking and screaming, and removed her from the room. Monica waited a few moments, glad she didn't hear a gunshot, though she suspected there would be one soon.

"Who are you?" Monica asked the man.

"My name is irrelevant. What I have to tell you is highly important and classified. The facility where I worked developed a bio-weapon meant to stop all brain activity of enemy combatants when infected. Animal trials were successful."

He stopped talking when his two escorts returned to his side. One whispered in his ear and he nodded. The two soldiers returned to their position on either side of him, awaiting further orders.

"We were preparing for human trials when an accident occurred. One of the vials broke and spilled its contents. Somehow, Mr. Williams became infected. You saw the end result. It killed him. The blood tests ran on him as well as you lot here show there has been some sort of mutation. It would seem the virus kills the body, but the brain is able to reanimate itself. Once reactivated, the individual is mindless and attacks anyone within range."

Monica stood up, between her fatigue, the headache, and now the damn heat in the room she'd had enough. "So what you're saying is there's no treatment, and we're going to end up like the private who just came in here throwing up blood? He attacked Mr. Jones!"

"That's exactly what I'm saying. As far as I know, it's now contained; no one else will be infected."

"So, this is the part where you wait to see which one of us turns in order to kill us, and those of us who don't turn you'll kill simply because we know the truth?" she asked.

The man's face didn't show one bit of emotion as he responded, "Yes, Doctor, that's the most likely scenario."

Frank sat on the floor as he watched the soldiers set up the quarantine zone. His head throbbed; he had a fever, and felt sick. Something started to rise in his stomach, and as he tried to stand, he began to vomit blood.

The soldiers saw what was happening and froze. Seconds later, every individual in the waiting room, as well as the nurses, began to do the same thing as Frank. The two soldiers went to draw their weapons, but didn't see the newly risen ICU patients exiting their rooms.

One soldier was attacked from behind, and bitten on the neck, his flesh torn open. The carotid artery sprayed blood everywhere, including the back of his partner.

Private Jack Hensen felt the warm spray on his back and turned to see a man in his seventies, his chest half open. The old man's eyes were entirely white, void of any other color. Behind the man an IV drip tottered along, various tubes and a catheter dangling off him.

Hensen watched as the old man bent down and began to feast on the neck of the fallen soldier, and gagged when he saw the flesh stretching and tearing off the neck of his slaughtered friend.

He aimed his gun, ready to shoot when a young woman approached him from the side. He thought she might be in shock at what she'd seen because she moved strangely. Then she looked up at him with milky-white eyes.

He lifted his shaking hand to shoot her, but was a moment too late. The woman ran at him, knocking him to the ground. Hensen tried to fight her off, but drool and other putrid smelling fluids were leaking out of her. He tried to avoid them and not gag.

She wouldn't give up, not even when he shot her in the chest. She couldn't be stopped. Then he felt something at his feet. He looked down and saw the doctor from the hallway chewing on his leg.

Private Jack Hensen knew death was imminent; he stopped fighting, and looked around. There were at least thirty infected people walking around, some running.

In seconds they would be all over the hospital, running out into the city. He knew there was no containing it.

It was only a matter of time before it escaped into the world.

Monica looked at the man who had essentially just told them they were going to die, and she felt sick. She was going to give him a piece of her mind, but before she could speak, she was forced to grab her stomach as a weird cramp seized her.

John started screaming for the soldiers to bring back Carly. He tossed Jenny to the side and charged the guard nearest him, wrestling him to the floor and grabbing the soldier's M16. He aimed it at the other solider and fired.

More fine pink mist floated into the air and up through the air vents. The orthopedic and maternity wards were connected to those vents.

John laughed like a maniac and shot the soldier he'd knocked over. Then looking up at the man who had condemned them all, he shot Mr. Jones in the back as he tried to flee the room.

Seconds later, the door burst open and everyone was surprised to see several soldiers enter the room, each of them covered in blood. They looked around, sniffed the air and then turned around. They began to run down the halls. When they reached the main doors, they forced them open, then faded into the night, screaming as they ran.

Monica thought about escaping, too, but then her vision blurred as the milky white film began to cover her eyes, and she expelled the contents of her stomach.

One at a time, everyone from the room began to sprint deeper into the hospital, looking for people to kill. The few soldiers who hadn't been infected were too scared to interfere.

Alarms were going off, lights were flashing, patients and zombies alike were scattered everywhere. Sleeping patients were waking up to infected people feeding on them.

Outside the hospital, the streets were filling with people running around attacking anyone within reach, seemingly unstoppable. At approximately four in the morning, the world had changed, and would never be the same again.

Monica ran down the street, following the route to her house. She couldn't stop thinking about her husband and how she was going to have him for dinner.

DAYS LIKE THIS

REBECCA SNOW

"Mom, can I borrow your car?" Amber—a typical, self-absorbed teenager—called, sliding her hand down the banister's polished wood.

She could hear her parents wrestling in the living room before she entered. Stepping into the carpeted room, she surveyed the scene. Her mother straddled her father and nuzzled his neck as he lounged on the leather couch. His hips bucked against his wife, seated above him.

"Stop it, you guys!" Amber said and wrinkled her nose. "I'm too young to see that."

Amber's mother bit into her father's neck. A torn artery sprayed a warm fountain of blood into the teenager's face. Her chin dropped to her chest as her eyes bulged from their sockets. "Oh my God, Mom, you're killing Dad!"

Her mother stopped eating, turned her head, and hissed at Amber, her eyes telling her daughter that she was next.

Amber, knowing to stay was to die, ran into the hall, grabbed her denim jacket from the coat rack, and the keys from the hook on the wall, and rammed face first into the door, stunning herself for a second.

She shook off her daze to hear footsteps behind her. Turning, she saw her mother and father coming for her, both bathed in blood.

Amber turned the knob and flung it open, toppling the tiny phone table that hadn't held a phone since the mid-nineties to the floor. Glancing over her shoulder, she saw her bloody parents stumbling into the yard. She mashed the buttons on the key alarm.

The car unlocked, locked, and unlocked again before the alarm shrilled, drowning out the screams that blanketed the neighborhood. She yanked the handle and got behind the wheel, slamming the door on her ankle. She added her own shrieks to the chorus of her surroundings.

"Stupid uncooperative doors," she hissed through clenched teeth.

Amber gawked through the windshield and saw her parents shuffling across the lawn as if she'd forgotten her lunch and they running it out to her. Trying to pull her bruised leg into the vehicle, she found that her foot wouldn't move. Fingers had gripped her swelling ankle.

Grabbing the ice scraper from the passenger seat, she slammed it onto the wrist. The fingers loosened, and she drew her foot inside just as her zombie mom reached the car. Amber slammed the door again, this time succeeding. Several of her mother's oozing fingers flopped into her lap.

"Great!" Amber yelled. "I just got these jeans. Thanks a lot, Mom!"

She put the key in the ignition and turned it. The engine coughed once before dying. She beat her fists on the dashboard as her father smeared his face across the glass. She pulled on the windshield washer lever. Bluish spray ran down the sides of his face and turned purple as it mixed with his blood. The wiper smacked him in the nose. Distracted, he rolled off the hood.

The engine sputtered to life. Throwing the sedan into reverse, Amber floored it and backed into a neighbor's yard. She gaped at the carnage in the rearview mirror. Cracked and shattered garden gnomes littered the once pristine lawn.

Returning to her escape, she swerved to avoid hitting the neighborhood troublemaker as he ran from a one-armed girl scout holding an open box of Thin Mints. Amber screamed when her cell phone chirped the theme from Jaws.

"Hello?" she said. "I'm kind of busy; my parents just tried to kill me. Can I…"

"Amber, it's Piper."

"Hey, girl. What's up?" Amber said as she maneuvered the car around a rolling baby carriage.

"Have you been outside?" Piper asked.

"Duh. I'm outside now." She rolled her eyes and dodged a fleeing postman.

"What's with all the crazies?" Piper asked.

"Don't know, but I'm going shopping. I need to de-stress after the stuff my parents put me through this morning. Want to come?"

"Abso-freankin-lutely!" Piper screamed. "Pick me up in five."

Amber snapped the phone closed, regretting the invitation. Piper wasn't in the popular crowd, and her house wasn't on the way to the mall. But a promise was a promise, so she turned left at the next stop sign and hummed as she drove.

A leaning mailbox marked the turn. Trees loomed over the car as it crept down Piper's winding dirt driveway.

The sprawling old mansion seemed to grow out of the vines. If Amber hadn't known the occupants, she would have bet money that a crazy witch with twenty-seven cats and a henchman named Damien lived there. Gravestones in the backyard peeked around the side of the house.

After parking the car, she walked up the creaking stairs and grabbed the brass doorknocker. She picked it up and dropped it several times, listening to the thuds echoing through the house. As she let go for the twelfth time, the door swung open by itself.

"A little slow, but it'll do," Amber said and stepped inside the darkened foyer. "Anyone home?"

A light flickered at the end of a long hallway. Stumbling toward it, Amber heard the door slam behind her. When she reached a lit kitchen, she realized that she hadn't had breakfast. She opened cupboards and unearthed an unopened box of Lucky Charms. Ripping the cardboard lid and stretching the plastic bag until it tore, she reached deep into the cereal bits.

"Score!" she said, pulling out a cellophane-wrapped action figure.

She shoved the toy into her pocket and crammed a handful of marshmallowy goodness into her mouth. She tried to call out to Piper but sprayed cereal onto the floor instead. A moan came from behind the basement door and she opened it. A pull chain swung like a noose from the ceiling. As she reached for it, a hand grabbed the collar of her shirt and pulled her back from the darkness.

"Don't you know not to go into the cellar?" Piper asked. She slammed and latched the door. "Hey, are those my Lucky Charms?"

"I heard a noise. I thought you were down there." Amber twisted as she tried to block her friend's view of the cereal box. "What Lucky Charms?"

Piper snatched the box from behind Amber's back.

"These Lucky Charms," she squeaked. "I was saving them. How could you do this to me? I thought you were my friend."

"I didn't know you were saving them. Your name wasn't on the box."

A loud thump shook the cellar door. Piper ignored it.

"Shouldn't you get that?" Amber asked, reaching for the latch.

"No," Piper said and smacked Amber's hand. "Let's just go."

Piper retrieved a tattered Army coat, a large black zipper bag that resembled a long briefcase, and a backpack from the closet.

"Ready?" Amber asked as she creaked open the front door.

"Drop!" Piper shrieked.

Amber fell to the floor and covered her head as a loud explosion shook the house. When she looked up, a crumpled body lay on the porch. Piper was holding a smoking rifle.

"All set," Piper smiled, gathered her bags and helped her friend to her feet.

"What?" Amber shouted, her ears ringing.

When they were inside the car, Amber turned on the radio, pressed the tuning button, and cranked up the volume. All she could hear was whispering talk radio until she reached a song at the end of the dial.

"High…way to Hell. I'm on the high…way to Hell," she warbled.

Piper switched off the noise.

"Hey, what was that for?" Amber asked when her ears popped.

"That was for eating my cereal," she said. "Now we're even. What are you getting at the mall, anyway?" She wiped the barrel of her rifle with a soft, blue rag.

"I was thinking about picking up a dress for the prom. Marcus asked me. Maybe try out some new shades of lipstick, too." Amber swerved to avoid hitting a sparking power line.

"Wait," Piper said, turning in her seat to look at her friend. "I thought you hated Marcus. You said he was an uber-dweeb."

"Dweebs are the new cool. Hadn't you heard?" Amber peeked at Piper to see she had bought the story. "Anyway, what did you want at the mall?"

"I might check out the bookstore. Pick up a few magazines. Nothing big."

Amber was glad that Piper had let her change the subject. Marcus was a four-foot-seven, chess-playing band geek. He had been the only one to ask Amber to the dance. Even the guy she was seeing from a rival school hadn't asked her. Granted, no one knew they were dating. She guessed they weren't really dating anyway, only steaming up his car windows after football games.

Amber drove the rest of the way in silence. Between animated corpses banging on the windshield and vehicles piling up on the sidewalks and medians, the road conditions were horrible.

When she pulled into the mall's parking lot, the emptiness surprised her. Most Saturday mornings, the place was packed. She slid the car into a great spot next to the elevator in the parking garage. Piper grabbed her bags and stepped out of the car.

"You're taking that thing into the mall?" Amber asked, motioning to the rifle case.

"I don't see why not. I've got a permit." Piper shrugged. "Anyway, I don't think anyone will care."

Piper pressed the elevator's call button. Amber watched the numbers light up and extinguish in succession. A deafening *ding*, almost as loud as Piper's rifle, announced the arrival of the elevator. The doors slid open, and the girls stepped inside.

"Now that's more like it," Amber said to the shiny, metal panels.

"Which floor?" Piper asked.

"Third. We can work our way down." Amber checked her reflection in the polished doors. "How come you didn't tell me I had blood all over my face?"

"I thought you were making a statement." Piper dug in her backpack, pulled out a small pack of hand wipes, and passed it to her soiled friend.

Amber read the ingredients and gasped. "This stuff will *ruin* my complexion, simply ruin it!"

Piper searched in her cavernous bag. "That should counteract any drying," she said and tossed a tube of lotion.

Amber threw the items back and watched as they bounced off Piper's chest and clattered to the floor.

"Hey, watch it," Piper said, annoyed. She retrieved the wayward items and returned them to her pack.

"I'll just pick some stuff up at the Clinique counter." Amber turned back to her hideous reflection and hoped she could remake her face before anyone recognized her.

The doors slid open on the vacant third floor. The glow of the emergency lights illuminated little more than a handful of floor tiles. From the open area in the middle of the floor, the girls could see light flooding the lower levels.

"I guess they haven't turned the lights on up here. We must be really early," Amber said as she stepped into the empty corridor and squinted at her surroundings.

"Let's go down one floor," Piper said, pressing her hand against the doors to prevent them from closing. "It's too quiet up here."

"This is the mall," Amber rolled her eyes. "There's nothing to be scared of."

In the distance, someone screamed. She jumped back into the elevator and Piper let the doors close. The two teenagers stood motionless and stared at each other until Piper said, "What do you think that was?"

"Maybe someone saw a sale tag at Neiman Marcus."

Piper shrugged and pressed the button for the second level. When the doors opened, three figures mashed themselves inside the small space. Before the girls could step off, one of the men slammed his hand on the 'close door' button.

"Hey, what do you think you're doing?" Amber asked the man.

"Where in the Sam Hill did you come from?" the man asked.

"Who are you to talk to my friend like that?" Piper demanded.

"What's going on?" another one of them asked.

"I think I'm going to be sick," the smallest man said.

"Then point it somewhere else," Amber said, pushing his face away from her chest.

"Are you going to let us out of here?" Piper asked as she tried to peel herself off the wall of the elevator.

"Not until we get up to the offices," the first man said. He pulled a key away from his belt and turned it, unlocking the upper floor. "Once we get up there, I'll lock this so none of them can use it."

"None of who?" Amber asked. "I want to wash my face."

"The zombies," the little man with the weak stomach said. "They're all over the mall. We've been working our way upstairs all morning."

"How do you know they're zombies?" Amber asked, cocking an eyebrow at the little man.

"I've never seen shoppers attack each other," he said shaking his head.

"Then you've never been in Best Buy at five in the morning the day after Thanksgiving."

"But there isn't a Best Buy in the mall, and it's April," the first man said. "I'm Paul." He motioned to the little man. "This is my brother Buddy. And this is Jim next to me." Jim grinned at Amber in spite of her blood-covered face.

"Why are you here?" Amber asked.

"Work," Paul said, jingling his keys.

"The lights on the third floor aren't on," Amber informed him. Paul gaped at her.

"What?" she said and shrugged.

Paul's gaze dropped to his hands and rose back to meet her hostile eyes. "We were making our opening rounds when one of the cashiers at The Shoe Factory screamed. We tried to help, but by the time I found the right key, they were waiting to ambush us." He took off his hat and looked at his shoes before adding, "They got Leroy."

The elevator bounced to a halt. The doors slid open to reveal a small, well-lit hallway carpeted in stained, industrial orange. When the group exited the elevator, Paul used his key to lock it to their floor.

"We haven't opened the main entrances, so the public can't get inside," Paul said. "However, some infected employees are locked inside the stores. Other employees that were here to open up this morning tried to help. Leroy and the shoe girls attacked them. I'm not sure how many are out there, but we should be safe here."

"And we can watch the security cameras. I'm not sure how we kill them though," Jim added, pointing at the bank of monitors as he flashed a leering smile at Amber.

She couldn't stop herself from returning the grin, even though she was more interested in Paul. He was hot, but rude. Maybe she could back out on Marcus and get Paul to take her to the prom.

"You shoot them in the head," Piper said.

"With what?" Buddy asked, cocking his head sideways.

"With those." Piper pointed at Buddy's holster.

"Oh, this?" Buddy grinned like a shy schoolgirl. "It's not real."

"They're props," Paul said. His upper lip curled into a sneer as he stared in Buddy's direction. "We can't carry real ones. Doofus here shot a mannequin."

Piper hugged her rifle case.

"Did the mannequin press charges?" Amber joked.

"We could probably get into Sears, grab some shovels, and bash a few skulls," Buddy said, as if he hadn't heard Paul's put-down.

"No, we can't," Paul said with a shake of his head. "The store is full of them. Sears opened early."

Amber glanced at one of the security screens and saw the Sears' gate collapse under a tidal wave of dead people. She thought she saw her aunt Janet and waved at the monitor. Everyone else turned to look.

"We're doomed," Buddy said, crumpling to the floor.

Piper dropped her backpack. She took off her Army jacket, revealing a handgun on each hip and two more in a shoulder holster. Grabbing her rifle, she strode to the emergency exit.

"I'll be right back," she said, one hand resting on the door.

"Wait," Paul said. "You can't go out that way."

"Just watch me." She shoved the door open and ran down the stairs.

An alarm shrieked…and shrieked…and shrieked.

"Can't you turn that thing off?" Amber yelled over the din.

Paul shook his head. "That's why I tried to stop her. We don't have a key," he said, his hands pressed over his ears. "Buddy lost it."

Amber stood in front of the screens and watched a zombie drop. Then another. And another. At one point, Piper passed in front of one of the cameras. A dark spot stained one of her sleeves.

"That had better not be *my* shirt, "Amber mumbled.

An hour later, nothing moved except for Piper weaving through the dropped bodies. She stumbled a little, so Amber figured she was tired after the slaughter. The alarm still sounded and Amber had her fingers in her ears when she felt a hand on her arm. Paul motioned for her to follow. They walked into the stairwell. The door closed behind them and the ceaseless buzzing diminished.

"Why didn't you tell me it was quieter out here?" Amber yelled.

"I didn't think you wanted to miss Piper's stunt," Paul said. "She's amazing, you know. Is she seeing anyone?"

She rolled her eyes and nodded. "Piper's got several boy-friends." she said, knowing that Piper hadn't had a date since going to a middle school dance with her brother. "I'm not dating anyone though." Amber blinked her gold-flecked, green eyes at Paul and smiled.

"Uh," he said and looked at his watch. "No thanks." A thump echoed up the stairwell. "Anyway, I think Jim has the hots for you." He motioned to the door with his chin before he trundled down the stairs.

Amber crashed back through the emergency exit and slammed the door behind her. Jim stared at the security monitors. The alarm still screamed inside the room. The picture on the screen showed Piper stepping in front of the stairwell camera just as Paul reached her. He embraced the quaking girl. Piper wrapped her arms around the man and buried her face in his neck, blood squirting around her mouth.

"Not again," Amber said when she saw Paul's mouth open in a scream. Piper pushed him to the wall and tore out his stomach. "I'm not staying here another minute." She ran inside the elevator and pressed the button. The doors didn't close.

Jim peered at her. "Want some company?"

"Not really." She pressed the button again.

"Do you want the key?" He held up a large, jingling ring.

"Yes." She held out her hand.

"Well then, you want company."

Jim grabbed Piper's backpack and stepped into the elevator. He turned a small silver key in the lock, and the doors began to close. Through the sliding panels, Amber saw Buddy curled into a ball, sucking his thumb.

"What about your friend?" she asked.

"He'd just drag us down, babe," he said and smiled at her.

She shrugged.

"So, where are we going?" he asked, shifting the weight of the backpack onto his shoulder.

"My family has a little cabin on a lake outside the city," Amber said. She pulled a tube of lip gloss from her pocket and slathered it on her puckered mouth. "I figure I'll head there until this thing blows over. At this time of year, no one's there. I should be there by dark."

"Don't you mean *we* should be there by dark?" Jim lifted his eyebrows.

The elevator doors slid open on the almost empty garage. Amber nodded her approval at the heavy panels.

"You wouldn't happen to have a blanket in your car, would you?" Jim asked. "I'm a little tired after all the chaos."

Amber walked to the trunk, wishing she were putting a long garment bag inside instead of rooting around for a travel blanket. She wanted to light a road flare and hurl it at Jim. But instead, when she found the blue and black Mexican throw, she tossed it to him.

"Thanks," he mumbled, diving into the backseat. "Wake me when we get there."

"Even my dad helps drive," Amber said. "And he's a narcoleptic."

Jim was snoring by the time Amber finished her sentence. Leaving the mall, she dodged bodies for the first twenty miles. Although she was tempted to stop and let a few into the back seat to teach Jim a lesson, she was afraid they'd ruin the upholstery. The amount of abandoned cars and corpses diminished as she drove farther from the city. When the monotony of Jim's snoring had driven Amber to her wit's end, she remembered the radio and leaned over to press the power button. The car jerked sideways. Something tumbled over the hood and rolled across the roof.

"What the hell!" she yelled, slamming on the brakes.

Jim grunted from his blanket cave. Amber threw an arm over the back of the passenger seat, turned to look out the rear window, and saw a body rolling in the road.

"Oh my God!" she yelled as she put the car into reverse.

When she reached the writhing form on the pavement, she rolled down her window and crossed her arms on the ledge.

"Hey, mister, you okay?"

Amber heard the man moan before he rolled onto his back. Blood covered his face, and his gas station uniform was torn. She screamed and rolled up her window when he thrust his right arm into the air and raised his thumb. His hand wavered above his body as the tires squealed on the pavement. She didn't care if she had run over him; it was a death wish to pick up hitchhikers.

After driving for another hour, she pulled off the road to rest. She made sure the doors were locked and let her head drop onto the steering wheel. She must have fallen asleep because her next moment of awareness involved a tapping at the window and a gut-wrenching scream; she realized the scream had come from her. The scream bubbled from her throat when she realized the man standing next to the car was smiling at her and looked exactly like the hitchhiker she'd run down many miles back.

"Get away!" she shouted and cranked over the engine.

The spinning tires spit gravel as she drove away from the side of the road. Glancing in the rearview mirror, she saw the man standing like a statue with his thumb in the air. A chill ran down her spine like the time someone had dropped a cupful of ice down her shirt. She must have been asleep longer than she'd thought, but when she looked at the clock, she realized she'd only been parked for ten minutes. She shook herself and checked the rear-view mirror once more to ensure the man wasn't following. He was gone.

The small towns Amber drove through looked deserted, but she didn't stop. The day faded, and the purples and pinks of sunset made her forget the current state of the world. A lone figure stood near the turn for the lake. The man's arm rose as she approached. Reaching into the passenger seat, her fingers closed around an ice scraper's plastic handle. She slammed a finger on the armrest, opening all the windows. As she passed, she hurled the scraper at the man in the gas station uniform. She laughed when it lodged in his skull and she smiled when he fell to the ground.

"Man, I hate hitchhikers," she said, turning the car toward the lake. "Wake up sleepyhead, we're almost there."

Empty fast food bags crackled. Jim snuffled and grunted. When Amber drove under the giant Hemlock trees that surrounded the cabin, a head popped up in the rearview mirror.

She screamed, startled.

"Are we there yet?" Jim asked with a grin.

"Yes, we're here, no thanks to you." She pressed the seatbelt release and pushed the belt from across her lap.

"Aw, come on. We're here now," he said. He raised his hand over the headrest and ruffled her hair. "Safe and sound."

"Don't touch my hair." She spun around and pointed a finger at him. After tossing a menacing glare into the backseat, she reached into the glove compartment and grabbed a hula girl key chain. The metal glinted in the dim glow of the dome light.

"I'm sure we'll find something relaxing to do," he said smirking, then got out of the car using the passenger door. When she joined him, he tried to put his arm around her, but she shrugged it off like an old sweater.

"Did you hear that?" Amber asked, stopping in her tracks.

"Hear what?" He pressed his lips onto her cheek.

She slapped him and pointed into the shadows. "Over there. I think someone's out there."

"Don't be silly," he snorted. "This is the safest place I've ever seen."

A twig snapped. Leaves rustled. A low growl rumbled from the darkness.

Jim's head snapped toward the noise. His nostrils flared. "Let's get inside." He took the keys from her, dragged her into the cabin, then slammed the door behind them.

Amber stared back at the closed door. "I guess that'll do."

A shadow passed by a pane of glass on her right.

"What was that?" Amber peeked through a ruffled curtain. Dust billowed into her nose and she sneezed.

"Shush," Jim hissed. "And drop that curtain before whatever's out there sees you."

She let go of the curtain as if it had burned her hand. Dropping to her knees, she tried to catch a glimpse through the small gap in the flowered cotton material. Jim grabbed her shoulder and yanked her into the center of the room.

"Why are you so scared?" she whispered.

"You wouldn't understand," he said. His body shook next to her.

"I wouldn't have understood zombies before today either." She patted his shoulder.

"How about we get something to eat? We'll talk about this later. Just don't turn on the lights," he said.

Amber heard the couch creak behind her as she felt her way to the kitchen. Opening a cupboard and reaching inside, she felt a disarray of boxes before something skittered over her fingers. Screeching, she drew her hand to her chest. She opened a drawer and sifted through rubber bands, coupons, paper clips, and birthday candles. The flashlight seemed safe in her grip until she flicked the switch and the dimness sputtered, sending the room back into darkness.

"I hope the batteries aren't undead, too," Amber mumbled.

Reaching back into the junk drawer, she found a lighter and grabbed the birthday candles. The tiny, flickering light was enough to see that the once stocked pantry had been ransacked. Chewed open boxes of food and mouse droppings coated the shelves. Amber grabbed an overturned cereal container and saw a dozen pairs of small red eyes reflected in the candle flame. She screamed, dropped the dripping, waxy stick, and ran back into the living room. She tumbled to the floor as her shin struck the coffee table.

"Can't you be quieter?" Jim said. "I'm trying to hear."

"I'm sorry, your highness, but you're being a royal pain." She rubbed her leg and tried not to cry. "My leg could be broken."

Slapping her hands on the carpet to get up, she bumped a chair leg, followed it up, and crawled onto the couch. The two refugees sat in silence until Amber couldn't stand it any longer. She shuffled back into the kitchen and retrieved the lighter, then held it above a can opener and a spoon.

She cranked the opener and dug into the can with the spoon. The beans tasted a little funny, but she was hungry. She scooped the last mouthful of beans in what seemed like just a few bites. She must have been starving. Not bothering with a cup, she stuck her mouth under the faucet and drank, ignoring the stagnant taste.

Something touched her shoulder, and when she opened her mouth to shout, a hand covered her mouth, stifling her. Jim turned her around to face him. In the moonlight, his eyes seemed to pulse. As he gazed at her, she lost the will to scream.

"Did you get something to eat?" he asked.

She nodded and stared up into his unblinking eyes.

"Do you want to know what was outside?"

She nodded again and continued to stare. He took her hand and led her to the couch. He maneuvered through the scattered furniture without a single collision. She couldn't see a thing. Her hand remained in his. Before he spoke, he touched her fingers to his lips.

Something inside Amber gurgled. She burped.

He released her hand and sniffed. "What did you eat? That smells rancid."

"I ate…" She took a breath and burped again, feeling some of her meal trying to escape. "Beans."

Her stomach churned and she sprinted in the direction of the bathroom. Knocking over a lamp, she slammed her forehead into the corner of the door.

"The doors are conspiring against me," she hissed.

She dropped to her knees and felt the fuzzy toilet rug before she found the matching seat cover and opened it. Retching into the bowl, the beans tasted worse the second time. Again, her stomach churned. She realized her dinner wasn't just coming up, it was finding any exit it could manage.

It took over an hour for her meal to leave her. She thought a shadow had passed outside the bathroom window, but she didn't care as she clutched her stomach and rocked on her throne.

When the worst was passed, Amber splashed water on her face. It felt like a bus had hit her and had then backed up to see what was under its tire. She didn't think the hitchhiker could have felt as bad as she did right now. He'd kept hitching. Her knees wobbled as she held onto the sink.

A knock at the bathroom door made her topple to the floor.

"Are you all right?" Jim called.

Amber opened the door and shuffled into the dark room. His hand closed on her arm immediately and he guided her to the couch. She saw movement outside the window next to the door and gasped as Jim pulled her down beside him.

"Did you see it?" he asked in a whisper.

"What was it?"

His eyes still pulsed.

"Don't freak out, but I think it's a werewolf," he said. "It caught my scent. I don't know how long it's been following us."

Amber opened her mouth to laugh when she saw a furry face at the window. An ice scraper's handle protruded from its skull. Jim pressed his hand to her mouth so she wouldn't scream. She whimpered instead.

He hugged her close. They watched the werewolf's head turn to face the road. Amber heard its paws thud across the porch planks before it dashed into the woods.

Jim let out a breath and released his hand from over her mouth. He struck a match. Amber squinted in the sudden brightness as a moan outside the front door broke the silence.

It was the rumbling groans of an undead horde.

"What do we do?" Amber looked into Jim's pulsing eyes as he held the match, wreathed in the circle of light.

Dead hands pounded the cabin walls. The front door shuddered and creaked.

She looked around the room for something to reinforce it but before she could move, rotting arms crashed through windowpanes. The moans grew louder as she ran to reinforce the door.

"I don't think I can take much more," she said, pressing her weight against the cracking boards of the front door. "Apocalyptic zombies, a psycho werewolf, hitchhikers that don't die, ravenous mice, and food poisoning. What's next? Vampires?"

The front door fell to the floor and the walking dead flooded the entryway.

"Now that you mention it." Jim stepped closer, his teeth glinting in the tiny flame. "I am a bit hungry."

SUPERBRAWL

DUSTIN STEVENS

The buzz in the air was palpable.

It began hours ago as the first few spectators straggled in, and had grown steadily ever since. Now, just minutes away from the start of the night, it had swelled into a tone that filled every last corner of the arena.

The sound rose up from a crowd that was as diverse as it was large. In the front rows sat middle-class businessmen, most of them wearing khaki slacks and collared shirts. They'd paid top dollar for the seats, and as the contest drew nearer, they'd spent a considerable amount of time shaking each other's hands and commenting on their good fortune at scoring such enviable seats.

Behind them was a contingent of families. Young boys perched on their father's knees, listening intently as the arena and the ring was explained to them. Young girls with chocolate and butter smeared across their faces from a bounty of pre-fight snacks.

Filling in the remainder of the seats behind them was the redneck crowd. Dressed in jeans and dingy flannels and t-shirts, many wore beards and were already working on their fourth or fifth beer of the night. Large pot-bellies protruded from the vast majority, with mullets and trucker's caps found on the rest.

Already they were restless and agitated, flinging insults and obscene gestures towards the empty ring in front of them.

The last section of the arena was a row of press boxes along the north and south walls. Encased in glass, the boxes bulged out from the ceiling and hung down into the arena. On the north end, the press boxes were filled with the world's elite. All were impeccably dressed and drinking cocktails, swapping stories and casting nervous glances down at the arena below them. A small army of servants ran back and forth, all hell bent on catering to their every whim.

On the south end, the boxes were elongated into two large rooms. On the left was for the press, filled with two lines of reporters all diligently bent over their laptops. Despite the fact that nothing had occurred yet, all were busy typing away. On the right was the announcing team for the night, two men seated in front of a full camera crew, overlooking the ring below.

The buzz hung in the air until exactly eight o' clock. Only then did the announcement team look into the cameras and begin their telecast.

"Good evening, ladies and gentlemen, and welcome to Superbrawl III. My name is Hector Scott and we're coming to you live from New Orleans, Louisiana," the man on the right began. He was a short man, standing just under five and a half feet tall, with receding strawberry blonde hair parted to the side and wearing a tuxedo. A bushy moustache was splashed across his upper lip and saggy jowls visibly shook as he talked. "Joining me here in the booth as always, former Mixed Martial Arts Champion Blaze."

Blaze smiled slowly and nodded his head at the camera. A set of gleaming white teeth peeked out against his black skin, several silver overlays shining brightly. He wore a white dress shirt with a design sewn on it in black and several long silver chains hung from his neck. His hair was trimmed into a wide Mohawk, and despite being indoors, he wore stylish black sunglasses. "That's reigning MMA Champion," Blaze pointed out in a low, gravelly voice.

"Yes, of course it is, my mistake," Scott said without breaking stride, bobbing his head ardently in agreement. "For those of you joining us for the first time, this is the third annual Superbrawl event, by far the largest contest on the Zombie Fighting Circuit each year."

"Yeah, that's right," Blaze inserted, leering into the camera. "To take you back a few years to human sports, this is like the World Series and Superbowl rolled into one."

"Right you are," Scott confirmed. "It all started just five years ago when Congress, concerned about the growing number of injuries in professional sports, shut down football, hockey and combat sports all with one fell swoop. Basketball and baseball soon followed, choosing to close their gates due to dwindling attendance and a revenue stream that was perpetually in the red."

Blaze nodded. "For two long years, the world suffered as athletes in their prime such as myself were forced to the sideline," he said, cocking an eyebrow at the camera above his sunglasses. "Finally, the visionary that is Mr. Marcellus Shine decided to do something about it."

"It's hard to believe the Zombie Fighting Circuit has come as far as it has," Scott said, beaming into the camera. "Just three short years ago we were broadcasting from high school gyms and small town fairgrounds. Now tonight, we're here in front of twenty thousand screaming fans and sending a live telecast out to over two million more."

"Congress may have been able to shut down contact sports for the living in this country, but there's not a damn thing they can do to zombies," Blaze said, showing off his silver-lined smile for the audience at home.

"And what a show we have planned here this evening," Scott said. "Tonight is the culmination of another grueling season and will feature our top four point winners from the Zombie Circuit, facing off in a winner take-all tournament. In the opening bout we have a pair of local boys with Dunc Guidry squaring off against

Beau Robichaud. Following that we'll see the top seed, Jade, go one-on-one with wild card entry The Hutt."

"And before the finals, a little something special for the folks at home," Blaze added with a sly grin. "The women's championship match, featuring Jasmine Cyr and Zydeco."

"And with that, let's take it down to Wiley Xavier, our ring announcer for the night."

At exactly ten minutes past eight, the red felt curtain from the back dressing room parted open and a tiny man with pale white skin and a bald head walked up to the ring. The buzz in the arena grew a decibel louder as he walked down the short walkway and climbed between the bottom two ropes into the ring. From the ceiling, a silver microphone was lowered straight down by a black extension cord.

Xavier caught the microphone with both hands and waited as the service technicians turned it on. It made a loud squeal that momentarily caused the crowd to wince, and around the room children reached to cover their ears. As soon as the sound died away, Xavier cleared his throat. "Good evening, ladies and gentlemen, and welcome to Superbrawl III!"

His voice was deep and baritone, reverberating off the rafters above. He barely got the first sentence out when thunderous applause erupted around him. "If you would, please rise and join me for the playing of our national anthem. Here to perform the honors this evening, being accompanied by Dunc Guidry, New Orleans very own Louis Armstrong!"

A series of whistles and screams went up around the room as the red felt curtain parted open again. Through it walked what was once a short black man, trumpet in hand. Chunks of flesh hung from his face and hands with long stretches of smooth white bone plainly evident. Long tendrils of moss and cobwebs hung from his ears and shoulders and he walked with his left foot out in front, dragging his right behind. A new white tuxedo covered most of his body, specs of bone and dirt dropping down onto it with every step.

Behind him walked a tall, skinny man with thinning gray hair, a long black cloak and a ghostly white pallor. His nose and chin both jutted out sharply from a sunken-in face and his eyes appeared as two black orbs deep-set in his face. As he strode forward, his lips moved in a barely perceptible rhythm and his right index finger remained outstretched, fixed on Armstrong.

With slow and laborious steps, Armstrong climbed into the ring, folding his rotted and decayed body between the second and third ropes and dragging himself to the middle. His face remained a blank mask as he stared forward at nothing in particular, not even noticing Xavier. He planted both feet in the middle of the ring and raised the trumpet to what remained of his lips.

Outside the ring, Guidry positioned himself on one of the two small landings on either side of it. Not once did his lips stop calling out the incantation or his finger leave Armstrong.

Using the bony remnants of his hands, Armstrong raised the trumpet to his lips and began to play the national anthem. The sound of the trumpet resonated throughout the arena, rising into the air and harmonizing perfectly with the sound of the crowd singing along. When finally the last note rang out from the trumpet, the crowd erupted again into applause.

The praise was lost on Armstrong as he slowly lowered the trumpet back to his side, and wearing the same catatonic mask, shuffled himself from the ring. Guidry remained close behind him every step of the way.

As they moved away from the ring, Scott turned to the cameras. "Wow, what a performance!" he exclaimed.

"Yeah, that's why he's the greatest," Blaze added simply, leering into the camera and bobbing his head nonchalantly. "The man's been dead forty years and he's still getting it done."

"That he is," Scott agreed. "And he looks great!"

"Yes, he certainly does," Blaze agreed.

"And you have to give it to Dunc Guidry," Scott added. "That kind of voodoo mastery is not the kind of thing you see everyday. It's that ability to control the dead that has him among the top four bokors going for a chance at the championship here tonight."

"Speaking of which, it looks like we're finally ready to get things started," Blaze said. As he spoke, both he and Scott turned to face the ring below.

Xavier waited until Armstrong and Guidry were completely backstage before stepping back up to the microphone. "And now for our first bout of this evening. Introducing, in the red corner from Ville Platte, Louisiana, Beau Robichaud!"

A swell of cheers erupted from the crowd as the red felt curtain swung open and a zombie standing nearly six feet tall strode through. Built like a whiskey barrel, his chest and stomach both rolled together in one long arc. He was bare-chested and bare-footed, wearing only a pair of black cut-off sweatpants. A heavy red grizzled beard hung down from his face and a thin thatch of red hair crossed the top of his head.

His eyes were locked straight ahead on the ring as he stumbled forward, heavy lines of blood leaking down from each of his ears and disappearing into his beard. A recent gunshot wound blossomed out from the left side of his chest, dark blood running down until it disappeared into the band of his sweatpants.

Behind him walked Robichaud, very nearly a living copy of his fighter. His beard was brown and hair slightly thicker, though he shared the same body type. Instead of sweatpants he wore bib overalls with no shirt underneath. With one hand he gave a quick wave to the crowd. The other he kept aimed at the zombie in front of him. He directed the zombie down inside the ring before settling himself onto the platform along the left side of it.

"And his opponent, coming to you from Chalmette, Louisiana, Dunc Guidry!"

Xavier's words still hung in the air as a storm of boos rang out in the arena. Men along the front rows gave thumbs down and voiced their displeasure while children behind them held their nose and made faces. In the back, rednecks yelled obscenities and tossed popcorn at the ring.

The red felt curtain parted again and through it walked a Mongolian zombie. He stood an inch or two above six feet and had thick shoulders and arms. A long black goatee hung down from his chin, cinched in the middle with a rubber band. His brown head was shaved clean, revealing an open wound that spread across his head like a spider's web. As he walked, dark blood dripped down the back of his neck and ran along his earlobe and onto his shoulder.

Behind him walked Guidry, still dressed in his long black cloak with the hood pulled up. He made no effort to acknowledge the crowd as he walked, keeping his entire focus trained on the man in front of him. Together they moved quickly for the ring, ignoring the shower of disdain raining down upon them.

"And it looks like we're ready to begin," Scott said, providing commentary for the fight as the cameras swooped in around the ring. "For those of you new to the sport of Zombie Fighting, the in-ring competitors are controlled by their respective bokors, or voodoo masters, outside the ring. The fight goes until one of the zombies is unable to continue."

"Or as I like to say, around here we literally mean sudden death," Blaze chimed in.

"Right you are," Scott said. "And with the sound of the bell, we're set to begin!"

The same glassy look remained in the eyes of the two zombies as their bokors summoned them to life. In unison, their bodies became as spry as they had been just weeks before when they were alive, and they began to circle each other slowly. As they moved, a trail of bloody spittle dripped onto the canvas beneath their feet.

Robichaud moved in first, his zombie charging in hard with a heavy overhand right. Guidry deftly slid his zombie to the side as Robichaud's stumbled by, slamming into the ropes and using the momentum to propel itself back towards his opponent. Again Guidry shifted his zombie to the side, this time throwing a hard elbow at Robichaud's zombie as it stepped by. The blow caught the zombie just below the ear, sending it reeling into the corner.

Guidry kept his zombie in the center of the ring as Robichaud straightened his zombie's skull atop its shoulders and circled back towards the center of the ring. Guidry's zombie stood completely motionless and waited for Robichaud's zombie to approach before shuffling two quick steps to the side and whistling a high thrust kick at its chest.

The strike caught Robichaud's zombie square in the chest, hurtling it back into the corner as blood and flakes of skin dropped to the mat in its wake. Without pause, Guidry sent his zombie into the corner after it, swinging with open handed palm strikes at Robichaud's zombie's head.

Chunks of loose skin and blood tore free from the zombie's head as the crowd moaned their displeasure loudly. Many stood and yelled at Robichaud while others simply booed as loud as they could.

Guidry continued pounding away at Robichaud's zombie with both hands until dull white skull showed from both sides of its head. A wide circle of blood, skin and red hair lay on the canvas around them and across Guidry's zombie's chest. For the first time, Guidry himself made the slightest show of emotion, the corner of his mouth curling up into a half-smile. He sent his zombie back three steps into the center of the ring and patiently waited for Robichaud to bring his fighter forward one last time. As soon as he did, Guidry shot another thrust kick at Robichaud's zombie, knocking the head clean from its shoulders. A loud moan went up from the crowd as the skull bounced back across the ring, through the ropes, and onto the floor.

A single plume of blood shot upward, out of the dismembered neck before the zombie went to its knees and fell flat. Ringside, Robichaud waved his arms angrily at Guidry and stomped back and forth across his platform. Across from him, Guidry bowed slightly before taking himself and his zombie back up the ramp to the backstage area.

Scott and Blaze both faced the cameras with large smiles. "And that, ladies and gentlemen, is why Dunc Guidry is one of the best in the world at what he does," Scott said.

"Absolutely," Blaze echoed. "What you saw right there was a very typical Guidry performance. He waited for his opening. When it finally presented itself, he went after it."

Behind them, a crew could be seen hastily cleaning the ring. Two men hefted the remains of Robichaud's zombie onto a cart and wheeled it away. Two more swept the ring clean.

"Wow, did he ever," Scott said. "The longer the season has gone on, the more we've seen Guidry expand his offensive arsenal. Tonight it appears to have grown again, introducing a bit of karate into the mix."

"What you saw was a man willing to do what it takes to win," Blaze said. "Plain and simple. A lot of these guys, like Robichaud, are brawlers. They're great bokors, but their background isn't in fighting."

"Speaking of brawlers," Scott said, "How about this next matchup? The Hutt going face-to-face with Jade."

"Oh my," Blaze smiled, shaking his head from side to side, his eyes wide with excitement. "We've got the biggest going up against the baddest. This one should be fun."

"Indeed it should," Scott agreed. "It appears that the ring is ready, so let's take it back down to Wiley for the call."

The microphone descended down from the rafters in a steady line, dropping straight down out of the darkness and ending in the outstretched hand of Xavier. "In our second bout of this evening, introducing first from Yendi, Ghana…The Hutt!"

Another shower of boos poured out of the crowd as the back-stage curtain parted and a large black zombie strode through, followed closely by an even larger black man. The zombie walked towards the ring with a bow-legged gait, his decaying limbs struggling to support his three hundred plus pounds of girth. His head was shaved completely clean and glinted under the bright overhead light. He was completely naked accept for a loincloth around his waist.

Behind him walked a man that closely mirrored him, only larger in every way. He stood almost seven feet tall and weighed close to four hundred pounds. He wore a pair of thick suspenders to hold up his shiny black pants and beneath them large tattoos covered much of his chest and arms. Slowly he made his way to the ring, pausing in his walk every few steps to stick his long tongue out of his mouth and yelled obscenities at the crowd. Each time he did, another burst of lusty boos rained down on him.

After several long minutes, The Hutt finally took his place on the left platform as Xavier stepped back up to the microphone. "And his opponent, hailing from The Valley, Anguilla…Jade!"

The crowd erupted into thunderous applause as a tall zombie topping seven feet entered. Its body was long and lean, much of the muscle from days among the living still intact. Long blonde hair fell down onto its shoulders and its skin was dark tan. If not for the patch of flesh missing from the left cheek and the blood dripping from its nose and mouth, it could almost pass for still being alive.

Following closely behind was its bokor, Jade. The reigning Zombie Fighting champion, Jade entered the arena with the air of a man on a mission. He was a couple of inches shorter and several pounds lighter than his fighter, though in every bit as good of shape. Chiseled arms protruded from his ribbed tank top and tribal tattoo bands were wrapped around either bicep. Short blonde hair was spiked out around his head, died a deep green hue.

"Oh my, do these two look like they mean business!" Scott exclaimed, an eager grin peeking out from beneath his moustache.

"No secret that there's no love-lost between The Hutt and Jade," Blaze added. "This is the third time these two have met, splitting them at one win each."

"And both times nearly coming to blows themselves," Scott said. "Who do you like in this matchup here?"

"Well, the smart money has to be on Jade. So far he's undefeated this season, using the same zombie in every single match," Blaze said. "On the flip side, The Hutt has shown up with his third fighter of the season."

"Yes, and did you see the size of that zombie?" Scott asked. "That has to easily be the biggest competitor we've ever seen on the Circuit."

"Well, just like in real life, bigger isn't necessarily better," Blaze said.

"Truer words have never been said, my friend," Scott added.

The bell sounded loudly throughout the arena as Jade's zombie began bouncing back and forth on the balls of its feet. Droplets of blood cascaded down from its mouth and onto the mat as dead eyes stared straight ahead.

Across from it, The Hutt's zombie slapped at its exposed chest and thighs. The rotting flesh beneath them appeared to visibly break down beneath the force of the blows, the sound ringing out into the air.

The two zombies stood measuring each other for several seconds before The Hutt broke the tension. He raised the arms of his zombie high in the air and charged forward, the bulbous body shaking with the movement. It covered the distance across the ring in several long, heavy strides, the ring shaking beneath its weight.

Jade's zombie continued to bounce back and forth for several seconds, waiting as The Hutt rushed in. Just before it arrived the zombie calmly stepped to the side, allowing the enormous opponent to slam into the ropes and be repelled back out into the ring.

Jade waited until The Hutt's zombie was in the middle of the ring before rushing forward and burying a thick shoulder into its midsection. The sound of old bones snapping rang out as Jade's zombie wrapped its long arms around The Hutt's and drove it back. A loud slapping sound erupted as the enormous zombie slammed back-first into the corner, matched a moment later by a loud cheer from the crowd.

In one fluid movement Jade's zombie climbed onto the middle rope and began driving overhand punches down into The Hutt's zombie's face. With each strike chunks of decaying flesh ripped clean, dropping down onto the mat and out into the first row. Several spectators picked up small pieces and held them up as souvenirs, others simply shied away.

The pounding continued for several long seconds before The Hutt's zombie reached up with two meaty hands and shoved the attacker away. The feet of Jade's zombie went out from beneath it as it fell back from the second rope, landing heavily on its back in the center of the ring. With two quick steps, The Hutt's zombie rushed forward and jumped high into the air. For a moment its enormous girth hung suspending in the air before crashing down on Jade's fighter.

A plume of bloody spray shot out as the force of The Hutt's fighter crashed to the mat. An audible groan went up from the crowd as The Hutt flexed one arm and sneered at Jade from his platform. "Not so bad now are you?" he called out, raising his zombie quickly to its feet before sending it crashing down with another heavy blow onto Jade's fighter.

Without responding, Jade kept his eyes locked on his fighter, his head rolling up as he peered down his nose with a snarl. Intensity roiled off of him as he waited for The Hutt's zombie to land before unleashing a vicious head butt to the bridge of its nose. A chunk of flesh tore free from his own zombie's forehead as The Hutt's zombie's nose crumbled beneath the blow.

A stream of blood and bone fragment poured from The Hutt's zombie's shattered nose as the force of the head-butt rolled him to the side. Quickly, Jade's fighter rolled from beneath it and snapped a hard kick to the side of the knee. A loud snapping sound rang out as it lashed at the knee a second and then a third time.

The Hutt tried to roll his zombie to its feet, but the knee refused to support its enormous weight. Using the ring side ropes it got as far as standing before the leg disintegrated and the zombie crumpled to the floor in a heap. With brutal efficiency Jade stepped forward and stomped hard on the opposite leg, snapping it mid-thigh. A shard of bone burst through the ashen flesh as The Hutt's zombie sat in the middle of the ring, unable to move.

Jade's zombie stared down at its opponent for several seconds before raising its gaze to The Hutt himself. It stayed that way for several long seconds as The Hutt quivered with fury, snarling and shaking his fists in anger. With one final snap kick, Jade's zombie slammed its foot under The Hutt's zombie's chin. The blow snapped the zombie's chin straight towards the ceiling, tearing a long gash along its neck. Slowly, the entire head fell back, coming to a stop against its shoulders, held up only by the remains of the spinal column and a single flap of skin.

The crowd exploded into raucous ovation as The Hutt stood on the edge of his platform and threatened to come into the ring after Jade. The angrier he became, the louder the crowd got, breaking into a chant of, "Jade! Jade! Jade!"

For his part, Jade and his zombie both stared at The Hutt, he with wild eyes and his zombie with the same impassive look it always wore. After several tense minutes, finally they climbed down and headed backstage.

"Whoo-hoo!" Scott practically spat out at the camera. "What a battle!"

"Yeah, like I said before the match started, bigger isn't always better," Blaze said, visibly pleased with his prediction.

Scott turned at the waist to display the clean-up crew struggling to heft the carcass of The Hutt's zombie onto the stainless steel cart resting alongside the ring behind him. All four of the men were straining mightily to heft the considerable bulk onto the cart. "That was most certainly the case here this evening."

"That one should go down as another chapter in the long rivalry of The Hutt and Jade," Blaze added.

"And more importantly, it sets up a championship match here this evening between local boy Dunc Guidry and reigning champion Jade," Scott said. He turned to Blaze and asked, "You've got to favor Jade in the final as well, don't you?"

"Oh absolutely," Blaze replied. "He's the two-time champion, he's been here before, he knows what to expect."

"But don't count out Guidry," Scott countered. "As we've already seen here this evening, he's definitely one of the up-and-coming bokors on the Zombie Fight Circuit today."

"That he is," Blaze said. A smile grew across his face, exposing his silver teeth. "But before we get to all that, we have one more bout on the docket."

"That's right," Scott agreed. "Time for us to shift gears a little bit to our women's division championship, which features Jasmine Cyr going toe-to-toe with Zydeco. What do you think of this match-up, Blaze?"

"I think obviously you have to like Jasmine Cyr here. Any discussion of women's zombie fighting begins and ends with her. Three years and she's never lost a match."

"This is true, but don't give up on Zydeco just yet," Scott cautioned. "A newcomer this year, she has taken the sport by storm, compiling an impressive 18-2 record this year. And both of those losses came at the hands of Cyr."

"But don't forget, those were both ugly losses," Blaze added gravely.

"Ladies and gentlemen, it's now time for the championship round of the night to begin!" Xavier paused momentarily for the inevitable rush of applause he knew would be coming. The crowd didn't disappoint.

"Introducing first, fighting out of Jacmel, Haiti…Zydeco!"

A medium-sized swell of applause filled the arena as an Amazonian zombie stepped down the runway. Long and lithe, she stood just a couple of inches short of six feet tall and her glossy-black hair reached halfway down her back. Her arms and legs were long and toned, her stomach hard. As she walked, a small trickle of blood leaked out from a thick laceration across her throat. Dark and red, it ran down her chest, soaking her yellow sports bra completely through.

Controlling her from behind was Zydeco, a diminutive black woman nearly a foot shorter than her fighter. Dressed in a long black dress that brushed the floor, she wore black fingernail polish and lipstick. Her hair was matted into heavy dreadlocks. She offered a single nod to either side in recognition of the crowd, walking her zombie directly to the ring and taking her place atop the right platform.

"And her opponent, by way of Mana, French Guiana, Jasmine Cyr!" An even louder surge of applause burst through the arena as a well-muscled woman parted the curtain and strode to the ring. Thick and beefy with arms of corded steel, she walked to the ring in a slow and steady gait. Wearing cowboy boots, jeans, and a blue bikini top, her bleach blonde hair fell about her shoulders as she strode forward. Across her stomach were three evenly spaced holes, each of them open and dripping blood. More blood ran from her nose and the sides of her mouth.

Behind her walked Cyr, strutting as if walking the runway in a beauty pageant. Her smooth, mocha-colored skin was completely flawless, framing a face with full lips and big dark eyes. Her black hair hung in ringlets about her face, and inch long fingernails curled from the end of her hands. A dress covered in rhinestones shimmered brightly as she walked to the ring, stopping just above the knee and giving way to perfectly sculpted calves. As she walked, she kept one hand extended in front of her to control her zombie, with the other she fluttered a wave at the crowd.

"I ask you, Blaze, is there a better showman in all of sports than Jasmine Cyr," Scott asked.

"You know, a few years ago I would have said I was the best showman alive," Blaze responded. "But now? No question it's Jasmine Cyr. Beauty and grace, she kicks ass and she looks good doing it."

"Right you are, Blaze, right you are," Scott agreed. "Just because she makes a living with zombies, her style and charm are still very much alive."

Xavier excused himself as the two fighters stood in the middle of the ring, measuring each other. Behind them, Zydeco and Cyr snuck looks at one another, each measuring the other. Small droplets of blood rained down from both fighters, spattering the mat around them as they prepared for the bout to begin.

With the sound of the bell, both zombies rushed forward, tying each other up in a tight headlock. Zydeco's zombie was several inches taller than Cyr's, though its body looked thin and frail next to the defined muscle of its opponent. The two turned in small circles for several seconds before Cyr's zombie broke free and pushed Zydeco's off the ropes.

The long legs of Zydeco's zombie moved gracefully as it bounced back and used the momentum from the ropes to rush forward at Cyr's.

For a moment it looked like Cyr's zombie would dodge to the side, before deciding at the last second to stand firm and slamming a thick shoulder into its opponent's chest. Cyr's zombie went down hard in the middle of the ring, landing flat on its back. A large smear of blood streaked its shoulder as it stood and watched its opponent roll to the ropes and climb back to its feet.

For a moment the two stood in the middle of the ring, sizing each other up before rushing forward again. This time Zydeco sent her zombie in with a different approach, leading with a hard one-two punch combination. Cyr managed to get her fighter out of the way of them, the thick zombie moving slowly from side to side.

Zydeco maneuvered her zombie in a third time, feigning another combination before backing off and unleashing a hard right hook. The shot caught Cyr's zombie just below the temple, tearing a hunk of flesh from its face and sending it out into the crowd with a spray of blood. Pale bone shown beneath tan skin as Zydeco stepped back in for another hook.

This time Cyr was ready and dropped her fighter to the ground, sending a straight palm thrust into the side of Zydeco's zombie's knee. The force of the shot bowed the joint backward making the zombie momentarily immobile as Cyr's zombie rose straight up with a wicked uppercut beneath the chin. Zydeco's zombie's head snapped up, gaping at the incision across its throat.

In one swift movement, Cyr brought her zombie upright and snapped its fingers straight into the gash. Blood dripped down its hands and along its forearms in long red tendrils, as it hooked its fingers along the inside of the neck. With a loud and guttural moan, it ripped its hands straight down, tearing away the throat of Zydeco's zombie. For a moment it remained immobile, before its chin smashed down into its collarbones. It fell to the mat in one slow arc, its forehead crumbling as it slammed into the canvas.

For several long seconds, Cyr's zombie stood and stared down at the carnage before raising its bloody arms into air and letting out another throaty moan. As it did so, more blood oozed from the bullet wounds across its stomach.

The crowd loved every second of it.

"And *that*, ladies and gentlemen, is why she's the best in the world!" Scott proclaimed. Behind him, Cyr paraded back and forth across her platform, waving to the crowd. Her bedazzled dress caught every stray ray of light in the room and sparkled brightly as she waved with one hand and commanded her zombie from the ring with the other.

"Three consecutive Zombie Fighting Circuit championships!" Blaze said. "There's even been talk of her joining the men's competition next season."

"I tell you what, I wouldn't be surprised at all to see that happen," Scott said. "If there's anyone capable of pulling it off, it would without a doubt be Jasmine Cyr. And speaking of the men's competition, that brings us to our main event here this evening."

"Yes, the moment we've all been waiting for," Blaze said, smiling brightly behind his sunglasses. "Time to see if we'll be crowning a second, three-time champion here tonight, or if the local boy will make good."

Flashbulbs began to erupt around the ring, illuminating the arena in a plume of artificial light. Slowly the microphone was lowered to the ring one last time as Xavier stepped forth and caught it in both hands. Around him, the mat was speckled with bloodstains.

"And now, it's time for our main event!" The words echoed from the far corners of the arena, the crowd rising to their feet in unison and cheering wildly. "Introducing the challenger, from nearby Chalmette, Louisiana. Dunc Guidry!"

The crowd jumped to their feet, their energy shifting from cheers to lusty booing as the curtain parted and the Mongolian zombie walked slowly to the ring. A few small streaks of blood crossed its thick chest and arms, the only signs of its previous bout. Blood continued to drip down from the tangle of open cuts carved into the back of its scalp, a few errant streaks reaching clear down to the band of its pants.

A moment later Guidry emerged, still wearing the hood on his robe flipped up as if he was some kind of ancient druid. His face was completely void of emotion as he walked the zombie to the ring and took his place on the left platform. No effort was made to acknowledge the torrent of booing raining down on him, or of the soda and popcorn hitting his robe.

"And his opponent, hailing from The Valley Anguilla, the reigning Zombie Fight Circuit Champion, Jade!"

Xavier extended Jade's name out several syllables as the crowd exploded with excitement. In unison they began chanting his name in rapid succession, many pumping their fists into the air in rhythm.

Jade's zombie stepped through first, shoving the heavy felt curtain to the side and bouncing back and forth on the balls of its feet. A new chunk of white bone was clearly visible on its forehead, matching the one on its cheek. Bloody spittle dripped from its chin as it swayed back and forth, long blonde hair bouncing across its shoulders.

A moment later Jade burst out behind it, keeping his eyes fixed on his zombie and matching the side-to-side bouncing as it walked.

Intensity almost visibly rolled off the zombie as its eyes grew wide and his tongue wagged out from his mouth as he walked. Veins bulged along his biceps and across his forearms as he bounded to the ring behind his fighter. They both took their places for the bout to begin, neither pausing their frenetic side-to-side movement.

"Dare I say it, Blaze, this could be the most intense I've ever seen Jade," Scott said.

"Without a doubt," Blaze agreed. "I don't know if that first bout with The Hutt gave him some extra juice going into this one, but I can't remember ever seeing Jade this outwardly excited before a match."

"You have to think that means bad things for Guidry, right?" Scott posed.

"Yes and no," Blaze said, "Yes and no. A huge part of this sport is the ability to control your zombie, and too much emotion can actually be counter-productive. We've never seen Jade this excited before, we'll have to see how it affects his game."

"One thing is for certain, too much emotion won't be a problem for Dunc Guidry," Scott said.

"Absolutely not," Blaze said. "The man looks like a statue down there. This building could be on fire right now and he wouldn't know it. We'll just have to see how that works out for him."

Scott nodded. "And with that, let's take it down to the ring," Scott said.

The entire crowd remained on their feet as the bell sounded. On one side Guidry's zombie stood, his large brown shape a motionless mass. Across from him, Jade's bounced from side to side, the overhead lights glinting off of its chiseled physique. At once they began to slowly circle one another.

Guidry made the first move, shuffling his zombie to the side and going for a quick high thrust kick. Jade's zombie slid by the kick and moved to the side, shooting a kick kidney punch out as it stepped by. The shot barely knocked the Mongolian off course as it came to a stop and slowly turned back around.

The two took their respective positions again, rotating and warily eyeing one another. Behind them, Guidry and Jade both locked in on their fighters, completely ignoring the pandemonium around them.

Guidry made the first move a second time, feigning another high thrust kick and waiting for Jade's zombie to slide to the side. As soon as it did, Guidry's zombie unleashed a hard sweep kick to the torso. The blow connected flush across Jade's zombie's flat abdomen, bending it over at the waist. In one quick move, the big

Mongolian stepped in and leveled a heavy elbow down across the back of the skull.

A flap of skin and long blonde hair fell to the mat as Jade's zombie went down face first. The moment it hit, Jade rolled it over onto its back just as Guidry sent his zombie down atop it. Using its knees to pin Jade's zombie to the mat, the Mongolian slammed hard punches down into the side of its head. Patches of skin flew off in both directions as blood streaked the long blonde hair and smeared itself across the mat.

The crowd called out in disdain as the blows continued to come down. Blood stained Guidry's zombie's fists and tufts of hair wafted up into the air.

From the right platform Jade let out a tortured cry and curled the legs of his fighter up into the air. He wrapped the feet of his zombie around Guidry's zombie's neck and snapped him backwards. In one quick movement his zombie was back on his feet. Most of the skin was gone from the sides of its face and above its ears, hanging in tatters from its head or scattered about the mat. Blood dripped down over its exposed skull and ran across its chest and arms.

The two circled each other again for only a moment before Jade shot his fighter forward, firing off two quick jabs and a blistering right hook. The first two jabs hit nothing but air, setting Guidry's zombie up for the hook. It connected with wicked viciousness, sending a spray of teeth and bloody spittle across the ring. As it connected, the crowd cheered wildly.

On the left platform Guidry stretched himself to full height, extending his arms out far in front of him. The energy in the arena rose again as the crowd leaned in, sensing the urgency in both combatants.

With a half-removed tooth still pressed between its lips, Guidry's zombie stepped forward and fired another sweep kick to the midsection. Again it connected fully, doubling Jade's zombie over at the waist. This time, Jade rolled it hard out of the way before the Mongolian could levy another heavy elbow down to the back of the head.

With a quick roll to its feet, Jade's zombie stood erect and moved forward, driving a straight heel kick to its opponent's stomach. The kick landed with full force, driving Guidry's zombie's hips back and its head forward. Stepping forward with one quick stride, Jade's zombie slammed a hard left hook into the opposite jaw. Another stream of teeth and blood shot across the ring in a wide arc.

Every person in the arena was on their feet cheering loudly as the two zombies circled each other again. Each bokor carefully measured the other; Jade's zombie feigned a kick and Guidry's feigned a punch. After several long seconds, Guidry's zombie took a quick shuffle step forward and swung out another hard sweep kick.

Jade was ready for this one as his zombie stepped forward and caught the kick before it could generate any power. It wrapped its upper body around the foot and drove its elbow down into the side of the knee, wrenching it violently to the side. Rising to full height it dropped another hard elbow to the joint, smashing it to a ninety-degree angle from the rest of the Mongolian's body. With one final, violent elbow it tore the lower half of the leg free.

The bottom half of the limb pulled free from the Mongolian's sweatpants as it toppled to the ground. A torrent of blood poured from the leg and out onto the mat as Guidry pushed the hood back from his head and rose onto his toes.

Jade's zombie held the bottom half of the leg in its hands and rotated it to grasp it around the ankle. Holding it like a club, it raised the leg high into the air and slammed it into the Mongolian's head.

Immediately, it fell back to the mat as Jade's zombie raised the leg and slammed it down hard again. Blood and bone scattered across the ring as Jade's zombie raised it one final time and slammed it down hard to the mat.

The Mongolian's face provided little resistance as the leg pounded it into the mat. The front of its skull caved in under the leg, every bit of brain and blood held within bursting out onto the mat around it. As it did, the bell sounded loudly overhead and the crowd broke out into pandemonium.

Jade's zombie left the leg across its opponent's face and raised its arms high into the air. A moment later Jade vaulted himself into the ring and both he and his zombie climbed to the second rope and preened to the crowd.

The crowd responded with thunderous ovation as just feet away, Guidry dropped to a knee and ran a hand over his face.

"Ladies and gentlemen, you're Superbrawl III champion…Jade!" Scott practically yelled at the camera. His face was bright red and beads of sweat had formed across his brow. He was visibly quivering with excitement.

"What a *match*!" Blaze exclaimed, smiling and shaking his head from side to side. "That is the kind of thing that legends are made of."

"And right now in the sport of zombie fighting, Jade is a living legend," Scott said.

"Yes he is," Blaze said. "But you've got to tip your hat to Dunc Guidry. He put up one hell of a fight, giving the champion everything he could handle. This is definitely a rivalry to watch going into the future."

"That it is," Scott agreed. "But for right now, the sport of zombie fighting belongs to Jade. For myself, my partner Blaze, Wiley

Xavier and all of us here in New Orleans, I thank you for tuning in tonight. It was everything any of us could have hoped for and we look forward to seeing you back here next season as Jade begins his push for a fourth consecutive Zombie Fight Circuit championship. Goodnight!"

The crowd remained on its feet, chanting the name of Jade over and over long after he and his zombie had retreated backstage. The crowd stayed long after the clean-up crew that was removing the remains of the Mongolian zombie from the ring and even past Guidry finally willing himself to his feet and stumbling backstage.

Not until the janitors began flipping off the lights did the crowd finally file out into the street, still chanting for their champion as they went.

Even after they were gone, a palpable buzz still hung in the air.

DEADLINE

CHANTAL BOUDREAU

Kimberly Johnson tapped impatiently on her steering wheel, waiting for the light to turn green. Her stomach churned with anxiety, desperate to make it back to her office. Why was it that whenever you were in a hurry, every traffic light you came to had just turned red?

"Come on...come on," she muttered under her breath. "Change, damn it!"

She chewed on her lower lip, a nervous habit she'd had since childhood. She'd known that when she decided to be indulgent and schedule that extra week of vacation, she would pay for it somehow.

No one took three weeks straight off in her office—no one. There was no written rule; she was senior enough that she had four weeks to use at her discretion, but anyone who valued their career prospects never dared to take more than two in a row, and that was considered pushing it. One week was the norm, and two weeks left you open to those wild dogs below you. The ones that were hankering for her position, or the vultures that viewed themselves as her peers, but wanted to weasel their way ahead of her in line for the next promotion.

She sighed, and gazed up in the rearview mirror, primping her ash-blonde hair. She was looking a little bedraggled, because of the rush she was in.

A buzz had started in the office a couple of days before she left for the Dominican, word of a new special project in the making. Kimberly was sure it was this particular item that was at the root of the most recent events—those recent events which now had her feeling so frantic.

She should be returning to work all tanned and relaxed, free of stress and ready to take on the world. Instead, she sat twitching in her seat and biting at her nails, the delay at the lights making her crazy.

Finally, after what seemed like an eternity, the light turned green. She gunned it. Her workplace was only a few minutes away; a converted warehouse on the outskirts of town, one that was gated for security. She hadn't even bothered to stop at her apartment and unpack, driving in straight from the airport. That was how concerned she was about getting back to her job.

"What have you assholes been doing behind my back?" she hissed, as she squealed around a corner.

Her cell phone skidded across the passenger seat where she'd tossed it. She'd taken it out of her purse, hoping to hear something from someone at some point, but at the moment it was as dead as her career prospects likely were.

Her phone had been that way for days: no calls, no text messages, nothing. She'd checked her email from the hotel, and there had been no movement there either. Her boss and co-workers were acting as if she'd dropped off the face of the planet.

She could only imagine a couple of reasons why they would be treating her like a leper; either that special 'confidential' project had really taken off while she was away, and they had decided to exclude her from it, because she hadn't been there from the get go, or even worse...her head was on the chopping block.

Kimberly could see the sign now, marking the dirt road leading up to the building. ***BIO-LOGICAL SOLUTIONS*** was clearly visible, in bold blues and reds. So was the chain-link fence surrounding the parking lot.

It was hard for her to believe she'd been working there for eight years. She'd started off as a young intern in one of the accounting offices, struggling her way further up the ladder by every means available to her, including an affair with one of the executives who was twice her age.

Until recently, it had paid off for her. She was currently one of the three executive assistants to the VP of finance at Bio-Logical and was usually aware of everything that was happening, or about to happen, within the business. That was why she knew about the anticipated special project.

Her sources assured her it was still in development, and that there wouldn't be any action on it for at least two more months. The problem was, in their line of business, sudden breakthroughs were not unheard of, and if you didn't jump on a patent as soon as the opportunity became available, someone else might steal it out from underneath you. It was a cut-throat industry. If that were the case, if they'd had a sudden breakthrough, they might have started the ball rolling without her, and if they did, there were plenty of her peers who would have demanded she be excluded from the remainder of the project.

Kimberly pulled up to the security booth with a screech of brakes and the crunch of gravel. She hurriedly rolled down her window, her eyes searching the dim interior of the booth for a familiar face.

"Carl? It's Kim. I'm back. Would you let me in, sweetie? I'm in a rush," she called out, even though she had yet to see a sign of the man in the shadows. There was no response, and the gate remained closed.

"Damn it!" she cursed under her breath and got out of the car. She dug through her purse frantically until she finally found her magnetized security card. "What a time to take a bathroom break, Carl. Why can't you be here when I need you?"

The man repulsed her. He was large, sweaty, and low on the totem pole, so he offered her no help with regards to advancing her career. She was friendly to him anyway, even flirtatious at times, specifically for occasions like this. Now she was wondering if it was worth it.

Kimberly swiped the card, hastily punched in her code, and pushed the button. Then she scrambled back into the driver's seat and slammed her door closed. The gate began to swing open.

"Thanks for nothing, Carl," she muttered, as she drove away.

She was startled by the number of cars in the parking lot, almost twice as many as she expected. She came to a jarring stop in her parking spot, staring around her in dismay. There were far too many people here for it to be business as usual. She'd been expecting to see the regulars who were there most afternoons, but allowing her blue-eyed gaze to drift about her surroundings, she also noted the majority of the morning shift there as well. This wasn't a good sign, she decided. Something was definitely going on, something big, and they had purposefully chosen to leave her out of the loop.

She swallowed hard, fighting back the lump of disappointment growing in her throat. Her fingers trembled slightly as she collected up her security pass, purse and cell phone from the passenger seat. She also reached into the back seat and grabbed her laptop, shaking as much from anger as from anxiety. How dare they exclude her after all she'd done for them?

Sliding out from behind the steering wheel, Kimberly stood up straight, cleared her throat, adjusted her suit jacket and patted back her hair. Taking a deep breath and assuring herself she could likely find better job prospects elsewhere, if necessary, she started towards the building. Her heels clicked noisily on the asphalt while she approached the door.

When she reached the entrance, she was met by a sight so shocking she almost fell over. There was one reserved parking spot that was hardly ever filled, despite being right next to the door. It was the spot designated for the president of Bio-Logical, a spot that was empty ninety-nine percent of the year, but there it was, the black Mercedes belonging to Ronald Collins. Kimberly's heart began to pound so hard she thought it was going to burst right out of her chest. If Mr. Collins was in the building, whatever was going on wasn't only big, it was monstrous.

Trying to get her knees to stop quaking, Kimberly swiped her card and awkwardly typed in her security code. Her fingers were so jittery she got it wrong the first time, and had to repeat the process. It felt as though she'd downed several espressos on her way in from the airport. She got it right on the second try, however, and the door clicked, allowing her access.

She stepped in, and was surprised to find herself surrounded by dim emergency lighting. That suggested the building was on generator power, and the lights would only be on in designated areas.

"What the hell!" she exclaimed.

There was nothing outside that would have caused a power outage. The weather was beautiful. Maybe, she wondered, there had been an accident nearby that had brought down some power lines, resulting in a black-out for every place on the grid.

Bio-Logical had materials and merchandise that required constant temperatures, be it refrigeration or a certain amount of heat, so if it weren't for the necessity of the generator, she might have found herself completely in the dark.

Kimberly sighed. This latest complication meant she wouldn't be able to use her PC at her desk, and she likely would have a lot of catching up to do. Thankfully her laptop had a six hour battery and she could run off of that to get whatever she needed done while she was there.

She stepped into the shadowy lobby, but the receptionist was nowhere in sight. In fact, the waiting area, which was normally crawling with people, was completely empty.

Oh, double hell! They're probably all holed up in one of the big boardrooms, she thought, pressing her palm to her forehead. *Going over the plans for our big press release, advertising campaign and all of the finance and sales details, no doubt. And I'm fucking missing it all. If I survive this train-wreck, I'm never going away for more than a week at a time ever again. I need to know where they are, so I can play catch-up.*

"Millie! Millie, where are you? I need to know where everyone is...I haven't been briefed yet!" she called out for the receptionist, her blue eyes flashing with impatience.

There was no response, although Kimberly thought she heard a faint noise from one of the corridors. She scowled and snorted.

Fine time to be taking a coffee break, you stupid bitch, she thought. "Millie! You aren't supposed to leave the reception desk without proper coverage. You know that! I'm gonna have to write you up for this, and you're still on your probationary period!"

There was still no response, and she groaned loudly and stomped down the hallway, vowing to find her co-workers, come hell or high water. She was making so much noise that she didn't hear the quiet shuffling and moaning behind her as the gray-mottled, rotting-fleshed petite woman, wearing a nametag that said, **Hi, my name is Millie,** shambled over to the space behind the reception desk. When she came to an abrupt halt near the printer, one of her mucus-covered brown eyes rolled out of its socket to hang against her skinless cheek by optic nerves.

Kimberly headed for her small office, one of three positioned outside of the large and extravagant office of Kevin Flatbush, her superior. She stopped at every door of every room on the way there, hoping to find someone who could give her some idea where everyone had disappeared to. She was starting to believe that she'd encountered some extreme practical joke, and maybe she was being punked, when she stepped into a doorway to an office where she hit a wall of stink. She drew her sleeve up to her face, gagging.

"Alden? Is that you?"

She was staring into one of the smaller boardrooms, where a lone figure in a white lab coat sat with his back to her. It was rather gloomy in the small room, lit only by a few runner lights along the wall, and its occupant was sagging in his chair amongst the shadows.

He appeared to be gazing at a whiteboard covered in figures written in red marker, at the far end of the room. Kimberly assumed they were schematics of some kind.

She was familiar with the man. He was one of the head scientists at the company, and had a problem with body odor. The funky little nerd had always reeked, but she was fairly certain he'd never smelled this bad before. Perhaps, she wondered, he'd been working with the logistics of their newest discovery for days, and hadn't bothered to return home to shower.

Considering how badly he normally stank, despite some attempt at grooming, she wouldn't be surprised if this newest high in stench originated from circumstances where all personal hygiene had been set aside. The fact that she'd been away for so long might have made her more sensitive to his putrid aroma as well.

"Sorry to disturb you, Alden," she coughed. "Where is everyone? You're the first soul I've seen since I came in today. I even missed Carl and Millie on the way in. Where's the party?" She tried to sound friendly and relaxed, but it was hard to disguise her anxiety.

Alden raised his hand very slowly, as if to silence her while he was attempting to concentrate, barely acknowledging she was there. The gesture made Kimberly's blood boil.

How dare he. Alden what's-his-name was giving *her* the cold shoulder? True, she'd dismissed him that way in the past, but as far as the smelly little troll was concerned, turnabout should certainly not be fair play where she was involved. Within the upper echelons of the company, she was far more important than he was—she was certain of it. Mr. Flatbush was going to hear of this, once she managed to get this whole mess sorted out.

Kimberly was about to express this opinion, and swivel on her heels before storming away, when she noticed one item on the whiteboard that stood out from all the others. It was the word 'deadline,' and it was underlined, and there was a date that matched the time when her calls, emails and text messages had stopped arriving. So maybe it was a conspiracy to push her out after all; no one had mentioned any of this to her while she was away.

There were other words on the board she recognized, but bore little significance to her. 'Anti-viral serum' she'd seen before, and 'host organism' as well. 'Ground zero' was another term she was familiar with, but she usually only associated that one with the 9/11 airplane incident. The ones she wasn't so sure of, aside from the plethora of numbers, mathematical symbols and Greek lettering, were: 'degenerative properties,' 'stasis-causing contagion,' and 'eventual parasitic breakdown.'

She shrugged and rolled her eyes. She had better things to do than wait for the egghead to finish pouring over this nonsense.

"Thanks a lot, Alden. I'll be sure to return the favor someday," Kimberly snapped sarcastically before retreating from the doorway, and returning to her search while on her way to her office.

After she'd stepped away, the scientist rose from his chair, ever so slowly, and moved to face where Kimberly had been a moment ago—if face was an appropriate term. He only had half of one now; the skin and some of the muscle was missing along his jaw line to the top of his brow. What was left of the flesh was pink and glistening, and oozing pus. What remained of his tongue had rotted and was mold-green in color. It hung out in the gap beside his teeth, where a cheek once existed. His chest cavity was exposed to the open air, maggots crawling within, the occasional one creeping too far forward and dropping to the floor. If she'd seen him before making her snide remark and turning away, she would have run screaming from the building.

With a quiet scraping, scuffing sound, what was once Alden lurched shakily after her.

Kimberly was half-sprinting down the corridor. She paused briefly at one of the larger boardrooms, one with an amphitheatre layout, but it was empty. She was both confused and frustrated. If she hadn't encountered Alden and seen the parking lot full of cars, she would have assumed that, for some reason, the place had been abandoned. Since that was not the case, why hadn't she come across anyone else? It didn't make sense.

She paused briefly at the washroom to primp and preen herself, reapplying her makeup and fluffing her hair in a controlled manner. Kimberly decided she would have to spend some time at her desk making calls and checking other people's schedules to find out what she'd missed, hopefully encountering Kevin, or one of his other two executive assistants. As long as it wasn't Paulina. The two of them had always had a bit of a rivalry going on, and it had become worse since Alec, the new intern, arrived.

Alec was a few years younger than both women, and the first real eye candy to come their way. Kimberly liked to believe he would prove to be as much of a stud as he was a looker, and she expected to be the first one to test that theory. Paulina, of course, felt the same way. Whoever won their battle of sex appeal would have the privilege of being able to gloat for weeks, and Kimberly hated to lose. Of course, there was always the possibility that Paulina had already taken advantage of Kimberly's absence to make her play. This idea irked Kimberly to no end.

"Three weeks," she muttered. "I shouldn't have taken three weeks. It made me miss the deadline."

Before reaching her desk, she had to pass the coffee machine, and she was hankering for a caffeine fix. She was tired from her flight, and one blow to her ego after another wasn't helping things any. She came to a stop in front of the coffee machine, which to her surprise was stone cold and filled with a dark sludge that was already growing a fuzzy, greenish-white film on the top. She gasped. Clearly, no one had bothered with the coffee for days.

Normally, she was the one to make sure that Kevin had a fresh pot available to him, but she couldn't imagine the others letting that task fall to neglect, especially not with an eager intern upon whom they could foist such a nuisance. Now she was really puzzled. She put the coffee pot down with an exhalation of disgust and proceeded to her tiny office empty-handed, past the rows of cubicles.

The offices surrounding hers were just as vacant as every other workspace that Kimberly had passed along the way. She sat at her desk, pulled out her laptop, and started going through her rolodex. She checked her emails—still nothing—then began to call those on the roster of her best and most regular sources of information. Every single call went to voicemail. No one was even picking up their calls. Either that or they were screening their calls and ignoring hers selectively.

I can't believe these jerks, she thought angrily. *At least they could have the decency to warn me that I'm totally fucked. I've always given them the heads-up when something bad was coming their way.*

She considered Alyssa in marketing. As was fairly common at Bio-Logical, she was having an affair with her boss. Hadn't Kimberly been the one to rat out the receptionist, the one prior to Millie, when she started getting too friendly with Alyssa's lunch ticket? Alyssa definitely owed her. If anyone should be answering her emails or picking up her calls, it should be that little hussy. What an ungrateful bitch.

Giving up on her efforts to make contact, Kimberly decided to go another route. If she was screwed one way or another, it wouldn't hurt to risk getting caught going through other people's things. She might miss something in the dim lighting, even with a thorough search, but it was worth a try.

She attacked Paulina's desk first, feeling the least hesitant about messing with her primary rival's things. All of Kimberly's efforts turned up nothing, so she switched her attention to Joe's desk instead, only a little more reluctant to dig through his desk and cabinets. That hunt didn't yield anything worthwhile either, except a note from Margaret, the head of communications, begging Joe to leave finance and come to work for her. Kevin would have to hear about that.

Since her two peers had nothing to offer, that left Kevin's office. Despite her desperate circumstances, she was still wary about intruding on his space. If anyone could still save her ass, it was him, and if he caught her, she would alienate him for sure. After a few false starts, desperation finally won over caution, and she delved into the stacks of paper he had on his desk with great enthusiasm.

She was there much longer than she planned. Kevin was usually such a neat freak, the typical anal number cruncher, well-organized and highly efficient. Surprisingly, it looked as though a tornado had laid waste to his desk. The papers on it were in a jumbled heap, juxtaposed to the usual order that would be there, and her superior had even dripped something a mustard yellow color onto some of the top sheets.

Kimberly was startled. Kevin never ate in his office, afraid of potential accidents that would result in some kind of spillage. She lifted one of the tainted leafs of paper to her nose, and recoiled in response. It didn't smell like mustard. In fact, it smelled kind of like Alden. Had he been through here? He and Kevin only spoke in project team meetings.

It was at that point that Kimberly's fingers settled on a coil bound report, with the word 'deadline,' and a familiar date on the cover. It had also been stamped 'confidential.' She hoped this was exactly what she was looking for. She carried it over to her desk, and made herself comfortable, nervously preparing to read it. She told herself she'd quickly jam it into one of her desk drawers if anyone came by.

She was only in the process of opening the cover when she heard a noise that made her jump and hurriedly shoved the report well out of sight. She glanced around. It was hard to see very well with the weak illumination from the runner lights, but Kimberly would have known the aesthetically pleasing outline of the man moving into the stockroom anywhere. It was Alec—finally, someone to talk to and maybe even flirt with.

With a calculating smile, she stood up and followed the hunky intern. As she approached the doorway, she noted that the interior of the stockroom was pitch-black. The emergency lighting didn't extend to the small storage area, as it wasn't deemed a necessary space for use during a power outage. While Alec might not be aware of this, being fairly new, she was sure he would have realized by now that the lights in the room weren't working. He did not, however, emerge.

Maybe, she hoped with a wicked grin, he'd seen her rise and follow him, and he was anticipating that she might join him in the darkness. Maybe he saw this as an opportunity to get close to her, on company time. She glanced down. She was wearing a skirt, it would be so easy to just slide down her thong panties and...

She scurried over to the stockroom, quite eager now, her heels thudding against the industrial gray carpet as she ran. When she reached the doorway, a horrid smell wafted from the dark space beyond, and blended with the barest hint of Alec's aftershave.

She grimaced. "Ugh! Alden...not here, too!" she groaned quietly.

Apparently the scientist had been through the finance section, and had managed to taint the storage area as well. Perhaps he'd come in search of markers for that whiteboard. The odor was so bad it almost made her want to vomit, but she wasn't about to let it deter her from the opportunity with Alec. Especially when Paulina was nowhere in sight. Swallowing her nausea, she sauntered into the blackness. It took a few moments for her eyes to adjust to the dark, and even then, Alec was nothing but a silhouette.

"Alec," she whispered seductively. "Were you hoping I might join you?"

He grunted in acknowledgement, she assumed, then moaned softly. The sound made her shiver in anticipation. That was all the encouragement she needed. She shimmied out of her panties and carelessly kicked them aside, then advanced wolfishly on him. She would beat Paulina to the punch.

He didn't resist as she pressed her body against his. He slowly brought his arm around to encircle her.

He's teasing me, she thought and leaned into him, finding his methods titillating. He was softer than his muscular build would have led her to believe. Perhaps appearances were deceiving.

Alec leaned down and grasped her arm, pulling it up to his face. He began nibbling on her skin.

"Ooooo," she giggled. "Kinky."

She didn't want to discourage him, but he was slobbering more than she would have liked, so she pulled her arm away, and nudged his chin towards her face.

"Kiss me," she demanded, pulling him within range.

He obliged, his lips pressing into hers. That was when she realized something was terribly wrong.

With his face right next to hers, she could now tell that the putrid smell, similar to rotting meat, hadn't come from Alden alone. Alec's lips were cold against hers, the flesh tattered, the teeth exposed in places, his entire mouth coated with a viscous slime that tasted horribly sour on her tongue. She couldn't stop herself from vomiting in response as she broke contact.

Kimberly never had the chance to scream. As Alec's jagged, pus-coated teeth clamped down over her lips and tongue, ripping them free from her face, her cry of terror came out only as a noisy gurgle.

CLEAN LIVING

RICHARD SALTER

We walk back to my place hand in hand. We don't say anything; there's really no need. Although we only met twenty minutes ago, already there is familiarity. We've found each other for one purpose: to feel something other than despair for a little while. She has no need to worry if I'm a rapist because really, why would I need to be? I have no need to worry that she's going to go crazy possessive on me and want to get married and shit because the bottom has really fallen out of the wedding industry.

Besides, we're both armed so what's the worst that can happen? I'm impressed by what she's packing. Sure it's just a handgun, but the Browning 9mm packs a punch and is super-easy to maintain. That's what you want these days, stuff that's reliable and easy to keep running.

We've reached my place. She follows me around the side of the house, to a flight of steps leading down to the basement apartment. I point out a hidden tripwire at the top so she can avoid it, and then I go first while she keeps watch. I'm checking the mirrors I have posted all over, looking for any signs of movement and listening for any telltale sounds. Nothing. I unlock the door. Warily, shotgun at the ready, I enter. She comes in behind me, still keeping a watchful eye out.

I close but don't lock the door so as not to hamper a hasty exit. I motion for the girl to wait there. I don't know the redhead's name—frankly I don't need to know. For now, I call her Becca. Mustn't let myself get distracted; need to check every room. I set up the bell over the door so I'll know if anyone opens it. Then I search room to room, which doesn't take long since there's only the kitchen/living area, a bedroom, a washroom and a couple of closets to worry about. Finally I'm satisfied we're alone and so I lock the door.

It's obvious I'm a lot cleaner than her. There's dirt streaked across her face, her hair is lank and greasy and her clothes smell terrible. I lead her to the washroom and start filling the bath with water from the tank upstairs. It's rainwater so of course it's freezing. I set out clean clothes for her—men's garments but it would look odd if I kept bras and panties about the place—and she gratefully strips out of her tattered clothes. She doesn't close the bathroom door—who would dare to do that?—so I get a good view of her firm breasts, slender torso and pleasantly curvy hips, and try not to notice her hairy legs and underarms. The carpet most definitely matches the drapes. I get a fresh razor and shampoo from my bathroom cabinet and hand it to her. She smiles, impossibly happy to see such simple things. She's naked in front of me, this girl I barely know. Like me, she's lost everything, so dignity is a distant memory. I look her over carefully as she turns around. Sure I'm enjoying the view, but at the same time I'm looking for evidence of bite marks.

Still we've not said a word to each other.

I stand and watch her to make sure she doesn't suddenly do something crazy like trying to eat me. She watches me the entire time, too, even while she's washing her hair, and for exactly the same reason.

Finally she gets out of the bath, shivering uncontrollably. I have a towel ready. I wrap her up in it and take her to the bedroom. She doesn't resist or hesitate. She needs this as much as I do.

Sex is a little awkward, after all we don't know what the other likes, but it's nice. I wear a condom of course—the last thing I need is an STD and the last thing she needs is a kid to worry about. As I'm kissing her shoulders, I'm imagining she's Becca. She's imagining I'm whoever she's lost. We're hungry for each other, despite our unfamiliarity. We need basic human contact—animal lust and the simple pleasure of touch and tongues and penetration. And for a little while, we both let down our defenses, we stop watching the door or worrying about what's waiting beyond it. We just *feel*.

When it's over, we lie together, still not talking, enjoying the tingling of our bodies and the feel of another person's skin in contact with our own.

I wake up and she's not beside me.

Shit shit shit! Stupid to fall asleep!

My shotgun is still there because I've wrapped bells around it so no one can move it without waking me. I unwrap the bells as quickly and quietly as I can. I move to the living area but she's not there either. It's dark outside now and the blackout screens aren't up. The light of the moon casts an eerie gloom, enough to see by. I don't dare fire up a gas lamp.

Really stupid, Carl, well done.

The door to the outside is unlocked. The dumb girl left while I was still asleep. She even took down the bell above the door quietly enough not to wake me. She's likely dead by now. Shit! She could have killed me, too. I check my network of mirrors. Something's moving up there, at street level. Is it her? Is she in trouble?

Every instinct tells me to bolt the door and stay inside. But she was nice and, as far as I can tell, she didn't steal anything. I can't believe I'm about to risk everything for a damn girl—I swear to God I should hack off my balls with an axe so I don't let this kind of thing ever happen again.

I open the door and slowly climb the steps, shotgun raised and ready. I'm checking the mirrors as I ascend and I can see someone on the porch of the house above my apartment. Since the original residents are long since dead, I guess it's either the redhead, a long lost uncle come to visit, or…

He's wearing a suit, torn and blood-streaked. His gray hair is matted and disheveled, and he's carrying a battered and bent golf umbrella with most of the fabric torn away. He looks at me somewhat confused, checking out my face, looking for the signs…

"Hey, buddy," he croaks in a hoarse voice. "Can you help me?"

I don't answer. His eyes are sunken. His cheeks are ashen. His stance is all wrong. The blood on his face and clothes is fresh.

"I don't know what's come over me," he says, moving jerkily towards me.

I take a step back. I glance at one of the mirrors to make sure I'm not about to walk backwards into a trap. There's no one else around. I turn my attention back to the man. He's closer now, holding out a hand. One finger is missing.

"I'm kind of lost," he says.

I should have blown his head off by now, but I'm transfixed by one tiny detail in this sea of wrong standing before me.

There's a small tuft of red hair stuck in his teeth.

While I'm distracted, he swings his umbrella and strikes the side of my head. I cry out and pull the trigger.

The crack of my shotgun shatters the night. The man's head explodes in a mess of brains, skull and gore, his headless body crashing to the ground. I stand and stare at the corpse for far too long.

This is all so fucked up! I'm so careful never to get into a situation where I have to fire my shotgun. I wish I had a silencer or something. I listen to the stillness for any signs I've attracted unwanted attention. Even though I hear nothing, it's time for plan B.

I hurl myself down the steps to my flat, open the door, grab my always-ready pack and head out again, only pausing to lock the door behind me. Then it's back up the steps and away at a full run.

This is why I set up a safe house. It's two blocks away, so at a brisk jog I can get there in five minutes. It's actually a pretty cool treehouse in someone's backyard. It's simple, unassuming, and high enough that I can see all around.

I reach it at a run, watching at all times to make sure I'm not followed. As I enter the backyard, I grab the pole that's clipped to the fence and break it free. When I reach the treehouse, I use the pole to snag a rope ladder. I ascend quickly, pulling the ladder and the pole up after me. There's not much room—but that's a good thing. There are no surprises waiting for me.

From my vantage point I can see in every window of the home to which the treehouse belongs, the street beyond the house, the entire backyard, and the neighbors' as well. There's no movement. I've stashed some food, water, another gun and binoculars up here. Another reason I chose this place as my second hangout: I can see my apartment from here.

There's nothing moving around my basement flat but I'm not taking any risks by going back so soon. As quietly as I can, I lower bells on ropes over the edge of the treehouse walls and then I scan the area one more time. Satisfied that no one has followed me, I settle down and try to get some sleep.

I miss carefree slumber the most I think, maybe even more than I miss Becca. I'm constantly starting awake at the slightest noise. It's exhausting. Whenever I'm reasonably safe I try to take naps but they never last for long. Those hours I slept after the redhead and I had sex—that's the most I've slept in a while.

As I start to drift off, I see Becca's face as I always do, but now I see the redhead's face, too. Great. That's all I need, another dead woman keeping me awake. I would have liked to see her again though. She was nice and she didn't steal anything.

The bells wake me up. It's morning and the sun is up, thankfully, so I don't have to move to see. Not moving is always the best policy. From where I sleep I can see three mirrors, all angled to reflect yet more mirrors showing the trunk of the tree and around the base. The bells chime softly again, but there's no one climbing up. I see a squirrel hanging from one of the ropes.

That's a relief.

I check my apartment again with the binoculars and there's no movement. The street is clear, too, so I climb down and head out. Daytime is much easier to navigate than night, though neither is safe. Still, if I keep to the center of the road and have my shotgun ready, I can handle anything fate might care to throw at me. Except a mob of course, but you usually hear them coming from a mile off.

When I get home, I can immediately tell that the events of the night before did draw attention. For one thing, the dead man has been eaten by predators. His mangled suit still remains along with his bones and his umbrella. There are signs someone tried to get into my apartment but it looks like they failed.

I open the door warily, though, and go through my usual routine twice just to make sure there's no one inside. Then I lock and bolt the door and head to the washroom. I take a dump and flush it away, then refill the toilet bowl with rainwater. Then I take a cold bath in silence, my shotgun never far from my hands. After that I stand in front of the mirror and assess the impact constant stress and lack of sleep is having on my body.

My hair seems a little grayer than it did yesterday. My eyes have the usual puffy bags underneath them. There's a nasty bruise on my cheek where the umbrella hit me, but thankfully it's not too painful. Since I'm not going to be looking for any female company for the next few days, I can forgo the shaving until it heals.

Despite the ravages of surviving, I'm still not bad looking. I'm not being conceited—you learn to accept and appreciate what you have and what you don't. For example, I can't carry a tune for shit. I can fire a gun though, and I can survive with no running water, no electricity, no modern conveniences and no grocery store to sell me a barbecue chicken and potato wedges for dinner. Also, I know a bunch of tricks on a skateboard but the damn things are too loud to use to get around. I used to race cars for fun, but now it's hard to find any gas to fill any of the abandoned vehicles littering the streets of Toronto. I can cycle fast, but the problem with bicycles is they move fast enough to attract attention and eventually you have to stop…

I sit down in front of my dead TV and pick up *The Great Gatsby*. When you're busy surviving, sometimes the hardest part is filling the time. Good thing I have a boatload of classics I never bothered to read before.

And this is what the majority of my days are like. Sitting, sleeping when I can, just surviving, keeping out of sight and out of the way. Waiting it out. Looking for things to make life easier and increase my chances of seeing tomorrow.

Because one day it will all be over. One day it will be safe to walk the streets, there will be gas to fill my car and a fully stocked grocery store selling barbecue chicken and potato wedges. One day I'll be able to find a woman who will help me forget Becca, and all of this. Maybe we can have kids and a mortgage and shit. You know, normal stuff. I miss normal stuff.

* * *

For two days I don't go out. On the second day, I'm just getting out of the bath when I hear the soft sound of a bell ringing. I stop moving. Someone has tripped one of the wires upstairs. As if to confirm it, I hear a floorboard creak above my head.

Noises like this should be scary as hell but actually I'm used to it. Upstairs is not hard to get into from outside. I hear sounds coming from up there all the time. Usually whoever it is will try the basement door and find it blocked off, so they'll give up. Sometimes they try and break it down but I've fixed a huge steel plate over it to stop that from happening. They might be 'Clean' folk, just looking for food or shelter. Or they might be looking to eat my brains. One time someone was up there for a couple of days while I stayed silent as a ghost downstairs. In the end I realized he'd taken up residence.

I crept up there from the outside and sliced the damn thing's head off with my katana sword before it had a chance to take a bite out of my face.

The really crazy fuckers aren't the problem because they're not thinking rationally. They don't tend to hang around for long. The Clean folk see there are bodies and rotting food and all sorts of shit—just like in every other house—and they don't want to stay. They might try harder to get into the basement, and if they're armed they're still a threat, but a manageable one. It's the smarter Crazies that are the real problem, the ones who haven't fallen all the way over the edge. They can still reason and think. Hell, they'll even hold a conversation with you about the stock market or the right wine to pair with filet mignon, right before they tear you apart with their teeth and hands and suck down your liver with a bottle of Chateau Margaux.

So the creaking goes on for half an hour and then fades away. In the meantime, I silently dress and pick up my book. I hope he'll go away but a soft ringing from beside me, triggered by the wire at the top of the steps outside, tells me otherwise. Seconds later I see feet move past the first ground-level window.

This is where I have to be careful.

I drop the book, grab my gun and position myself in front of the door. If he's determined enough to break it down—and it'll take some doing—I will only have seconds to pull the trigger. If I miss, I'm dead. If I don't kill him with one shot, I'm dead. If he's dressed like Coco the Clown and I get distracted, I'm dead.

The door handle turns and is released. There's thumping as my visitor throws himself against the wood a few times. Then he goes back to the windows. From my position I can see bits of him but I know he can't see me. The figure peers through the glass. It's hard to tell for certain but I think he's Clean. Doesn't make a huge difference either way. I hold my ground.

Moments later, he's gone.

I stay perfectly still for a full half hour. Sometimes they come back. Other times, you go to investigate to find them just leaving the house opposite. Then it's a 12-gauge slug to the head time and another night in the treehouse. Once I'm satisfied he's really gone, I return to my book.

It's been five days since I left my apartment and I'm going a little stir crazy. I have a stomach bug maybe, because since I ate I threw up a couple of times. Cold canned food tastes like shit so it's hardly surprising I can't keep it down, but I'm really hoping I'm not getting sick. The redhead may have been free of the most dangerous infection but she might have passed on something less deadly.

I guess it's time to head outside. Maybe the cool air will clear the fog in my head from lack of sleep.

I don't *need* anything because periodically I head out in search of stuff to hoard so that I never run out. My place is piled high with cans of food, bottles of water, toiletries, ammunition and other bits and pieces I've found that might come in handy, all carefully hidden out of sight of the windows.

Sometimes I'll come across a mirror that's ideal for the network around the apartment or the treehouse, or sometimes I'll find a huge supply of candy bars that were locked up somewhere and went undiscovered until now. Shit, without chocolate I'd blow my own head off right now. Good thing I have a ton of toothbrushes and toothpaste so my teeth don't fall out, and a set of compact gym equipment to keep those calories burning.

The real problem is going to be winter.

The first winter without gas for the furnace is going to be interesting so I'm stocking up now. Warm clothing will be the key, but I need to figure out a way to at least take the chill off the water. Once the rain turns to snow I'll need to warm it enough to avoid hypothermia. I've collected paraffin lamps and the like, but really I need to come up with a way to heat water in bulk without burning the whole place down. I also need to stock up the treehouse with enough warm clothes to survive minus thirty degrees C temperatures and a wind chill that'll turn me into a Popsicle treat for Crazies.

The cold is a good thing, though. The Crazies and the mobs— they won't be thinking straight enough to worry about keeping warm. I'm hoping the cold will kill them off, like it does the hornets each year at least until the spring. Sure it'll be hard to keep my fingers from falling off, but it'll be even worse for the zomb…

Whoa, nearly said it. Can't quite bring myself to use *that* word. To me it feels cheap, like a Friday night low-budget horror flick. Something that's not real, just for safe-scares. I chuckle to myself as I strap on my body armor. I believe I can outlive this problem and live to see kids play in the streets again and cars jammed on the 401 every rush hour. But despite knowing that as long as I'm careful, I can survive, I'm still scared shitless half the time. I don't want to be eaten. Even more, I don't want to become one of *them*.

There's a special gun, kept in my nightstand, always loaded with just one bullet, just in case that ever happens. If I'm infected, I vow to use it before I turn. It may be minutes or months before the virus takes hold of me, but I won't wait to find out.

Sometimes I contemplate using the gun now.

But no. I can survive and I will.

Before I go out, I open a can of beans. The smell turns my stomach and I fight the urge to hurl. Christ I'm hungry though! I could really go for a steak about now. My mind drifts off to happier times in the local steakhouse Becca and I used to go to all the time. I really miss their prime rib. I've tried hunting wild animals, raccoons and the like, but it's hard to do without making a lot of noise. Perhaps I'll get lucky this time and see a cow walking down the street, just waiting for me to slaughter it, drag its carcass down my steps and…then what? Cook small pieces of it over a camping stove? Say to hell with it, fire up the generator and cook a whole cut of meat? Tempting for sure, but it would be my last meal.

I scratch at my scraggly beard, wondering if I should shave it off first. Nah, no point. I'm not looking for any company today. So I strap on my backpack filled with ammunition and survival essentials and tie a bunch of rolled-up canvas bags to my belt so I have something to carry my spoils home in.

Checking the mirrors outside and holding my gun at the ready, I head out of the door and up the steps. As I ascend, I trip and smack my jaw on the step. Stupid idiot! What the hell? Thankfully the pain subsides quickly, and other than a slight clicking when I open and close my mouth, I recover quickly. The noise hasn't attracted any movement in the street so I take a deep breath and walk north.

I've been in every direction, to every mall and grocery store and to most of the houses in the area. Last time I went to the biggest strip mall I wasn't looking for winter clothing, so it's worth going back and seeing if there's anything left.

It takes me an hour to get there. I pass abandoned cars that are useless to me. I've already popped the trunks of most of them and taken what I find inside. Most have some gas left in them, but the noise and speed would draw attention—eventually I'd have to stop. Skeletons litter the street, picked clean by scavengers. Broken windows, battered paintwork and damaged walls are features of every house I pass, and the grass and vegetation is overgrown in front of all of them.

As I move out of the housing area and into the commercial zone, I start to see people.

They are mostly, if not all, alone. All carry weapons. They make eye contact with me long enough to assess my threat level, then move on. No one speaks. No one offers to help if someone falls from exhaustion or lack of food. We all keep our distance from each other. We're all trying to survive and there isn't much room for trust or charity.

I catch the eye of a pretty girl with blonde hair. She's carrying an enormous machete. Sex is still a primal urge in all of us and it's a good way to bury the hurt. Sometimes I get lucky. I'm not interested today, my stomach is too unsettled and I'm still tense after what happened to the redhead. But the blonde is checking me out and no doubt noticing that I'm cleaner than most, despite the week's growth on my face. The promise of a bath with some shampoo is something worth the cost of admission for many women, who probably don't have a bunch of rain barrels hidden on the roof of their house like I do. She turns away, moving off towards a hardware store in a hurry. Her reaction isn't unusual—everyone's been burned.

The Crazies are here, too. Not many of them, not enough to cause panic, but a few. They're still sentient enough to know if they try to attack anyone they'll get a bullet between the eyes. They stare madly at each Clean person in turn, looking for someone with their guard down.

Sometimes I see them eat each other but I think they prefer us. Some folks are obviously infected but don't seem to have realized it. The urge to eat flesh hasn't become all consuming yet but it's only a matter of time. One man is wearing a 'The end is nigh' sandwich board and ringing a bell, telling everyone to repent. One look in his eyes is enough to tell me his end is long since nigh.

As I pass a shoe store I keep my distance from one of the Crazies beside the doors. He's crouched on the ground, tearing flesh from a human forearm that's no longer attached to its owner. Half his face is missing so I can see the meat in his mouth through his ruined cheek. I watch as the bloody chunks are chewed up by rotten teeth before disappearing down his throat. Feeling queasy, I turn my gaze to the interior of the store through the shattered windows. There are several of them inside, ripping apart the rest of the unlucky woman like a pack of lions around a fallen gazelle. I don't feel upset about it; this is how life is. I'm glad it's her and not me.

One of the Crazies is running, which is unusual. He must be so far gone he doesn't see the guns raised in alarm as he approaches. He's liable to get shot dead—or even more dead than he already is—if anyone considers him threatening enough.

I stare at him for a moment, at the blood and drool dripping from his open mouth, at the wild-eyed sunken pits in his skull, at his left arm clearly broken and hanging loose by his side, at the ragged clothing and single remaining shoe. I consider putting him out of his misery but it would be a waste of ammo and might draw the attention of the Crazies in the shoe store.

Then I pause. He's not running *towards* anyone. He's running *away*.

I step out into the parking lot full of abandoned cars. My eyes fix on a point beyond the fleeing Crazy. I load a shell into my shotgun.

Cha-chink...

Others have already worked it out for themselves. You don't survive this long without knowing the signs. I'm tensed and ready to run but I have to be sure I flee in the right direction.

I can hear them now: a crowd, screaming and yelling, still at a distance but drawing closer with alarming speed. Worryingly, we can hear car engines.

Folks drop whatever they have scavenged and start running. Even the Crazies abandon their macabre feast and flee. I can't be concerned with anyone else. It's time to leave.

The cars arrive first, smashing through abandoned vehicles at the far end of the large parking lot. Crazies who still have enough wits about them to drive are the only ones who use cars now. They don't care who hears them and it's not an issue if they run out of gas or break down in the middle of a bad-place-to-be.

Of course we're all running in the other direction, all hoping we're not the slowest of the group and that some one else will be picked off first. What we don't expect is the bicycles.

Shit, the Crazies are actually getting *smarter*.

The bikes are so quiet that we don't even realize what's happening until they're upon us. We were all focused on the engines behind us as we flee in the opposite direction, right towards...

We're now in deep shit.

People are ripped apart by monsters on bicycles, which is as surreal as it is horrifying. They leap from their seats and tackle the panicked Clean, tearing flesh from bone before a single shot can be fired. One is coming at me. I just have time to aim my shotgun and…

BOOM!

Cha-chink…

The dead thing's bike skids to a halt at my feet and I'm on it in seconds, peddling hard to try to get away. I haven't cycled in a while but I was pretty good. Already I'm more effort to kill than the others, so I'm being largely ignored. Most of the riders are now on their feet, gorging on human flesh. The sandwich board Crazy is being eaten too—Clean or not there is no safety from the 'Mob'. They will eat anything that moves. The cars have stopped and more monsters are jumping out.

I cycle past the pretty blonde who is running from a Crazy. She reaches out to me, imploring me to help her. I know full well that I can't out pedal these creatures with a passenger. All I can do is swing my shotgun around and

BOOM!

There's a hole in her pursuer's face. I carry on without looking back. This is as much charity as I can afford.

I pedal hard, leaving the strip mall and heading out onto an empty street. As far as I can tell I'm the only escapee. Behind me I hear screams and engines and gunfire. The whirr-whirr-whirr sound of my furious peddling and my ragged breathing start to drown out the carnage. Wait, is that…? There's an engine behind me! A car is chasing me and I don't need to look around to see who is driving. There's no way I can outrun them so I head for the entrance to a footpath that's too narrow for cars. The bike wheels squeal as I turn and enter the alleyway, and sure enough I hear the screech of car brakes behind me. The doors open, then I hear loud hooting and hollering. They're chasing me on foot.

I hate riding on such a narrow path. There's no time to see any dangers on either side and I'm rapidly approaching the next street, which means I could burst out into the middle of a horde of Crazies. There's no turning back so I plow on.

I'm in luck. As I emerge onto the wide street, no one is in sight. I slide to a halt at the far side of the road and look back towards the footpath. There are three of them, none armed with guns thankfully. They do have knives. I check my shotgun—five cartridges are loaded. It should be enough. I contemplate trying to outride them but I know I will tire soon given the energy I've expended getting this far and the pounding of my heart. The bastards won't slow down until they've got me.

Now that they're out of the alleyway, they fan out, coming at me with terrifying speed.

Cha-chink…

BOOM!

One of them drops with a gaping hole where its chest used to be.

Cha-chink…

BOOM!

Second one loses its head. Third one is nearly on me. Should I move? I'd never get up to speed quick enough. No choice.

Cha-chink…

BOOM!

I only get his shoulder.

Ah son of a…

The bastard is on me now, all teeth and snarling. This is the closest I've ever gotten to one of them and it smells like death. Oh God it's strong…trying to keep its teeth away from my face. Its hands are clawing at me. Thank God for my body armor.

I smash its nose in with the butt of my shotgun—blood spurts everywhere, but still it comes at me. Die you fucker! My shotgun flies from my grasp but I refuse to be eaten. I will *not* be eaten! Its mouth snaps shut perilously close to my right ear. I can hear its wet breathing, fluid-filled lungs gasping at me. There's barely any skin left at all on its face.

Got it!

My hand closes around the reassuring grip of my compact Beretta. I place the sole of my boot in the creature's chest and push with all my remaining strength, hurling it away. It recovers with blinding speed and comes at me again. I whip the gun around and empty the entire magazine into the ugly fucker's head.

Eventually, it stops moving.

I stand there, breathing so hard I'm amazed the entire Mob doesn't hear me and come running.

I look at all three of the dead bastards, wondering how in the hell they got so organized. All of them were clearly so far gone that all they were thinking about was food. None of them could possibly have their shit together enough to drive a car.

Which leaves one question.

I'm aware of him before he gets within ten feet of me. I turn slowly, realizing that I'm facing a killing-machine smart enough to know the difference between a brake pedal and a clutch. The driver has a gun pointed at me, a Colt if I'm not mistaken. I'm about to be shot and then eaten. He'll probably put a bullet in each leg so that he can eat me alive. They seem to prefer live meat.

Since when did the saner ones start hanging with Mobs?

I'm so tired I can barely stand. I think I'm going to be sick. The gun in my hand is empty and I'll never get a spare clip loaded in time. My shotgun with its two remaining cartridges is lying three feet away.

"You know what?" I say. "How about you and me team up? If you can tame the Crazies, then why not work with a Clean? We could catch you a lot of food that way, and in return I get your protection. What do you say?"

I'm babbling—what are we going to do? Sit down and draw up a contract? I'm wondering if I can get to my sword in time.

His words are slurry but betray a foreign, perhaps English accent. He sounds kind of pissed off, like his gradual transformation into a walking corpse has interrupted his golfing schedule.

"Have you looked in the mirror lately?"

Then he walks away.

I stand there for some time, only moving to pick up my shotgun in case he returns. He doesn't. It will be dark soon—I have to get home.

What did he mean? Did the Crazy break my skin? Am I infected?

I check myself all over. My clothes are torn but the body armor has taken the force of the onslaught. There are scratches on my hands but they're from the sidewalk, not the monster's teeth. Perhaps some of its blood and spittle got in my mouth or eyes. I pick up the bike and pedal as fast as my exhausted legs will allow. Two blocks from my home, I abandon the bike and reload my shotgun.

Cha-chink…

I hurry to my apartment. I do all my usual checks—outside and inside—as quickly as I can, then I put up the blackout shutters and fire up a paraffin lamp. I tear off every item of clothing I'm wearing and examine every inch of my torso, legs and arms using two handheld mirrors.

Beyond the odd explainable scratches, I am none the worse for my ordeal. The creature didn't break my skin.

I stare at my ashen face and suddenly step back in shock.

My pale skin can be explained by the trauma of what I've just been through. My tired-looking eyes can be blamed on lack of decent sleep and regular state of high stress. Even my graying hair can be put down to the simple passage of time.

What terrifies me, what really fills my pants with crap, is that one side of my jaw is detached.

My mouth hangs limply on the injured side. What's more, a huge welt on the skin of my cheek is partially visible beneath my patchy beard. With horror I realize I can actually put a finger inside my mouth through a tiny hole that has opened up.

How have I not noticed a broken jaw? I must have done it when I tripped on the steps. How did I not feel it? Why am I not feeling it now? How did I get a damn hole in my head?

There is only one explanation.

To be so far gone that I can't feel the pain of a broken jaw, *to have not even noticed it at all* — I must have been infected weeks ago. But that's not possible — before today I never had a close-quarters fight with a Crazy and I've certainly never been bitten. Why is the skin on my cheek so carved up? I didn't do that on the steps. How did I get infected? When?

Who cares how and when? The fact of it is: my survival has been for nothing. No wonder I was craving meat. No wonder I felt so sick. No wonder the blonde chick hurried away when she saw my broken damn face.

While I'm still sane, I walk over to my nightstand, open it and take out the handgun. It's a beautiful piece of work, hand crafted and made forty years ago by a friend of the family. My dad gave it to me and taught me how to shoot with it.

I don't want to die. I've worked too hard, lived too long. I'm supposed to be a survivor, dammit! I'm supposed to outlast the apocalypse and get a mortgage. Who the hell is going to lend me money now?

I picture a banker with a briefcase and an umbrella, walking away from me while I implore him to lend me money and sell life insurance to a dead man. Afterlife insurance? See, I'm still thinking up dumb stuff—I can't be one of them!

And then it hits me, or I remember it hitting me. The man at the door who ate the pretty redhead who was nice and didn't steal anything. He swung his umbrella and…it had just a bruise then, but now I can finally brush those hard to reach back teeth!

Shit. So even then I was infected.

Perhaps I got it from the redhead. Have I been wrong all along about how it spreads? Maybe it's like the flu: you can catch it from the air or a door handle. Maybe it takes minutes to change some people and six months for others, but we all have it and will all turn eventually. Maybe every person on the planet is infected and it's only a matter of time…

Maybe it's time to use the gun. I walk to the nightstand and pull it open. The gun sits there, daring me to use it. I pick it up, place it against my skull and close my eyes.

Wait, I can't use this. I was going to use the gun if I got bitten, *before* I turned into one of them.

I place the handgun carefully back in the nightstand, close the drawer and pick up my shotgun instead.

BOOM!

DEADHEADS

TIM J. FINN

Tanner exited the gunmetal gray barracks carrying a Styrofoam cup of steaming coffee. He first sipped it, then gulped and enjoyed the burn as it poured down his throat. He hoped the hot liquid would numb his taste buds in case he needed to operate on any messy ones that night. He stared at the three men grouped outside the doors of the barracks. They swayed in place and moaned to each other. Their still pinkish skin and only slightly sunken eyes marked them as recent additions to the ranks of the eaters. The skin would soon turn pale and gray and their eyes hollow. The gross changes started if they managed to exist long term. He remembered an old restaurant jingle: the meat falls off the bone.

Tanner strode past the barbed wire surrounding the camp's holding pen. Three stanchions of lights illuminated the yard inside the wire. A group evenly distributed between men and women huddled on the brown grass. Two men walked to the wire when Tanner passed. One of them spat at him.

"Traitor. You're a traitor to the human race!"

"Collaborator, that's what you are," the second man said. "Do you feel good about it, collaborator?"

Tanner flipped his middle finger at them. "Eat me. The human resistance is deader than they are. You're just too stupid to see it. This time tomorrow, I'll be alive and kicking, and you two will be dissolving in one of their stomachs."

"And do you feel good about that, collaborator?"

Tanner waved his finger at the men and continued around the barbed wire to a small, split-level structure. Fumes wafted from the smoke stacks attached to its back. He paused to stare at the blast furnaces reflections that glinted off the partially soot-blackened windows. A line queued at the open double doors of the building. The members of the line groaned as they shambled around the doors. He recalled how no one had realized until it was too late that the eaters communicated with each other by moaning.

He waited as the line shuffled aside to allow him access into the split level. Florescent tubes suspended from the ceiling lit up a room the size of two end zones. A waist high stainless steel table sat directly under one of the lights. Hand tools and surgical instruments ran in parallel lines across it. A stocky man hovered over a straight-back wooden chair next to the table. Safety goggles and a surgical mask obscured his features. He wore a full rubber apron with a couple of pockets stitched in its front. Black, white and red streaks stained it. Bloodied latex gloves covered his arms up to the elbows.

"How goes it, Robbins," Tanner asked.

Robbins removed the goggles and tugged the mask from his mouth. "Well, now that you're here and I don't have to look into any more eater heads, it goes all right." He stripped off the gloves, exposing his hairy hands, and dropped them in a metal waste basket under the table, then tossed the mask into a cloth hamper next to the sink opposite the table. He washed his hands and spoke to Tanner as he dried them with a couple of paper towels. "There's one left from my last batch." He gestured to a utility cart a few feet from the sink. A metal half sphere perched on the corner of it. "Flashdance is probably finishing up the next batch. She's working a double today. Maybe so she can see more of you," Robbins said.

"Hey, what can I say, the woman loves me," Tanner smiled.

"In your dreams. I'll see you tomorrow. I got one of the last Buds in existence waiting for me. I put it on ice just before my shift. It should be nice and ice cold now. Have fun, if you call any of this fun."

"You sound like the resistance. This beats being food, or always being on the run."

Tanner donned the apron while he watched Robbins exit, then slipped on gloves and a mask as a corpulent man shuffled into the room. The man dropped into the chair next to Tanner.

"I guess your eater buddies clued you in on things. And nice, no hair for me to worry about," the man said.

Tanner picked up a scalpel and squinted at the man's bald head. Once he'd needed a magic marker, but constant practice now allowed him to simply eyeball the proper spot. He cut into the man's forehead and a couple of pasty blood drops popped from the incision. He sliced along the circumference of the man's skull, cutting apart skin until he reached the back of the head, then pulled out the scalpel and cut a similar line on the opposite side. He pulled back the skin and grimaced at the clamminess he felt through the gloves. After draping the loose epidermis against the neck, he patted the exposed bone.

"Say good bye, top cat."

Tanner lifted a bone saw from the table and turned it on. He hefted the saw as it whirred and placed it against the fat man's skull. Blade scraped against bone as the saw ground into the skull. Tanner steadied it as moist chips spewed out. The saw crunched to a halt as the blade stuck halfway through the skull, so he wrenched it free and leaned in to press with his full weight. With a steady, monotonous grinding, the saw cleaved through the bone until it burst out the back of the head. The shorn, half-skull spun on the floor and rolled under the table. Tanner retrieved it and dangled the half skull in front of the man.

"Want to save it for sentimental reasons?"

The man stared up at him with glazed eyes.

"Yeah, I didn't think so."

Tanner tossed the half skull in the trash can. He wiped bone flecks from his goggles and peered into the fat man's open skull. A thin sheen of mucus stretched across the blackish-gray brain inside. The brain shifted back and forth with a moist pop as bright crimson veins pulsated through it.

"All you eater brains look alike."

Tanner lifted the metal half sphere from the cart and positioned it directly above the man's head. He gingerly lowered the partial orb into the man's skull, then picked up a wooden mallet and chisel. He inserted the chisel between bone and metal and banged with the mallet, forcing the edges of the half sphere into the skull. He pursed his lips as he perused the man's noggin. Gripping the mallet with both hands, he pounded the metal half orb several times.

"There you go, nice and snug as a bug in a rug now." He turned as a short, curvy women pushed in a squeaking utility cart filled with half spheres. She wore jeans and a faded red tank top. A black and red bandana stained with soot and sweat hung around her neck. A welder's masked rested atop her crew-cut, dirty blonde hair.

"Hi ya, Flashdance," Tanner said.

Thompson, the last overnight cap maker, had christened her with the nickname when she first apprenticed with him. He said her outfit reminded him of the old movie about an aspiring dancer who worked as a welder. Thompson passed away soon after that, leaving instructions for his body to be burned in the furnaces to prevent his reanimation.

"Looks like I got here just in time. I'll take the empty back with me," she said.

"But if you leave now, you'll miss another example of my expert needle work."

"Seen it. I have another batch in the oven anyway. See you in a bit." She snagged the empty cart and wheeled it out. Tanner ogled her departing buttocks as they strained against the jeans and wished for a fortuitous tear. He lusted after shorter women, considering 'short' a synonym for 'sexy.' *Thank heaven for little girls*, he often said.

He unspooled a line of thread from the wheel on the table and clipped it free with steel scissors, then slid the goggles onto his forehead and threaded a needle from the tiny oblong box on the table. He placed his palm under loose skin resting on the fat man's head and flipped the dermis over the metal half sphere, then slapped the skin to smooth out any ripples.

Tanner remembered when it contented the eaters to want the cap uncovered, but somewhere along the line they acquired a human sense of vanity. He pinched the skin above the man's cheek and inserted the needle. Pulling the thread through the hole to tie together the loose skin, he pricked more holes and wound the thread around the fat man's head. When finished, he clipped away the excess and tied a knot in the slack ends.

"Once the stitches dissolve, you'll have a nice scar to show your eater friends. And you won't be dead when you get shot in the head."

Tanner waved to the doorway. The fat man slowly rose and shambled out the open door. A redheaded woman shuffled in and sat in the chair next. Tanner gathered her hair and cinched it with an elastic, then picked up the scalpel and mentally measured her skull.

Startled, he jerked upright, startled by a series of thumps on the walls. Angry moans and howls followed the thuds. Tanner backpedaled as several members of the outside line stomped into the room. A man in a three-piece suit cradled a thin teen with unkempt black hair. He dropped the youth at Tanner's feet and the boy's head bounced on the concrete floor. The bumping produced a metallic rattle inside the youth's skull. Tanner looked at the suited man and shrugged. The man growled and pointed to the boy's head. Tanner knelt and observed a circular perforation in a cluster of pimples on the teen's forehead. Drying gray pus leaked from the wound. He inserted his finger into the hole and nearly snagged the latex on the jagged metal he felt beneath the youth's skin. Pulling back when his finger, he touched damp gelatin.

He looked up at the man in the suit. The man growled and pointed again. Tanner wielded the scalpel and cut along a white scar running around the boy's head. When finished, he slid the scalpel into one of his apron's pockets and grabbed the boy's mass of hair, then yanked back and lifted up the teen's scalp.

A dented half sphere rolled around inside the youth's cranium. Upon closer examination of the orb, he saw a ragged hole in the front of it. Something had punctured it. Tanner crammed his finger in and lifted out the sphere. He wrinkled his nose at the fetid stench emanating from the teen's head. He winched as he probed the residue of the boy's brain, then pulled out a small, round metal cylinder with a dented nose. He recognized it as one of the human resistance's homemade bullets.

"How the hell..." Tanner rose to his feet as Flashdance stumbled into the room. Two men with pale skin and hollow eyes followed her. One of the men shoved her and she nearly fell against Tanner. He held the damaged half sphere and bullet in front of her.

"So it's finally come home to roost," she said, eying the items in his hands.

"You know about this? What the hell did you do, Flashdance?"

"I waited a while, until everything was nice and settled. Then I started using what you might call substandard material. These bastards thought they were safe, but surprise, surprise, the resistance isn't as dead as you think, you collaborating son-of-a-bitch!"

"Do you know what you've done?" Tanner asked. "They can't tell differences; they'll blame the whole camp. We've both heard stories about what they do in that case."

"You know what, Tanner? I don't care," she said. "Collaborators should die, and anyone else will eventually probably wind up as food anyway. And you know what else? I'm goddamn sick and tired of it all. The whole damn game. So let's get it started. Come on, freaks." She waved her arm in front of the two men who followed her. "Go ahead and do it. Just do it!"

The men drooled as they opened their mouths and chomped on her arm with their rotting yellow teeth. She grinned at Tanner while they tore out bloody chunks of flesh. The group in front of Tanner lurched towards him. He ducked under their outstretched arms and ran for the open double doors. Tanner stopped short when he reached the outside. A growling crowd squatted on the ground, chewing on pieces of skin and sinew. A blonde in a string bikini stuffed a still beating heart in her mouth. She splashed blood over chin as she attempted to swallow the organ whole. A boy in a football uniform and a girl dressed as a cheerleader chowed on opposite ends of a large intestine. They chewed until their mouths met in the center. A biker ripped gory pieces from the severed arm he held. The arm ended in a hairy hand clutching a half empty bottle of Bud Light. Tanner skirted the group and raced towards the barracks. He slowed when he passed the holding pen. The pen's gate hung loose on torn fastenings, and a snarling crowd surrounded living men and woman inside the barbed wire.

Two of the women knelt in prayer and a bearded man swore at the approaching mass. Tanner quickened his step as he reached the barracks. Another growling crowd dragged people from the building. They bit and chewed as they pulled the barrack's inhabitants out onto the rapidly reddening grass.

Several of the barrack's former occupants wore bathrobes and wiped sleep from their eyes. A Hispanic man in boxers kicked at a girl with pigtails who held onto his right ankle. The girl snapped her jaws on his flailing feet and gnawed off his toes.

Tanner ran around the barracks and headed for the motor pool. Two of the trucks rested on their sides. Half a dozen people huddled in the flatbed of the lone, upright truck. Growling men and women crawled onto the vehicle's back, front and sides. A muscular man in a red speedo groped inside the cab. He clutched the head of a black man behind the wheel and wrenched it from his neck. Blood sprayed the truck's windshield. The muscular man held the black man's head by its hair and fastened his mouth on one cheek. He twirled the head and ripped skin strips from it with his teeth.

Tanner backed away from the motor pool. He ran past the barracks and flattened himself against the wall of the adjacent mess hall. He gasped for breath as he listened to the alternating growls and screams around him. He slid the scalpel from his apron pocket. The eaters only liked feeding off a living body. Escape from the camp seemed impossible. Even if he succeeded, the outside world waited with less than desirable possibilities. He placed the scalpel against his right eye. Thompson was right. Who wanted to become an eater? He shrieked as he jabbed the scalpel through his eye and pressed it deep into the socket. Turning and facing the steel wall of the mess hall, he heard growling and stamping feet approach as he stepped back a dozen paces. Either this or become dinner. Tanner ran and slammed face first into the steel wall, driving the scalpel deep into his brain. He felt blinding pain for a second, then felt nothing as he dropped to the ground.

TWO WRONGS DON'T MAKE A RIGHT

AARON RAYNER

It was only the static crackle of the radio breaking through the silence of the cab that woke me. I couldn't even remember falling asleep. I'd been drinking harder lately. It was all I could do to try and escape the pain and guilt I felt every waking hour. If only it would drown out the nightmares.

I began to rub the sleep from my eyes and instinctively reached for the hip flask in my overall pocket, almost forgetting that Shayne was sitting next to me. Lucky for me, his face was buried in today's paper. I don't know why, but I'd thought about Curtis Reynolds so much more lately.

The image on his face before he died was all I could see in my mind. I thought less and less about what he'd done or took from me; maybe it was just the sleepless nights and double shifts?

"This is dispatch," a voice cut in from the radio, snapping me back. "I need an available bus to attend a possible fatality at Priory Park, repeat, Priory Park, over."

"Great, I got an hour left on shift and we have to visit that shithole," Shayne complained. "Well, I guess we're up then, chief." He folded the paper and tucked it into the glove box. "That's the life of a paramedic."

I wanted to answer, but I my throat started to close up, so I only nodded.

"Hey, Rick! You awake, buddy?" he called out, slapping my leg.

"Yeah, course. I'll…I'll call it in," I told him.

"Hey, don't worry, man, old Shayne will look after you in there."

Shayne had been on the job for almost as long as I had, and like me, he'd watched this town corrode around us, seen the cancer take hold of everything, turning picturesque places like Priory Park to the breeding ground of human depravity it had become. I guess the thought of wading through a river of broken bottles and discarded needles didn't appeal to him. I had my own reasons for not wanting to go there.

"Dispatch, this is Rick, we got that call, ETA five minutes," I said, then hung up the receiver.

As we drove through the quiet, dark early morning streets with the blue light on the dash strobing to red, I couldn't help but cast my mind back to when I came face to face with Reynolds. I'd begun to follow him at night. I'd watch him score his junk, before heading back to the park to get his fix. I had a lot to drink that night, but I never meant to kill him; I just wanted him to know what he'd taken from me.

I knew exactly where to find him. When I arrived, a layer of mist covered everything. I could barely see the trees in front of me. The night was so quiet, not even the wind breathed. I found him slumped against a tree. He looked so helpless lying in front of me, the dirty syringe still buried in his arm. I remember how the anger began to course through my veins, like the heroine coursed through his.

Before I attacked, I told him it was because of him, every night my wife and child called to me in my sleep, begging me to save them. I'm not sure if he understood what I was saying. Any consciousness he felt quickly faded when I sent the first blow raining down on his face. I can't remember how many times I struck him, but when it was over, he was dead.

"We're almost there, Rick," Shayne said, breaking my chain of thought.

"Yeah, great," I felt the knot in my stomach start to tighten.

"Don't worry, my friend, I know just how you feel. This is the last fucking place I want to be."

"It's not that…I just…" I trailed off.

"It's just what?"

"Nothing. Like you said, it's the last place I want to be."

"You okay?"

"Yeah, I'm fine," I lied.

"I don't know, man. You sure you're okay?"

"Honestly, I'm fine."

"Okay, man, if you say so. You know you can talk to me, right?"

"I know. Now let's get this over and done with." I wanted to tell him so much, but I couldn't.

I could already see the faint blue and red glow of more police car lights skirting the distant tree tops as we came to a stop. I was glad they'd arrived before us; we couldn't have risked going in alone. When I opened my door, the smell hit me like a brick wall. I'd smelled it dozens of times over the years, but had never gotten used to it. The warm humid night air only seemed to magnify the stench.

"Jesus," Shayne said coughing, trying to clear the taste of the smell from his throat. "I thought it was a possible fatality. It smells like they've been dead for weeks."

"I know," I said and fumbled for my response bag in the back of the van. I began thinking back to a call we'd attended two weeks ago. The man had died alone in his apartment. He'd been there for weeks before the smell drove neighbors to make the call. He'd probably lived there for years, but no friends or family came to identify the body. I felt a knot grip my stomach, wondering if that's how I'd end up. Maybe it's what I deserved.

"You ready, Rick?" Shayne called, snapping me back.

"Yeah, I'm coming," I said, almost choking on a mouthful of vodka I'd just stolen from my hip flask.

As we passed through the park's entrance, the smell worsened. The warm night made it hang thick in the air, and a light breeze had picked up, carrying it onto us. The weight of the bag that draped over my shoulder was nothing compared to the guilt weighing on my mind.

With every step I took, the image of Reynolds' face become clearer in my head. I could almost picture him slumped at the bottom of every tree we passed, the smell of death getting stronger the closer we got. Further in, the park's lighting became sporadic, a combination of neglect and vandalism.

Our flashlights barely cut through the thick trees and bushes. Shayne's light darted back and forth as he nervously looked around. I couldn't blame him, the place was too quiet.

There was normally always some drunk talking to himself or a fire burning. You might have been able to smell the smoke had it not been for the scent of a thousand decaying corpses carried on the breeze. Neither of us spoke as we made our way in further, then up a small incline and onto the park's deteriorating path. It's loose and uneven bricks meant I had to concentrate to keep my footing. At the top, the path began to slope down and partially disappear beneath the weeds and moss that had begun to reclaim it.

When we reached the bottom, the police car came into sight. It's blue and red lights whirled silently as they reflected off the water's edge. I began to feel an emptiness in my heart. I remembered how the sun used to reflect off its clear water, and how the ducks swam and dived beneath the surface.

I would hold my son and wife close while they threw bread to them. Sometimes, I would just sit and watch them as they both smiled and laughed, feeling the warm summer sun on my face. But all that floats now on the water's surface is debris. Shallow murky water now laps over abandoned shopping trolleys and other discarded junk. I'd begun to feel the pain seeping into my heart, and I could feel my hands start to shake, but somehow, I kept myself from breaking down.

"Where's the police then?" Shayne whispered, his words cutting through the stillness of the night." Well, where are they?" His voice was just above a whisper this time.

"They have to be around here somewhere," I said. "Why don't you call out?"

"What, and have every junkie in earshot hear us. No chance. I vote we wait here."

I was just about to call out myself when I heard a noise. I wasn't sure at first, but it sounded like the breaking of branches. It was too hard to tell which direction it was coming from; it sounded like it was all around us.

"Hello!" Shayne called out, more out of being startled. "You called for a medic?"

No one answered, but the noise began to pick up speed. It was getting closer, and I could hear the sound of brittle branches being snapped; heavy footsteps followed. Shayne stared at me blankly. Whoever was crashing through the trees was getting closer. I hadn't realized it, but I was frozen to the spot. I was staring straight ahead when someone broke through the treeline and onto the path in front of us.

"Shit!" I heard Shayne say, startled next to me, but I was too scared to move. All I saw was Reynolds' ghost gliding towards me, the poor light and shadows playing tricks. It was only as

Shayne raised his flashlight that I could see it was a police officer. But something was wrong.

"Thank God," the officer said in a tight voice. I could see he was clutching his arm, and as he stepped closer, I saw blood on it.

"Are you all right?" I asked, moving towards him as his legs began to buckle. I got to him just in time to catch his fall. "What happened to you?" I asked as I strained under his weight.

"We need to go," the officer said, his voice weak and breathless.

I called over to Shayne as I struggled to keep him upright.

"Just…just hurry!" the man begged, letting out a groan of agony. I felt his weight shift and he became unsteady on his feet. I did all I could to hold onto him, but I lost my grip and my hand slid on his blood-soaked arm. My right knee took the full force of the fall and struck hard against the jagged and broken bricks. I tried to get up again, but my right leg wouldn't straighten. The sudden sharp pain that shot through it caused me to scream. I could feel the shard of glass protruding with my hand before I saw it. The bleeding began instantly.

"Rick, you all right?" Shayne called.

I struggled to reply. Even the slightest movement caused the serrated edges of the glass to cut even further into my knee.

"Rick!"

"Yeah, I'm…I'm okay," I said and gritted my teeth. "But I can't move my leg."

"Okay, Rick, call it in and get some backup, I'll deal with this," he said and began to tend to the injured officer.

I tried several times to get through to dispatch but all I got was static. I figured the fall must have damaged my radio. I tried my cell phone, but the park was a dead zone.

"It's no good, my radio's out, and the network's dead. What about you?"

"Shit! Me neither," he said, checking the display on his cell phone and hearing the static on the radio. "Can you give me some light over here? I need to check him over!" Shayne called.

The flashlight's beam danced off the ground as I did my best to stop my hand from shaking. Every slight movement only seemed to intensify my pain. As the beam settled, I could see the officer's wound glistening with fresh blood.

Shayne franticly tore open a pressure bandage and pressed it firmly on the man's arm. I could see the sweat beading on the officer's brow. Suddenly, I heard the trees around me come to life and two more people appeared on the pathway in front of me. In the dim light I could just about make them out. The smaller of the two, who seemed to sway drunkenly, was female; the dim light behind her cast a silhouette around her long, unkempt hair, and what looked like a tattered old mini-skirt. The other figure stood almost a foot taller. His torn shirt and vest hung loosely off his torso.

"Over here!" Shayne shouted to them. "Rick, how bad is that leg?"

"It hurts like hell."

"Damn, I could really use you, man, I need to see if one of these new arrivals has a phone that works."

"I'll keep an eye on him," I said and went to the officer.

I slowly began to drag myself across to the injured man on the ground, gritting my teeth as I clawed my hands through the soft mud. When I reached him, I heard a dull heavy thud as the man in the vest lost his footing. That was when the smell hit me. I watched as Shayne cupped his hand over his mouth. The man that had fallen began to clumsily try and right himself. His arms and legs began to thrash about, but it was like he was too drunk to remember how to stand.

Shayne tried to help him up when the woman tripped over the fallen man's legs and landed awkwardly on both of them, her head striking Shayne's, before rolling a few feet down the small embankment towards me. She didn't move at first, her body lying face down, motionless. I heard Shayne groan slightly as he started to rub the side of his head.

"You all right, pal?" I called.

"Yeah I'm good. She just caught me on the temple. How is she?"

When I looked down, the woman was moving. I noticed her eyes staring straight at me. I was close enough for me to see her mouth was gaping open. Thin strands of saliva trickled down her chin. Her eyes looked white and lifeless. I was about to ask if she was hurt, when out of the corner of my eye, I saw the officer start to move.

His arms and legs began to twitch, before a violent spasm took hold of his entire body. I looked down to see his eyes wide with fear, staring straight into mine. He started to convulse, forcing what looked like a mixture of blood and vomit out of his mouth. I moved to get him on his side to stop him from aspirating on it, but his hand grasped hold of my overalls. I tried to work myself free when the fallen woman's hand latched onto the officer's face. She slowly began to pull herself towards him. Suddenly, I heard an agonizing scream cut through the air.

"He's got my fucking arm!" Shayne shouted, as the man in the vest bit into it.

I tried to yank myself free to get to Shayne, when I heard the wet crunch next to me. The woman had joined in and they looked like two lovers caught in an embrace. It was only as the woman jolted her head back that I saw the gaping hole in Shayne's face. Small threads of skin and sinew were still attached as she began devouring the mouthful.

The officer continued to convulse on the ground, oblivious to what was happening. I edged myself back, almost blacking out from the pain in my knee. I turned toward Shayne. It all happened so fast; he must have lost his footing. The man in the vest was right on top of him. Shayne's arms and legs flailed wildly as the man tore free a mouthful of Shayne's throat. I heard Shayne's voice gurgle as he tried to let out a scream. I ignored the pain in my knee and got to my feet. I moved as fast as I could, dragging my injured leg behind me. By the time I reached him, Shayne had managed to push the man off and get free.

"Shayne!" I shouted and collapsed beside him; he didn't answer. I could see the blood slowly pumping from his torn neck. "Come on, buddy." I desperately clasped my hand around the wound, trying to get him to respond, but he wouldn't.

For a few seconds it all went silent around me. I just stared into Shayne's eyes and watched as he slipped away. It was only the hand grabbing my foot that snapped me back. Shayne's attacker began to claw his way forward, his bony and jagged fingers gouging their way into my lower leg. I couldn't believe what was happening; the events of the last few minutes had left me numb and unable to react. I just stared, helpless, looking into his vacant, milky eyes.

I could smell the faint metallic scent of blood that dripped off his lips over the stench of decay. His hands began to work their way up my leg before clutching at my bloodied knee. The pain caused me to instinctively recoil my leg back and bring the other crashing into his face.

I crawled backwards a few feet over Shayne's lifeless body until it was between me and the attacker, who by now was slowly dragging himself up again. His eyes were still fixed on me. His mouth opened, and he let out a low, rasping moan. It was followed by another, but this one came from my left.

I turned to see the woman stumbling forward, her unsteady legs bowing, arms outstretched. She ignored the wounded officer who now lay motionless and continued towards me. My mind was screaming for me to run, but my body refused to move. She was just inches away when something in me began to push the fear aside. A shrill cry of agony escaped me as I got to my feet and began to move away. I headed towards the trees in the hope that I could lose them. Every painful step I took was matched by every unsteady one of theirs.

The wet, dew-covered leaves began to slap against me as I retreated deeper into the foliage. I could hear them still coming, their clumsy bodies colliding with the branches. I soon became swallowed in the darkness and shadows of the trees. I carried on, the branches tearing at my exposed skin, and what felt like bullets impacting on my injured knee as I navigated my way through the pitch-black and over uneven ground.

I stopped to listen.

I could hear them crashing blindly behind me, but I'd managed to put a little distance between us. I nestled myself between a copse of small trees, hoping to catch my breath. All I could hear was the blood pumping in my ears and my heavy breathing.

Suddenly, someone broke through the bushes in front of me. I felt their heavy footsteps through the ground as they charged past me and headed off into the distance.

I held my hand over my mouth to try and silence my breathing. Before long, I heard twigs and fallen branches being broken underfoot and caught their stench as the two attackers shambled by me, then stumbled away.

I knew I had to move; I was losing too much blood. If I didn't make it back to the ambulance soon, I wouldn't make it out alive. I backtracked and soon broke through the treeline to where

Shayne's lifeless body was, but as I got closer I could see it was convulsing. I didn't understand. I'd watched him die.

I was about to reach him when someone collided with me from behind, knocking every ounce of breath from my body. We both fell to a heap on the ground. A flash of colors shot before my eyes as the back of my head struck the soft earth. It only lasted for a second, but before I had a chance to move, the body of the police officer was on me. His jaw snapped shut, just missing my face. I somehow managed to place my elbow underneath his chin and keep him from latching onto me. I stared into his eyes, shocked. Bitter-smelling saliva leaked from his open mouth and onto my face. His grip never let up. My arm began to fatigue and I was struggling to get air into my already burning lungs. I punched at his face furiously with my opposite hand, but he never even flinched.

By now I could feel his weight becoming too much as his face moved closer to mine, his mouth opening and closing in a frenzy, hands trying desperately to pull me even nearer. I turned my head, trying to put a few inches between us, when I saw 'it' lying there; its silver beam stretching across the patchy grass. I reached out and felt the cold metal cylinder on my fingertips, and with one final stretch it was clasped firmly in my hand.

Before he was able to bite again, I swung the heavy flashlight down. I heard and felt a dull, wet thump as it struck his head, and then another when I hit him again. The impact of the second blow caused his skull to give way. His body crumpled. I tried to move and get him off, but I couldn't. My body felt too weak and my eyes heavy. The thud of my heart beating in my chest began to sound distant.

I passed out.

The wind lightly rustled through the leaves and tree tops, as the sun pushed towards the early morning sky. I managed to roll the dead officer's body off me. The light breeze sent a shiver through me as it cooled against the blood on my leg. I slowly sat up, trying to remember everything that had happened. Maybe it was a dream, I thought, before I caught the two of them out of the corner of my eye. They stumbled out of the treeline straight towards me.

As the wind blew, I caught the smell of decay. I forced myself up, my leg shaking unsteadily as it took my weight. I moved as best I could, but the glass had pushed further into my knee during my struggle. It was bleeding heavily now, but I could do nothing for it. I slowly shuffled out of the park.

My head swam as I covered the last few yards to the ambulance, its blue and red light flashing silently as the first rays of the sun hit the dilapidated houses across the street. I could feel the bile beginning to rise in my stomach as the blood drained from my face. I stumbled forward and collided with the bumper and began to vomit. The smell of partially digested food and vodka only forced me to vomit more. I wiped the residue from my mouth, tears falling from my eyes.

When I focused, I could see them still lumbering behind me, only now there was someone else with them, someone I knew all to well. It was Shayne. His medic's overalls—now blood-soaked— flashed in the sun as he came at me, knocking aside the other two in his path. The woman fell to the ground while the man in the vest managed to keep his balance and carry on.

The bile was still burning the back of my throat as I tried to call out to him. There was no reply. I knew deep down he was gone. Whatever had happened to these people had happened to Shayne. Using the side of the vehicle for support, I staggered to the driver's door.

"Shit!" I cursed out loud, realizing the door was locked.

I fumbled for the keys in my pocket, and heard Shayne getting closer. My hands were shaking as I tried to get the key in the door, but I opened it just in time. I pulled myself into the driver's seat with my bad leg trailing behind.

Ignoring the pain, I forced myself in and slammed the door closed, slapping the lock down with my hand. Shayne's face slammed into the window a moment later, spreading a greasy smear of blood and spittle across the glass. He started biting at the glass. All I could do was stare helplessly into the vacant, lifeless eyes of what had once been my friend. He was soon joined by the other two, who in turn began to claw and chew at the glass, leaving equally disgusting stains.

I tried to put the key into the ignition but as it slid in, I twisted it wrong in my panic and it broke. I couldn't leave; not by driving away. I was trapped.

The sound of pounding fists became deafening as they relentlessly beat on the windows; the glass would break soon, especially when one of them picked up a rock and began using it as a bludgeon.

I began to ease myself into the back of the van, all the while fighting off the waves of unconsciousness that washed over my tired and battered body.

The sounds around me started to become distant, and before I closed my eyes, I watched the sunlight spill in through the breaking windows and began to think about my wife and child. I remembered so clearly the smile on Curtis Reynolds' face as he walked free from court, his friends and family throwing their arms around him in celebration.

All I could see was Lisa and Noah's lifeless bodies lying dead in the morgue. I just wanted him to feel what I felt inside that day: dead. It was supposed to take away my pain; take away the nightmares, but it just made them worse. Every day I thought about taking my own life in the hope that maybe I'd be with them again, but I couldn't. It's not what they would have wanted.

Finally, I passed out from blood loss, never to awaken.

When I opened my eyes it was day. The curtains moved as the warm summer air blew around the room. I could smell and feel my wife's perfect brown hair as she lay sleeping next to me. Noah moved closer into my shoulder and I held him tight, his soft breath hitting my check as he slept.

I whispered softly to them, telling them I loved them both, and begged for their forgiveness.

Then, for the first time since their death, I prayed. I begged God to not let me wake, but instead to let me lie here with them.

If only for a little while.

MAD

MAX BOOTH III

This will be a report on the Creutzfeldt-Jakob disease (CJD) epidemic that has penetrated the unincorporated community of Jonesville, Butte County, California; population 425,000.

The date is May 31, 2016. My name is Brian Fitzgerald, head researcher for the CDC team recruited to investigate the Jonesville Prion Contamination, and as of this writing, I have no idea who is infected and who isn't. I don't know who is still alive, or dead. As a matter of fact, I'm not even certain if I will still be sane by this time tomorrow—or for that matter, in a couple hours. I just don't know.

I'll begin this report by apologizing for not checking in sooner. I realize that our first priority was designing a plan of action for the city council, but by the time I finish relaying the following events, you'll understand that this has proven to be more difficult than any of us could have ever thought possible.

At this moment, I'm barricaded in my hotel room; a dresser has been pushed against the door, although I don't know how long this will last. Fortunately, the room is on the third floor, otherwise I would have had to do the same for the window. I'm sitting behind a large Mahogany desk; present in front of me is a uniform gooseneck lamp, a bottle of Jack Daniels three quarters of the way empty, the word processor which I'm currently typing this report on, and a Beretta M9. The pistol's magazine is currently housing thirteen out of fifteen bullets. I would be lying if I said I wasn't aware of the use of those two missing bullets; a man—a man of science, no less—was killed this morning by my own hand. I fired two shots off; one in his chest, the other in his head. I'm not proud of this, but my job is to report to you every fact and this, I feel, is a pretty important fact.

The facts are this: three months ago a CJD report was sent in by a local Jonesville mortician. While this in itself is a very rare incident, the Centers for Disease Control didn't act right away as they should have. However, three weeks ago, we received another report by the same mortician—who, understandably enough, was quite concerned—of *another* case of Creutzfeldt-Jakob disease. Another unusual detail in these cases was the victims' ages, both of whom were in their early twenties—whereas most of those who suffer from CJD are in their sixties and up. Discovering the extremely young ages of both cases and how close together the deaths were, the CDC was given enough reason to issue an investigative team out on the site.

I was the leader of that investigation. As of now, I cannot account for the whereabouts of most of my team. I know some of them are dead, and others I can only pray, have escaped from the area.

Given the young ages of the two victims, we were able to determine that the form of disease was, in fact, a new variant of CJD—vCJD; a type of Creutzfeldt-Jakob disease that affects people considerably below the average age of those who suffer from CJD. This diagnosis quickly became the concern for our entire team, as all indications pointed toward the consumption of a possible beef contamination—and as until now, there had only been one case of vCJD being contacted this way in the United States. In the entire world, there has been over one hundred and fifty people infected by contaminated beef, all primarily in the UK.

In new variant CJD, the disease can be spread through exposure to brain or nervous system tissue—usually through medical procedures—or in other cases, by contaminated beef. It has been unknown whether or not one can become infected with CJD through blood or plasma; previous studies on animals have suggested contaminated blood may transmit the disease, although this hasn't been ascertained with humans—up until now.

Here, barricaded in my hotel room, the screams of the crazed continue pouring in from outside, I can state without a doubt in my mind that the disease can indeed be transmitted by blood. I have witnessed its ability from first-hand experience, along with witnessing many other things that I wish could be erased from memory. I've seen what this disease can do. The pistol on my desk is enough proof of that.

When we arrived in Jonesville, we didn't fear for our own safety. There was no reason to: this disease isn't airborne, or travel through water and casual contact. In fact, the one person most in danger of becoming infected with such a disease would have been the mortician himself from having performed the autopsy of two such victims, although we didn't anticipate such an unlikely reaction at the time. We didn't anticipate much of anything that would follow. How could we?

Considering that both victims had contracted vCJD, we couldn't simply rely on coincidence as an explanation. Therefore, I issued a portion of my team to purchase a few pounds of beef from the local supermarkets, and to test it for any nefarious activity. Sure enough, the next day they returned to me and reported that they'd bought a pound of meat from each market within a five miles radius, and every one of them tested positive for bovine spongiform encephalopathy—or as it's better known; mad cow disease. As its nickname explains rather bluntly, BSE is a disease that only affects cattle; symptoms would include obnoxious drooling, unreasonable fear, grinding of teeth, consistent staggering, and unusual aggression toward fellow animals. It makes them quite literally 'mad.'

Now, if a human were to ingest the meat of a cow riddled with BSE, then that human would become infected as well; only when we're talking about humans, the disease is instead now called vCJD, as previously mentioned. The symptoms are pretty similar to mad cow disease, only a lot more powerful: the victim suffers from a rapidly progressive form of dementia; uncontrollable crying and/or screaming; severe personality changes such as impaired memory, judgment, thinking and vision; insomnia; depression; occasional blindness, and all around a series of strange sensations. Initially, the infected individual might experience problems with muscle coordination, and as time passes, it will progress into strong muscle jerks called myoclonus; eventually, they'll lose the ability to move and speak altogether and end up in a coma. It's true that some of these symptoms are quite identical to other neurological disorders like Alzheimer's and Huntington's disease, but CJD differs with unique brain tissue changes seen at the autopsy and by more rapid deterioration of a person's abilities than these other diseases. Like the cows, the humans will be turned completely mad.

Once receiving the BSE test results, I immediately contacted every market within the city and ordered them to pull all stocks of beef from their shelves. Of course, most of them didn't want to oblige willingly, but after some empty threats and questionable declarations, I was finally able to convince them all that I was in fact being serious: all of the beef in the city would be considered contaminated until further tests could be carried out. I understood how this would affect profits, but I was left with little choice.

Afterward, I gave my team instructions to collect more product from the grocery stores and follow through with more testing. While they did this, I—and a few others in my group—headed back to the city morgue, where we commenced to studying the two vCJD victims, whom had already been isolated in their own little room thanks to the mortician.

The mortician was an odd man; he would begin to join us in analyzing the situation, only to abruptly change the conversation around to his mother, now dead, but he assured us many times that she'd been an excellent cook. Then he would continue to talk about the two cadavers until stopping mid-sentence, having forgotten what he was going to say. At the time, we all figured he'd just been an old man in need of an early retirement. On retrospect, however, I was a fool not to notice the signs. They were so obvious, and I failed to see them. Although, even if I had realized what was wrong with the mortician, there was nothing I could have done to save him; he was already dying—as was everyone else in the city. We may have stopped the sale of beef, but we'd arrived too late; they never had a chance.

There was no saving them.

Back at the morgue, my associates and I went to work on the corpses without a moment's waste. Their brains had become almost deformed looking; under the microscope, their brain tissue appeared to be violated with innumerable holes drilled into the cortex, giving it the resemblance of a sponge. It was the trademark feature of transmissible spongiform encephalopathy—otherwise known as prion disease. I had already anticipated this discovery, and though never seeing a brain like this firsthand, I'd certainly read my share of information about the matter.

The prion, an infectious protein, is unlike any other bacteria or virus known to man; while normal infectious agents require some kind of nucleic acid to exist (DNA, RNA, or both), the prion protein doesn't contain any such gene. Transmissible spongiform encephalopathy, the diseases caused by these prions—which both of the victims had suffered from—can be associated with four characteristics: spongiform change, neuronal loss, astrocytosis, and amyloid plaque.

There are two kinds of the prion protein (PrP): properly-folded (PrP-C; meaning common or cellular) and disease-linked and misfolded (PrP-SC; named after scrapie, the first known prion disease). The PrP-SC enters a healthy organism and right away makes itself at home; meaning, the prion will begin to convert normal PrP-C into a diseased state; these newly adapted proteins will then go on to convert more and more protein, which only proceed to do the very same thing, triggering a chain reaction that produces an immense volume of the abnormal prion form. This mass of misfolded proteins interrupts all cell function and subsequently causes cell death; alterations in conformation puts an end to the protein's ability to undergo digestion. It's all maintained by invading the brain and producing itself in one surreal, self-sustaining feedback loop.

Such structural stability means these prions are incredibly resistant to heat, chemicals, and even radiation. They can't be inactivated with disinfection measures used to destroy other disease-causing agents. There is, in fact, no way of stopping them. There is no cure. There is no anything. Once they're in, there is no getting them back out.

The next morning, I began to make rounds at doctor offices inquiring over any unusual patients. I was quite mortified to discover there had been more than just a few recent diagnoses of borderline dementia, as well as more patients who were suffering from some of the other very same symptoms that those with CJD suffer from. I collected a handful of these patients and brought them back to the hospital, where I put them on top priority for treatment.

We gave them the whole nine yards: spinal taps to rule out other more common cases of dementia; electroencephalograms to record brain patterns; computerized tomography of the brain to help rule out the probability that the symptoms were the result from a stroke or brain tumor; and MRIs, which can often reveal characteristic patterns of brain degeneration that can help diagnose CJD. All of these results started to lean toward an outcome I didn't want to think about, but nothing was for sure—at least not then. The only way to truly confirm a case of CJD is either by a brain biopsy or an autopsy, and since these patients were still alive, we decided to go with the former.

I already knew what the biopsies would say before we even did it. I'd had this feeling in my gut that entire morning; a feeling like there was a storm coming, and everything would drown in its wake. It was a sensation I'd been experiencing since first arriving in the city. Nothing good would come from my stay here, and the biopsy results proved just that.

Of course, I was right: the results came back positive for vCJD—and sure enough, when we took another biopsy of another patient the following week, these results reported positive as well. By then, we'd already set up roadblocks around the area. We didn't know how many people in the city were infected, and there was no way to tell; it wasn't like we could go around giving door-to-door brain biopsies. No one knows how all the city's beef products became infected like it did, but it doesn't mean this is only happening here; other shipments of meat could also be contaminated, and they're being consumed right now as I type this. I urge you to order mandatory BSE tests for all of the United States. There is nothing else I can do about the matter except finish this report. I don't even have a phone to call for help now. I just have this word processor that lacks an Internet connection. Truthfully, I haven't thought about how I'm going to send this report out until now, but I am sure one of your men will come across it—I just hope it's not too late by the time you do.

I'm pretty sure I'm infected, by the way. I don't know if I made that clear. I haven't been feeling very good all day. I've been careful, too. I've defended myself well; no blood has gotten on me, no brain tissue, no gore, no anything. My best guess would be back when I first arrived here and was experimenting with the brains of the first two cadavers. Perhaps I was neglectful. I don't know. It doesn't really matter now, I suppose. I'm finding it harder to make my fingers type the keys I want to type. I'm growing tired of typing. Typing…

It's around five in the evening now. I dozed off for a while. It didn't help; the situation is still the same. There is no sleeping and waking up to a better tomorrow. The prion is still alive, still in me, still in us all. If I look out my window, I can see the occasional pedestrian running wildly down the street. On the curb, next to a streetlamp, there is a puddle of blood; it's so dark and thick looking. You can see crimson footsteps leading away from the puddle, disappearing behind a family restaurant. I dined at that restaurant a few times during the three weeks I've been stationed here. I made sure not to order anything with beef. Like that's really helped, right?

I don't remember ever reading a CJD case where the victim lashed out with violence before. Something is different with this case. I regret to admit I don't know what that is. There was simply not enough time for proper testing. The normal incubation period for CJD should be years—in most cases, even decades—yet with this mutated version of vCJD, people begin showing symptoms in as little as a few *hours* after being infected. Some last longer, some even shorter. It just doesn't make any sense.

As I've previously mentioned, this disease can indeed be transmitted through blood. I'm able to determine this from an incident three days ago, when this entire situation really began to spin out of control. I was leaving the hospital with a few other members of my team at the time. We boarded the elevator and discovered the mortician leaning against the floor buttons. He was just standing there, staring at his feet, and sobbing silently. For some reason, there was a line of blood streaming from out of the corner of his lips—I can only assume he'd been chewing on his tongue. We tried calling his name but he didn't respond. Then one of my associates laid a hand on his shoulder, and the mortician snapped out of his daze at once. He looked up at my associate with a pair of these miserable foggy eyes, and before any of us knew what was wrong, he opened his mouth and ripped a good chunk of flesh from my associate's neck. There was much scream-ing then, and lots of blood, so much blood. The mortician was crazy. He started lashing out at us all. Blood squirted from my associate's neck. Perhaps some of it got in my mouth or my eyes; that would also be a perfectly reasonable explanation for my probable infection.

It took quite a struggle, but we were finally able to subdue him. We knocked him out by repeatedly banging his skull against the elevator door—barbaric, yes, but also very effective. We got the attention of the authorities and they chained the mortician to a bedpost up in one of the hospital rooms. My associate was also admitted to a room, although his injury wasn't as damaging as it appeared in the elevator; all it took was a few stitches and he was fine. He was able to check himself out that very night.

Unfortunately, I wouldn't be given the chance to examine the mortician any further than I was able to in the elevator, for things only began to escalate from there. Apparently, a large sum of the city's population was infected, just like I'd feared, and for some reason, they all began to show symptoms almost simultaneously. Unlike other CJD cases, they were all associated with an abnormal rage; almost as if this new prion form destroys serotonins as well, turning them all into these crazed killing machines.

Since then, the streets haven't been safe to walk. The infected are everywhere, it seems. I've watched survivors stumbling around outside confused, only to be attacked moments later by a drooling lunatic. I tried to warn them from my window but it only distracted the infected long enough for one of them to sneak up on the survivors. God knows how the roadblocks are handling all of this. Have they broken free of the city? Have they migrated toward other populations? I don't know. Is this just an isolated event, or is this happening in other places besides Jonesville? What the hell has happened?

This isn't coincidental. Something disrupted the city's beef supply with BSE-infected cattle carcasses. We're talking hundreds upon hundreds of pounds of beef—all contaminated. Such a disaster should have been impossible, and yet it's happened, and the results are miles beyond the normal definition of terror. I'm left with the only conclusion that outside parties must be responsible; perhaps a foreign group of terrorists who had the access and the ability to infiltrate the country's beef supply—a group that, somehow, have managed to escape our radars. Such an attack would have taken years of formation, and precise action to carry it out successfully; and somehow, they have. If this is only the beginning, God only knows what else they have in store for us. The possibilities are cataclysmic.

I became separated from most of my team just last night, when a large group of infected burst into the hospital and began attacking everyone. We'd all gathered in the cafeteria, eating dinner, when the crazies came storming through the doors, lunging anyone within reach. I witnessed from my table as one of my associates had a large pipe driven through her face, while another one was bashed in the skull with a brick; others were bitten, clawed, torn apart, and all around dismembered. Many, though, were able to flee the scene. I don't know where they are now; I can only hope they're safe. The infected jumped at me as well, but I managed to defend myself without being injured. I can very vividly recall one gentleman was able to tackle me to the floor, and despite holding the man's hands back while he wrestled on top of me, he still tried to snap at me with his teeth.

Long thin lines of blood were dripping from his mouth, and if I hadn't thrown him off me in time, then it would have undoubtedly spilled into my own opened mouth. There was a broken chair leg nearby that I swung at the rest of the attackers as I fled from the building, along with the only other survivor in the room. It was my associate whom had previously been bitten by the conformed mortician.

We managed to board ourselves up in my hotel room, having first confiscated the aforementioned Beretta M9 from a dead policeman's holster. I don't think either one of us slept much all night. We haven't really said much to each other either. What is there to say? There is nothing. We just stayed up here listening to the screaming and the crying and the killing. It's madness.

In the morning I woke up, having finally nodded off at sunrise, and discovered my associate kneeled down in front of me, just watching me like I was some kind of mysterious creature. For a moment I feared the worst, that I'd turned into one of the crazies roaming around outside, that I'd become one of them, one of those monsters. But it didn't take long to realize that the monster wasn't me, it was *him*. His arms were jerking, his teeth chattering frantically. I looked him in the eyes and asked if he was okay. He didn't hear me. A single tear rolled down his cheek, then he screamed into my face and backhanded me across the jaw as hard as he could. I fell to the floor, my mouth bleeding almost instantly, and fumbled for the pistol in my jacket pocket. I knew what needed to be done and didn't intend on wasting any time. He started to charge toward me, screaming madly, and I raised the gun. Two deafening bangs later and I was the only living soul left in the hotel room. Now it all smells so rancid, I can't bear it anymore. I'm sitting at my desk, looking at the corpse across the room and it all makes me want to vomit, but if I do, it will just make it smell worse and I just want to leave this place. I want to go home…

Where no one is killing anyone…no one is infected, it's my home…this is a strange land, I don't know these people, these people are going to kill me, they've killed me, look at the gun on the desk, it will kill me like it's killed my associate, whom I don't even know the name of…

Everyone's dead… I don't know, they're all dead maybe… maybe they are dead yes, maybe… Still no one understands. I don't understand what has happened here in this place, this strange land…I don't know this place. I don't these things.

I don't know…getting harder to type, screen is blurry.

I can't stand this much longer. *I swear to God I don't* want this… I can't do it. There's so much sweat I keep sweating… I don't know why I don't know why anything and no one does…

Why would they… They are just infected too. *They* are all in-fected… We are and you are and I am and he is and she is and the world is and everyone is…infected…

There's no more whiskey left in my bottle. I think I might go look and find some more and maybe I will find a way, a car with the keys in it, and leave this place for good and everything will be okay. I can see my family, they're waiting for me.

The thing is, I don't know what the thing is… It's too hard to type now… I think I am going to… I don't remember my mother's name. What is her name? I want to talk to her…where is she…why am, I am here She wore a pink dress…with…flowers.

I remember her now… There are more outside…

ORDER UP

SCOTT T. GOUDSWARD

Darrell glared at the morning sun streaming through the open skylight. The light hurt his eyes like a baby migraine, so he reached up for the pull cord on the ceiling fan and switched off the overheads—less light equaled less pain.

His right arm ached and leaked fluids from the bite wounds and phantom tendrils itched. He swore he could still feel his missing fingers. Even the chill of his absent wedding ring was there. Trails of gore dripped on the stained tiled floor.

Through the window came noises—noises that burned. People talked and laughed, the clink of silverware on plates and spoons against coffee mugs, and it all pissed him off, angered him to the point of becoming ravenous.

He reached for the stereo, ripped out the audio cables, and smashed the power button with a spatula. The music that was piped into the diner stopped, but no one seemed to notice. The pain in his head eased up a little bit. He limped over to the grill, scowled, and wiped his sleeve across his mouth.

"Hot damn," he grumbled. "Somethin' smells good."

He pried another chunk of meat from the slab on the grill-top with the edge of the metal spatula and flipped it onto a plate. He set the implement down in front of the grill, as rivulets of grease rolled off it. With his good hand, he reached for the can of bacon fat and chucked another spoonful on the hissing grill. He turned a quick eye to the diner behind him, packed with customers with a small line outside. They were waiting for the 'Big Bacon Breakfast.' Four buttermilk pancakes with bacon in the batter, four eggs any style—cooked in bacon fat—a double side of bacon, grits or oatmeal, served with crumbled bacon and orange juice.

Through the window to the main room of the Silverline Diner, Betty worked the counter of twelve barstools. Alice worked the booths; four on either side of the entrance. Billy worked the register, the phone, and took the takeout orders.

Darrell reached to the window for the pile of slips with his good arm; what was left of the other hung limp at his side. He hid his eyes under the brim of a stained baseball cap and spread the order tickets out on the counter.

A groan escaped his pale lips as he pulled another chunk of meat free from the slab on the grill. The last man on Darrell's crew was Phillip. He was the dishwasher, busboy and a slacker who currently resided on the grill-top and sizzled in a puddle of bacon fat and lard on the hot grill; bacon fat for the taste and lard to crisp him up.

Phillip groaned and Darrell slapped him with the flat of the spatula, leaving a rectangular mark on his cheek. Phillip's eyes were solid gray and unblinking, his lips were burnt and covered with blistering scars. What remained of his arms and legs now boiled in a pot on the stove, with an herb pouch, two halved onions and a carrot.

Darrell cracked half a dozen eggs on the grill and flipped them quick and cool, it was all reflex to him. He slid them on plates with 'Phillip Hash' and placed them in the window. He slapped a small metal bell with the spatula and growled, "Order up!"

Betty peered through the window at him. Darrell turned quick so she wouldn't see him in his current state. Phillip, the rat bastard, had bitten him good, but the transformation wasn't complete yet. Darrell knew he was dying and his body changing, but over there on the grill, Phillip was getting what he deserved. There wouldn't be much left of him soon, unless Darrell opened up his belly for the rest of the hungry mouths he needed to feed.

Darrell stumbled backwards and dropped his spatula, it clanged against the floor. He tripped up and landed ass over elbow on the floor. Slowly, he picked himself up; everything was turning gray and groggy. He wanted to sleep, just for a few minutes, but there were too many people in the dining room.

"You need some help on the grill, boss?" Billy called and scribbled another order onto a notepad. He slipped the phone off the hook and hoped Darrell didn't notice.

"No."

"Just holler if you need anything," Billy said. He handed Betty a handful of orders on her way back to the coffee pots.

"No."

"Sure is chatty this morning," Alice said. She pulled a pencil from the back of her ear and wrote some numbers on her pad. She ripped off the page and slid it to a man at the counter with a sly smile and a wink.

"We're super busy and that douche Phillip is nowhere to be found," Billy said.

"I don't know why Darrell keeps him on staff. We'll be bussing our own stations soon," Alice said.

"Things don't let up soon out here I won't be able to get pies made for lunch," Betty added and handed a handful of cash and receipts to Billy.

"Order up!"

Two more plates appeared in the window. Betty checked the tickets and grabbed them, then she winced at the presentation and handed them off to Alice. Darrell wasn't even trying anymore, just throwing the food on the plates lazily.

Darrell turned back to the window and watched the customers eat their food. They chewed on Phillip; some took second looks at the meat, others didn't notice after covering it with ketchup. He smiled and wiped black bile from his lips. The bite wound on his good arm oozed brackish blood down his wrist, over his fingers and splattered on the floor. His bad arm, gone at the elbow and well gnawed on, had developed a smell.

Darrell turned back to Phillip on the grill and waved the spatula threateningly at him. He grabbed the order slips from the window, spread them out on the counter, and put more eggs on the grill. Phillip moaned and was slapped again with the spatula for the interruption.

While the eggs sizzled, he dropped toast and bagels in the industrial toaster and added salt and pepper to the boiling pot on the stove. He went to the walk-in for the pancake batter and then crumpled crispy bacon into the batter bowl. He poured out sixteen circles of batter on the grill and topped them off with a splash of Phillip's blood for good measure.

Six hours earlier.

Phillip slammed the screen door of the diner and stomped out into the alleyway, as the first light peeked out from behind gold and red clouds. He dropped four plastic bags of garbage on the ground and reached for the dumpster's lid. A soft growl oozed out from the inside. Phillip pressed his hand against the side and found it warm to the touch. He looked back to the diner's door and thought for an instant about going to get Darrell. Through the rusted holes in the side of the green dumpster he heard movement.

"Ah hell," Phillip muttered. "I hate it when raccoons get in there."

"What's the hold-up out there? I got booths in here to be bussed and dishes that need to be washed. And the juice glasses ain't goin' to clean themselves!" Darrell yelled.

"Yeah, yeah hold on, Darrell." Phillip pulled up a stack of milk crates from the side of the dumpster and sat down. He flipped off Darrell, knowing full well the man couldn't see him. With the skill of a ninja, he flipped the cigarette out from behind his ear and lit it as it settled on his lips. He sucked in the smoke and let it out slow. Another growl from the dumpster was followed by another yell from the kitchen. Through the screen door, he heard Darrell wailing on the grill with his spatulas, his weapon of choice. He wielded them like samurai swords.

"You better not be smoking out there," Darrell warned.

Phillip flipped him off again and slipped the cigarette into the corner of his mouth. "There's something in the dumpster, an animal or something."

"If it ain't human, kill it and get your fat ass back in here."

"Always a joy," Phillip whispered. He grabbed the corner of the black plastic lid, flipped it up and backpedaled. A soft green light pulsed out from the inside. The growling became louder and more assertive, like a mother bear protecting her cubs. Except bears didn't glow green, at least not that he remembered.

Phillip picked up a rock and prepared to smash whatever was in the bottom of the dumpster into paste. He peered in, wiped a lock of greasy hair from his eyes, and jumped back, the rock sliding from his grasp.

A homeless man looked up at him; the green glow came from a rock imbedded in his chest, the skin, bone and clothes fused to the outside of it. The bum's eyes were solid white, and purple and gray veins crisscrossed the surface.

"What are you?" Phillip whispered.

The bum slipped and tumbled out of the dumpster, his head bouncing off the cracked pavement. Blood oozed out from between his teeth as a chunk of his tongue plopped out his mouth.

"Look, pal, I don't want no trouble. Just be on your way and find a gutter to sleep in," Phillip said. The bum staggered closer and grabbed at Phillip, who easily side-stepped away.

"Just be on your way, mister."

The homeless man, his clothes in tatters, hair matted to his skull, and missing a shoe, lashed out at Phillip. He grabbed Phillip's arm and bit it just above the wrist. Teeth scraped against bone. Phillip screamed and ripped his arm free from the bum's mouth, as blood poured from the jagged hole. Phillip fell backwards, trying to cover the wound, blood gushing from between his fingers.

"You're a dead man, you old bastard." Phillip reached for the rock he'd dropped, his hand slick with blood. Picking it up, he brought the rock down on the bum's head over and over, until the skull shattered and the brains within were showing. One final blow and the bum stopped moving and growling—stopped everything and died.

Phillip stood up and tore the sleeve of the corpse's shirt and staggered to the milk crates to sit down. He wrapped the dirty cloth around his wound and reached for his cigarette, which was still burning on the ground in front of the dumpster.

He looked up to see Darrell standing in the doorway of the diner, two spatulas held white-knuckled in each hand, ready to attack him.

"What do you think you're doing out here?"

"Taking a break," Phillip gasped. He struggled with each breath, the cigarette forgotten, though locked between his fingers.

"Oh, really. It's not break time now, is it? What's that guy doing there?" Darrell motioned with a spatula at the dead bum.

"That's who was in the dumpster. The crazy jerk took a bite out of me so I kicked his ass."

Darrell stared at the body. "If you killed that guy, then what's making his chest glow green? Forget it, I don't care. Now get back to work!"

"Not yet. Look, you can dock me, Darrell." The cigarette slipped out from between Phillip's fingers and his head rolled back. He didn't feel very good. He closed his eyes.

"Listen to me and listen good, Phillip. I'm not payin' for your smoking habit. Now get to the hospital and get cleaned up, then get back here before the morning rush."

Phillip's head suddenly snapped up and he locked eyes with Darrell.

"Take one step towards me and you're fired," Darrell warned, waving a spatula like a weapon.

Phillip jumped up, scattering the milk crates behind him, and rushed Darrell. They collided and fell over in a great writhing ball of limbs. Expletives flew from Darrell's mouth, and spit and blood came from Phillip's.

Darrell screamed and stopped fighting when Phillip bit into his arm right below the elbow. He cried out in pain and beat Phillip with the spatula. When Darrell tried to stand, his forearm was still in Phillip's mouth.

Darrell ran for the back door to the diner, clutching the stump of his arm, his blood gushing out with each step. He was reaching for the door handle when Phillip took a bite out of his good arm and they tumbled together into the kitchen. No one out front seemed to notice the crash or if they did, they didn't care. People who came to the diner were used to the spats between Phillip and Darrell. They would fight often.

Darrell extricated himself from Phillip and stood up, then leaned against the metal door to the walk-in. With his good arm, he grabbed the stainless steel meat tenderizer off a nearby shelf and beat Phillip with it, until the man stopped moving.

Darrell dropped the bloody utensil and slid to the floor. Tears welled up and rolled down his cheeks, and mixed with the blood on his face to run in gory rivulets. He grabbed at the stump of his arm and tried to stop the bleeding; it wasn't slowing. He could feel his body slowing, his functions shutting down. With a last act of defiance, he reached for the meat cleaver as Phillip's fingers twitched.

"Order up!" Darrell growled and slid another three plates through the window. Alice grimaced and shook her head. She looked at Darrell, but he turned away.

"Honey, we can't serve this, it's disgusting." She eyeballed the plate. The hash and egg whites were running together, and garnish was dropped haphazardly in the middle of the runny yolks; the toast wasn't buttered.

"Serve it or you're fired!" came the response.

Alice shrugged and handed off the plates.

"If you see Phillip, I got three buckets of dishes and booths that need to be bussed," she said.

Darrell turned away and looked at the order tickets on the counter. His vision was blurred, the words all jumbled together. He reached to scratch his arm and remembered it was mostly gone. He walked out of the kitchen and outside to the back alley. Once there, he picked up his arm, which was lying in a puddle of gore. He stared at it like it was a grotesque trophy, then went back inside. He put it on a shelf in the walk-in fridge next to the tomatoes and carrots.

A strange and powerful hunger overtook him; none of the food in the walk-in looked appealing, in fact, it all looked like poison.

He spun around and slammed the door closed. After spitting into the pot of Phillip stock, he returned to the grill and a sizzling Phillip. The meat would be the afternoon stew if anyone was still alive. Phillip's dead eyes darted back and forth in confusion as he looked around the kitchen.

Darrell licked his lips and staggered over to him, and with the spatula he pried another piece of meat from Phillip's thigh and greedily ripped chunks from it and gobbled it down. The hunger within him ebbed and flowed, and Darrell smiled and lowered the heat on the grill. Phillip was a good medium rare.

"Order in!" Alice hollered through the window.

Darrell took the tickets and started to cook. He cooked through the rush, feeding himself with handfuls of meat ripped from Phillip's torso and leg stumps.

When enough of the body was gone, he grabbed the sharpening stone and drove it through Phillip's skull until it scraped against the grill on the other side. He pulled on Phillip's shirt and yanked the carcass off the grill top.

Darrell slid his stump into his apron in a make-shift sling to hide the ravaged arm and went to the window. The diner was still crowded; people moved slower, some slouched over in the booths. Not so much chit-chat now.

Darrell grinned wickedly. His gums had begun to rot, his teeth turning yellow. Billy still bussed the tables, Alice wiped down the counter, and Betty made coffee. All was as it should be.

"Soon," Darrell grumbled as a smile played across his lips.

"You say something, Darrell?" Betty asked.

"Need you back here. I cut myself bad."

Betty hustled to the kitchen door, wiping her hands on her apron. She burst through the door, and before she could scream, Darrell smashed in her skull with a frying pan.

She crumpled to the floor, her head bouncing off the tiles. Without a second thought, Darrell fell on her. He bit into her neck and ripped out her throat, blood gushing over his lips as he chewed. She started to spasm, and on the second mouthful she went still. Darrel gnawed on her cheek bone. He ate his fill, then wiped his mouth and neck on her apron to clean up.

Someone groaned from the dining room. He stood up as quick as he could and went to the swinging door leading into the diner. He watched Billy checking on a sick customer, and then jump back in surprise.

He dropped the tub of dishes in his hands. Broken glass and dishes exploded across the floor, and bits of eggs and toast flew off in every direction. If anyone in the diner was still alive, they would have cheered or clapped, which was something they did whenever a dish or glass was broken.

Alice screamed from behind the counter as her customers reached out and grabbed for her. Darrell smiled from his vantage point and ran a pasty tongue across his lips. He went back into the kitchen, the swinging door hitting him in the back on the way in. He grabbed Betty's corpse by the hair and dragged her to the window. With the cleaver, he cut off her arm. When she started to stir, Darrell pushed her out into the main room of the diner.

While the diners came back to re-life, Darrell chewed on Betty's bicep like a theater-goer in a movie with popcorn as he watched the tableaux.

Then he went outside and dragged the dead bum in. From the bum's chest cavity the meteorite hummed and pulsed with green light. Darrell continued to watch through the window as Billy was dragged under a table and ripped apart. Greedy, clawed hands reached into his abdomen for the fresh hot organs within.

"He won't be coming back," Darrell whispered with a smile.

Alice was pulled over the counter and forced onto the floor. The stools swiveled on their posts as she slid by them. Her blood splashed on the red vinyl cushions as she was eaten alive.

Darrell exited the kitchen with the gore-encrusted meteorite in hand. He looked over the remnants of his employees on the floor, then surveyed the dining room like a king in his great hall. His zombie minions were spread out before him. When he tried to say something, two of his teeth slid out of his diseased gums and clattered to the floor. He decided to stay silent after that.

When the last of the customers had died and reanimated, then everyone had left the diner to feast on the people outside, Darrell dragged himself to the front door and changed the sign from **OPEN** to **CLOSED**.

JUSTICE IS SERVED

BENNIE L. NEWSOME

"Honorable Judge Bailey…zombies of the jury. Despite what it may look like, I'm not here to condemn anyone. My duty is not to prosecute the defendant, but to uphold justice on behalf of the victim."

The smooth talking lawyer, Mr. Greg Fitzgerald, paced before the courtroom with his ragged head bowed as if he was in deep contemplation. His pale, rotten hands were clasped behind his back, and his best suit—tattered and stained with dirt and blood—made a rustling sound whenever he moved.

Mr. Fitzgerald looked up and fixed the jury with his bloodshot, bulging eyes. "My client, Mr. Bryan Donahue, was a kind zombie and a pillar to the community. He had the rest of his afterlife to look forward to, until *this man*…"

The zombified lawyer pointed an accusing finger at a living human being who was gagged, hog-tied, and seated at the defendant's designated area. The beleaguered man's eyes were wide and filled with fright. He made whimpering noises around the cloth in his mouth, but no one paid him any attention—except to glare at him whenever the prosecutor mentioned him in his opening argument.

"This man approached the victim, randomly, and fired two bullets into the zombie's head. The defendant committed this heinous act, simply because…he's anti-zombie."

The victim's wife, *twice* widowed despite being married only once, began to sob. Low whispers suddenly filled the courtroom as the zombie jurors talked amongst themselves. Those sitting in the spectators' pews began to quietly voice their outrage. Even the zombified judge shifted uncomfortably.

"I have here in my hand," Mr. Fitzgerald said while holding up a book, "material that was found on the defendant's person at the time of his arrest. It is full of slanderous stories propagated by the humans. They depict us zombies as heartless savages who must be stopped at all cost. The title of this book is *Headshots Only*. The back cover proceeds to instruct humans to, and I quote, 'Grab your gun, take aim, and make sure it's a headshot!' End quote. And that is exactly what the defendant did."

More whispered conversations arose and mingled with the frightened gasps.

"Ever since our Great Awakening, or what the prejudice humans refer to as the 'zombie apocalypse,' we have treated our living counterparts with nothing but compassion and respect. We've even gone as far as to give them their own land to do with as they please."

A zombie in the spectators' area muttered, "Free-range humans." That statement caused a few chuckles to arise.

Mr. Fitzgerald continued by asking, "And how do they repay us? They create propaganda such as this, and gun down our innocent. Well, I for one am fed up. As I said before, I'm not here to condemn this human. I'm here to uphold justice for the victim who is no longer with us. I'm here to speak for Mr. Bryan Donahue, who can not speak for himself."

On the night in question, Bryan Donahue was impatiently waiting in the dead room—a zombie's equivalent to a human's living room. His wife, Diane Donahue, had been in the bathroom for over an hour, primping needlessly.

Bryan lifted his arm, with its torn flesh and exposed ulna bone, and glanced at his analog watch. The hands on the clock declared that it was 8:13, which meant that they should have left about ten minutes ago. "Diane! We need to be leaving if we're gonna make that movie!"

The bathroom door creaked open and he heard his wife's voice come from the hallway. "I'm coming, I'm coming. I just wanna make sure I look decent."

"Who're you trying to impress?" Bryan asked, sounding a bit agitated. "My opinion should be the only one that matters and I'm saying that you're fine just like you are. Now let's go!"

He heard the muffled sound of high heels thumping on carpet, a noise that caused him to let out a frustrated sigh. *We're just going to the movies then out to eat. Why in the world is she wearing heels?*

A moment later, Diane stepped into the dead room and came to a stop. "So, what do you think?"

Bryan quickly gave his wife a once over.

It was obvious that the female zombie had used the flatirons on her hair, because it was nice and straight. He noticed a bit of whiteness creeping into his wife's hair, another side effect of being dead, but for the most part, her hair was still luxurious and gray. Her pallid skin clung to her facial structure, while her milky white eyes bulged from their sockets. A human being would most likely vomit at the sight, but Bryan thought she was beautiful. From her nose that was nothing more than two holes in her face, to her rotting teeth that were visible due to the lack of lips.

"You're sexy," he said as he scanned her boney, insect gnawed body, which was clothed in her favorite tattered dress. He was no longer sure what color it was supposed to be, but the material was now a purplish-brown. His eyes came to a stop at her skeleton-like feet, which were adorned by a pair of scuffed high heels.

"Are you sure you wanna wear those heels? You always talking 'bout how they hurt your feet."

"I'll be fine," Diane said, but Bryan knew she would be singing a different tune about an hour into their outing. "So you really think I look okay? You don't think this dress is too tight on me? I feel like I might've gained a bit of weight."

With a sigh, Bryan rose from the couch to retrieve his keys and wallet from the side table. "Well," he said as he placed the items in his pocket. "You'll be the first zombie I've ever heard of that gained weight instead of shedding it. Let's go."

"All right," Diane said while making her way to the front door.

As he fell in step behind his wife, he casually smacked her on her butt. Where cushiony flesh used to be, there was nothing but skin and bone.

Diane giggled "All right now! You better cut that out before you get something started."

"That'll be the day," he muttered.

Back in the courtroom, Mr. Fitzgerald addressed the jury.

"Although it was brief, that tale should have allowed you to get a feel for what kind of zombie Bryan Donahue was, which was kind and loving. And I know what many of you are thinking. Bryan died at the ripe old age of eight-five, and then went on to be twenty-five years dead. You're probably thinking that he'd lived a full life and then some, but that is not the issue. What *is* the issue is that Bryan Donahue was everything to that zombie sitting right over there."

Mrs. Donahue suddenly started weeping, which was all sound and no tears. Mr. Fitzgerald's paralegal quickly slid over to console the heartbroken dead woman.

She couldn't have had better timing, the lawyer thought happily.

"He was her lover, her friend, her spouse, and most importantly, he was her soul mate. Now it's all gone. There's life and there's resurrection, but there is no third coming. Mr. Bryan Donahue is now lost to us forever."

Twinkling stars sat in the heavens, and the full moon chased the Donahues' car as they drove through the city. It was a little after eight o' clock on a Tuesday night, which meant a lot of zombies were just awaking to get their routine started. Traffic was full of impatient living dead who were rushing to get to work, already at work, or just riding around to complete errands. There were even undead pedestrians moving about on the sidewalk.

Bryan and Diane, however, were retired and had no need to rush anywhere.

Bryan sounded the car's horn because of a pedestrian in the crosswalk. "MY LIGHT IS GREEN, YOU MORON! WHY THE HELL ARE YOU...? Oh! And he's just shuffling across the street like he has all the time in the world."

The walking zombie turned toward Bryan and flipped him the bird.

"WHAT? FUCK YOU TOO, BUDDY!"

"Bryan, just calm down," Diane whispered. "It's not like the movie theater will be crowded. It's almost nine at night. Everyone is either at work or headed there."

Bryan sighed. "It's not about the movie. It's the principle of the whole thing. If we're expected to show some consideration toward pedestrians, then they should show some to us drivers. He didn't have any business walking across the street against the light. He's lucky I didn't knock his ass three ways to Sunday."

"Well, don't get so riled up. You remember what your doctor said about your blood pressure?"

Bryan quickly glanced at his wife, then returned his eyes to the road. "Blood pressure? I don't have any flowing blood!"

Diane started giggling and Bryan soon joined her.

"High blood pressure did me in the first time. It can't get me a second time," he added.

Eventually, the married couple made their way across town and sat down in the theater just in time to catch the previews. When the advertisements and trailers for upcoming movies were over, they watched a movie starring Bryan's favorite actor, a zombified Johnny Walton. Bryan had been elated the day Johnny Walton died, because movies with living actors were prohibited in public places. Even if a zombie was caught hording Blu-Rays and DVD's of live actors, they could be slapped with five thousand dollars in fines, or ten years in a federal penitentiary.

After the movie, which Bryan gave two putrid thumbs up, the undead couple went to a Golden Horseshoe for their all-you-can-eat buffet.

They stood at the serving station, eyeballing a few dishes. "I don't know what I wanna start with first," Bryan said. "There's so much to choose from."

"Well, I think I'll start with a liver and a bit of the small intestines," Diane said and reached for a pair of tongs.

He made a disgusted face while observing his wife. "Ugh!"

"Ugh, what? Liver and intestines are good for you."

He shook his head and returned his attention to the choices before him. "I'll stick with a few tongues and a couple of eyeballs." After he scooped those items onto his dish, he looked up and down the service station, searching for something. "Why don't I see any thighs? That's one of the main reasons I came here. I was told they have the best human thighs around."

Diane tilted her head to the right. "You have to go down there and talk to the butcher. They have to hack that off for you fresh."

"All right!" Bryan exclaimed as he hurried in the direction his wife indicated. "That's why they're the best."

The gagged and bound defendant peed his pants when Fitzgerald started talking about the selections at Golden Horseshoes' all-you-can-eat buffet.

The lawyer looked over at the pale man and smiled a gruesome, lipless smile.

"The humans say that we're nothing but a bunch of savages," Mr. Fitzgerald said. "A blight to the world. Why? Because we eat human flesh? How is that any different from what humans do to pigs and cows, just to name a few of their victims. At least we don't walk around wearing human skin for clothing! All of a sudden, the humans fall to the bottom of the food chain and now they have a problem with the consumption of flesh."

Mr. Fitzgerald rushed over to the defendant's table, stopped in front of the terrified man, and banged his fist on the wooden surface. He brought his face down, leveled with the human's, and asked, "HOW WOULD YOU LIKE IT IF A PORTLY PIG CREPT UP ON YOU AND PUT A BULLET THROUGH *YOUR* SKULL, HUH? MR. HEADSHOTS ONLY!" He lowered his voice "You want to know something? To me you're nothing more than a portly pig, ripe for slaughter."

The defense attorney jumped to his feet. "Objection your honor!"

"Sustained!" cried the judge, with his decaying flesh and yellowish-white wig.

Mr. Fitzgerald stood erect once more and turned to face the judge, then the jury. "I apologize. But I become so *damn* angry when I come across those who don't even flinch at the thought of taking another's life…afterlife."

A few handclaps could be heard coming from the rear of the courtroom, near the double doors.

"Mr. Bryan Donahue was just trying to enjoy himself. He'd taken his wife out to a movie and dinner. Then he was going to wrap the wonderful evening up by visiting the park. The park where the *defendant* was waiting like the coward he is. Waiting to ambush a helpless Mr. and Mrs. Donahue."

Just like Mr. Fitzgerald said, when the movie and dinner was over, Bryan and Diane made their way to Railroad Park. A warm, spring breeze swept across the streetlamp-lit landscape, causing the leaves of nearby trees to whisper in their own strange vernacular. Bryan reveled in the peaceful scene, but Diane was too preoccupied to enjoy nature's wonderment.

"I told you heels were a bad idea?" Bryan said as he observed his wife.

She had her bare, right foot resting atop the thigh of her left leg and was in the middle of massaging the hurting limb.

"How was I supposed to know you were going to suggest we walk through the park?"

"You're the one who said you were getting fa…"

Before Bryan could finish his sentence, Diane's head snapped up and she fixed him with a murderous stare.

"Fa…farther along…in your, uh, weight gain," he said hesitantly. "What did you think I was going to say?"

"Uh-huh," she said before returning her attention to her foot. "The word you were about to say is grounds for a divorce."

"Woman, please! In our vows, we said till death do us part. Guess what? We're dead, I did my part. As far as the two of us are concerned, I'm single and allowed to mingle."

"Well, you just try it and see what happens," Diane said with a laugh.

Bryan smiled at her last statement, then watched as a group of zombie kids went stampeding by. One of the boys happened to stumble, causing his right eye to fall out of its socket.

"Aw man!" the undead child groaned before coming to a stop. He went perfectly still and carefully looked for his eyeball as if he was searching for a hard- to-spot contact lens.

Instead of being where the kid thought it might be, the squishy orb was in the process of rolling across the sidewalk, gathering dirt as it went. Within a matter of seconds, the item came to rest at Bryan's feet. The old zombie bent over, moaning all the way because of his stiff joints, then picked up the child's lost eye.

"Here you go," Bryan called.

The kid looked up, and with his remaining eye saw what Bryan's held in his hand. "Thank you, mister!" He trotted over to the bench where the zombified couple sat, and retrieved his eye. He held up the orb while repeating his thanks, then ran off to catch up with his friends.

Bryan watched the boy go. "That's a sad sight."

"What's that?" his wife asked. She had alternated feet and was still rubbing and squeezing.

"I think it's sad that that boy couldn't have been no more than nine-years-old when he died. He's so young. There's no way he got to experience life before it was taken away from him."

"I suppose you're right, but this world is no longer a safe place for humans," Diane stated. "He's better off being one of us."

Out of the blue, the magnificent evening took a dramatic turn for the worse. In Diane's mind, the sudden shift would be forever marked by the phrase, "Give me all of your money, now!"

Her first instinct was to let out a startled cry at the sound of the gruff, hostile voice. Bryan spun around, reflexively, then became nervous after seeing a gun pointed right at his head. "Now just calm down," Bryan told the man, while raising his hands in a gesture of surrender.

Diane continued her whimpering.

"I don't have any money on me, but I think we might be able to work…"

"SHUT THE HELL UP!" the hooded mugger screamed. It didn't take him long to remember where he was, and he quickly lowered his voice. "Shut up! I don't wanna hear that you don't have any cash! Just give me your wallet and let me be the judge of that!"

Bryan haltingly nodded his grotesque head and said, "All right. I'm going for my wallet, slowly. Don't do anything you'll regret."

"HEY! WHAT ARE YOU DOING OVER THERE?" It was another one of the park's patrons.

The mugger's head abruptly turned in the direction of the shout, and when he did, the gun went off! The bullet tore through Bryan's skull, and knocked him flat on the park bench.

Diane placed her hands on the sides of her face and started screaming in horror. Any zombies in the area who either heard the gunshot, or witnessed the shooting, quickly fled.

"Shit!" the gunman yelled after realizing what he'd done.

Deciding there was no turning back, he fired another round into Bryan's head just to make sure there would be no movement, then proceeded to rifle through his moth-eaten pockets.

The killer located the wallet and pulled it free before sprinting for the shadows.

Diane was left howling next to her husband, who was deceased for the second and final time.

* * *

The trial had barely begun, but Mr. Fitzgerald could already tell that the case was all but won. Like the good orator he was, he stood quietly and let the last bit of Bryan Donahue's tragic story sink into the minds of those present.

He let a few seconds slip by, and after seeing the sufficient number of forlorn expressions, or angry scowls—he really couldn't tell one from the other, because they were after all, zombie faces—the lawyer began to bring his argument to a close.

"If we were to take the gag from this…*human's* mouth, he would probably bore us to a second death with tales of hardship. He'll most likely tell us how hard life is on the human reservations, how food is scarce, or that jobs are almost nonexistent. Well, I'm sure Mrs. Donahue wouldn't be willing to exchange her husband's afterlife for pitiful excuses. And I for one am not willing to exchange the afterlife of one of our own for excuses.

"We have brought with us tonight, signed affidavits along with several witnesses that can attest to what occurred that faithful night. We found Bryan Donahue's empty wallet in the human's possession along with the murder weapon. I'm not asking you to prosecute this human to the full extent of the law—no. I'm asking you to *uphold justice* to the full extent of the law."

Mr. Greg Fitzgerald went to take his seat.

An awkward moment of silence followed, then the judge said, "Well…uh, Mr. Thompson, we're ready for your opening argument."

The zombie known as Mr. Thompson looked around the hostile courtroom, cleared his dry throat, and slowly rose to his feet. "Uhm, I don't see any…any reason to carry this on any further. I move we find my client guilty."

The human defendant's brown eyes, the only ones in the courtroom that were full of life, suddenly went wide. He started shaking his head furiously and emitting muffled screams from behind his gag, but then, what did he really expect from a court-appointed attorney?

The judge nodded his head as if he totally understood and agreed with the defense attorney. When the defendant's lawyer sat back down, Judge Bailey turned toward the jury filled with zombies "Well, I guess you all can retire to the jurors' chamber and…"

"That's not necessary," one of the zombies said and stood up. "We the jury find the defendant…guilty of all charges."

The courtroom suddenly became filled with excited voices.

The bound defendant went berserk, but once again, what did he expect? Technically, they were not a jury of his peers.

"Order! Order in the court!" the judge yelled and banged his gavel. "Settle down, people!"

The noise lowered considerably, then disappeared altogether before Judge Bailey turned his glare to the weeping human. "You have been charged with petty theft and first degree murder. Because of your people's hatred toward the zombie race, I think we should make an example out of you. I sentence you to be devoured by those you hate so much. Ladies and gentlemen, justice is served."

The man's sentence was made official after the judge banged his gavel a final time.

Before the human defendant could figure out what had just taken place in the kangaroo court, his attorney leaned over and took a large bite out of his shoulder. The man howled in pain and quickly wrenched away, blood splattering onto the floor.

If facial expressions had names, the man would have been wearing a 'what the hell?' on his face when he turned to stare at his zombie lawyer. The blood that dribbled down the monster's mouth and chin explained it all.

The man, who was hog-tied and gagged, scooted away from his good-for-nothing attorney. However, the zombie to his right was just a small percentage of the problem. After glancing all around him, the man noticed there were several others on the move as well. The fearsome-looking judge was also making his way over the podium, heading in the guilty man's direction. All of the jurors were coming for him, along with the spectators to his rear and the prosecution team on his left.

Please don't! he thought but couldn't quite convey it because of the cloth in his mouth. With no other options before him, he fell onto his side, rolled until he hit the floor, then inch wormed his way under the defense table.

From where he lay, beneath the table, he could see legs surrounding him. Some were covered in torn pants, others in ragged dresses. Then there were the terrifying growls that nearly drowned out his frantic thoughts.

Unexpectedly, one of the zombies gripped the extremely heavy table and threw it halfway across the room, leaving the guilty man exposed. He suddenly began to scream for aid while flailing on the floor like a fish out of water, then his efforts were subdued by the wave of zombies that washed over him.

Justice had been served.

CLUB DEAD: ZOMBIE ISLAND

DANE T. HATCHELL

"I didn't think the line could move any slower, but I was wrong," Nancy said, lugging her seventy-pound suitcase forward another six inches. Looking for sympathy and a word of encouragement, she turned to her boyfriend, Rod, behind her.

Rod, sporting an Australian style olive green jacura, his sunglasses pulled low on his brow, ignored her. He was lost in a world of thrashing guitars and pounding drums mixing between his ears from his iPod.

She gave him an elbow to the ribs, and while pointing to her ears, she mouthed the words, *I'm talking to you*.

Jerking the ear buds out, he left them dangling down his chest. "What? I'm on vacation!"

Nancy rolled her eyes and turned back around.

"It's called 'Island time,' you have to get used to it," Lisa told Nancy. "If they'd serve us cocktails while we were in line it wouldn't be so bad."

"No problem, mon, soon come," Truett said to Lisa, his wife. "Everything is no problem, just ask the locals. You want service? *No problem*. You want it right now? *No problem*. You've been waiting for thirty minutes for them to pour you a drink? *No problem*. If you try to get these locals to hurry, it only makes them go slower. It took me a few trips to the islands before I figured out what *no problem* was code for. It means, *fuck you*."

"This is the smallest airport I've ever been to in my life," Bo said to his girlfriend, Natalie, who was right in the middle of taking a swig of a homemade tonic for a burst of energy after the flight over to the tiny Caribbean island.

"Hey, I've got an idea how we can pass the time," Truett said. "This is a French resort, right? And, you know how those French women all go topless on the beach, right? Well, we can play a game and imagine what all the women around us will look like topless!"

Responding to Truett's suggestion as if it were a subconscious command, Rod and Bo's roaming eyes went to work with robotic precision, targeting women both young and old alike, mentally freeing them of shirts and braziers.

Their three female companions looked at each other and shook their heads in unison, learning long ago that boys never really grow up.

Finally passing through immigration, the three couples and nearly one hundred others climbed aboard the vans waiting to take them for the three minute ride to Club Caribe. It took longer to load the passengers and their carry-ons than the drive itself to the resort receiving area.

Once at the resort, the captain of the village, Barke, offered a brief welcoming on stage after the guests seated themselves in the outside theater. Wearing a pink shirt and matching sneakers, he concluded his introduction with a warm invitation to meet back at that very theater each night at ten o' clock for live entertainment. The *Goes*, what the activity directors working at the village were called because they were 'always on the go,' performed song and dance routines for those wishing the fun to continue into the wee hours of the morning.

"And be sure, ladies and gentlemen, to be here tonight for our special zombie extravaganza. Your Goes will *rise* from the dead and dance, telling the story of their transformation, and of the loved ones they leave behind. It is our most popular show, and it will play only one time this week."

Bo leaned over to Truett. "That ought to be right up your alley," he said, knowing that Truett was geeky in that sort of way.

Afterward, the Goes led the guests to their assigned rooms after grouping them together according to location. The resort stretched across eighty acres, with the farthest room taking a full ten minutes to reach.

The island itself was the quintessential definition of a tropical paradise. Sandy white beaches kissed by the deepest of clear blue sea, invited the weary guests a chance to explore and relax, recharging the batteries of the soul. Bright Caribbean yellow, blue, and green rooms offset in triangular patterns gave each a spectacular ocean view.

After unpacking, the three couples met in front of the dive center for a late lunch at the dining room on the above level. A balding man exited through double doors dressed in a blue-colored rash guard to greet them.

"Ah, new arrivals! Welcome to Club Caribe. My name is Jean-Luc. I am the Dive Master and head of all of Club Caribe's water activities. Perhaps my new friends here will be spending some time under the waters of the Caribbean with me, no? Discovering the wonders of oceanic life, from the smallest anemone, to the great hammerhead sharks that lurk in the deep."

"We we, mon-*sewer*," Truett said.

"Ah, parlez-vous Français?"

"No, just funning with ya. My buddy Rod over there will be taking a few dives though. He's Canadian. You need to end every sentence with 'ay?' or he won't understand you."

"Really? How strange."

"No, not really, just funning with ya. Right now we're waiting to go to lunch."

From around Jean-Luc's legs, a small chicken with the coloring of dark rust stepped from the dive center, pecking at bits of debris on the concrete.

"Oh look, a chicken," Lisa said, bending down to pet it. "Hey, little chicky, aren't you cute."

"By any chance is its name, *le dîner de poulet gagnant gagnant?*" Truett asked.

"No, monsieur. Her name is not 'winner winner chicken dinner.' She is my pet, Calimero. A sad tale is hers. My sister is an activist for PETA. She rescued a dozen eggs from a French bioengineering facility in Paris. There is no telling what horrors awaited these poor innocent creatures of God had they hatched into a life filled with knives and needles. I incubated them here at the club. Alas, she was the only one to survive." Jean-Luc reached down to pick up Calimero.

Spying the hand coming towards her, the chicken thrust its head forward and gave him a peck on the soft skin between his thumb and forefinger.

"*Sacrebleu!*" Jean-Luc said, jerking his hand away.

"Maybe you should have named her 'Pecker'," Truett joked.

"Monsieur, my chicken is normally calm, cool, and collected. She is merely upset over your incessant prattle. Now, if you will excuse me, it is time for my Calimero to have a nap. I wish you to enjoy the lunch. We have chicken nuggets swimming in a pool of ketchup to delight someone of self acclaimed esteem such as yourself." Jean-Luc snatched the chicken up without further incident, slamming closed the door to the dive center behind him.

Truett looked over to see the other staring at him with obvious irritation. He raised his hands to his shoulders. "What I'd say to piss him off?"

Nancy looked over at Lisa. "How do you put up with *that*?"

Lisa sighed, "I'll give you my answer in French…champagne!"

* * *

Emile navigated the dive boat from the cockpit located on the upper deck. The stars twinkled above like illuminated diamonds on black velvet, as the sweet sounds of steel drums warmed the air in the background, playing over the radio.

"Hey, Emile, what's the name of the site we'll be diving at tonight?" Rod asked, calling up from the bow.

"The sea…I'm taking you to the sea. Ha-ha! Always with the questions, you guests. I am the boat captain. You place your trust in me. I will show you a time that you will never forget," Emile said, with his thick St. Lucian accent. He was a hulking, intimidating man to look at, but he was a gentle giant, and loved to tease.

Diesel fumes mingling with the constant sway of the boat had Rod contemplating hanging his head over the side but he fought off the nausea. The party of eight divers and two dive team members huddled in the stern, excitingly reminiscing over previous dive adventures, each story topping the one told before. A lovely Italian couple, Roberto and Louisa, had traveled the most, and delighted the others with photos of professional quality on their iPad.

The roar from the engine subsided, allowing Emile to call down to Lauren to hook the mooring line to the buoy. She hopped to attention, still dressed in her Goes attire; a pink shirt and white shorts. Tonight she wouldn't have the duty and privilege to dive with the team. Recent dental work required her to have her mouth wired shut for a minimum of six weeks, preventing her from breathing from a regulator underwater. Thankfully, it didn't prevent her from enjoying a few drinks after work though a straw.

Once the boat was secure, Lauren joined Jean-Luc midway through his instructional, as Emile climbed down the ladder and began suiting up for the dive.

Dabbing his brow with a soft towel, Jean-Luc excused himself while taking a sip of water. "The darkness of the waters will make you consume more air from your tank than you normally do in the daytime. You will understand why once you dive, as you can only see where your light shines. Your imagination will run wild as to what sea monster awaits nearby to attack. Be not afraid, there is nothing to fear. Emile and I will be there to guide you along the way. Now, everyone suit-up."

Lauren grabbed a tank for Jean-Luc and brought it over to him. "Are you okay? You're sweating, and it's not from the heat. You don't look so good."

"A touch of fever, perhaps. It is breaking."

"Don't go. Emile can handle it."

"Yes, he could. However, safety rules will not allow. For a group this size, we both have to go, or four will have to remain on the boat."

Jean-Luc took the tank and strapped it around his chest. Lauren knew he was right and there would be no talking him out of going. Every employee of Club Caribe made individual sacrifices in order to fulfill the obligations to their job. It would take more than a little fever for Jean-Luc to deny four guests an exciting night dive.

Bodies splashed over the side of the boat, the beams of the flashlights mingling with the blue waters turning the surface a mystic green. Rod felt almost immediate relief once off the boat and in a free float above the frigate wreck, his head no longer hostage of the cascading waves. He mouthed a difficult smile, and followed Emile and the others to the forty foot destination below.

Last in was Jean-Luc, breathing so heavily that he was afraid his tank wouldn't last the length of the dive. He, too, expected salvation once below the surface, the waters purging the impurities his body now secreted.

The dark depths wrapped him like a shroud, bringing confusion instead. The lights from the others loomed beneath him, seemingly an unreachable distance as his arms and legs refused to obey his commands and he began to convulse. Adrift in a world of indescribable beauty, the most hideous of transformations came over him, as he first lost consciousness, then passed into death.

One full minute after his heart took its final beat, the dead man's eyes opened to a world of new possibilities. After shedding the cumbersome air tank and mask, the newly-born zombie drifted downward under the cover of darkness, until coming to rest alongside a lone diver scanning coral for tiny creatures that hid during the day.

Two naked female legs stretched from wetsuit shorts down to their scuba fins, their knees bending slightly forward, calf muscles plump with meaty goodness. Jean-Luc crawled on the ocean floor using his hands, stealthily moving towards his prey.

Finding it tempting as a leg of roasted lamb, Jean-Luc grabbed onto the leg securely and ferociously torn into the bare flesh with his teeth.

The diver impulsively attempted to jerk free from her attacker, screaming while desperately trying to keep the regulator from escaping her mouth. Bubbles flooded from the mouthpiece in the woman's vain attempt to call for help. The flashlight fell from her hand as she reached down to fight the creature gnawing away on her calf.

Blood from the anterior artery pulsed into the water, sending out a silent signal that something was hurt and unable to defend itself. Fish swarmed to the newly-opened buffet.

She was doubly surprised when her fingers encountered hair and a human head as she fought to pull the attacker free. Her imagination ran wild with images of mutated humans from Atlantis seeking revenge on modern man for polluting the beautiful ocean waters.

Jean-Luc followed the meaty trail up to her thigh, and was well into devouring it, when her body went limp, her blood leaving in enough quantity to take her life with it. Leaving the dead body for the sea to reclaim, Jean-Luc gazed through the water, looking for his next victim.

By this time, Emile, Rod, and another diver had grouped together and were heading towards the flashlight abandoned on the ocean floor. Jean-Luc sensed a new source of food swimming his way, and headed straight for them. Several different species of hungry fish invaded the area, including a shiver of hammerhead sharks. The other three divers were too engrossed in a three foot spiny lobster to notice Jean-Luc's attack, and the dangers that were swimming circles around them.

Emile swam as fast as he could towards Jean-Luc, when he saw that he was without a mask and air tank. He couldn't imagine what had happened for him to be without his gear, and he fished out his spare regulator, ready to hand it to Jean-Luc when they met.

Rod and his companion looked at each other, not believing what they were seeing. They were even more surprised when Emile stopped kicking his fins and attempted to reverse course when Jean-Luc was only a few feet away from him.

It was the blank look in Jean-Luc's eyes, or the strand of femoral vein wedged between his lower teeth dangling from the side of his mouth, that stopped Emile cold, filling his bowels with hollow terror.

The two men met with Jean-Luc grabbing the flaying arms of Emile, seeking to draw him into a sweet embrace. Emile, outweighing Jean-Luc by a hundred pounds, had met his match against dead muscle reanimated by a power no longer limited by imprints of memory. Jean-Luc sank his teeth deep into his friend's neck, feeling the fast beat of the jugular pulsating in his mouth as he chewed down. The chunk of meat pulled free and found a new home in the zombie's stomach.

Rod and the other diver witnessed it all in the beam of their flashlights. Before either had a chance to fight or flee, the female diver first attacked by Jean-Luc—now reanimated— snuck up behind Rod and bit off his left ear.

Turning and facing his attacker, shining the light at what just bit him, Rod witnessed the woman he'd met on the boat that introduced herself as Gisele, chow down on his ear like it were a huge wad of bubble gum. He thought she was attractive then, but now, the distant stare that death brings and the wicked expression of human meat satisfaction on her face made her look like the ugliest woman in the world.

A hammerhead shark swam between Roberto and Louisa, just inches above the spiny lobster. They followed it with their lights, surprised, but relieved that it didn't stick around. The relief faded when the shark joined its companions circling above, and their lights illuminated over fifty of the nasty beasts.

The wall of sharks descended, the bodies disappearing in a frenzy of flesh, bone, and blood. Jean-Luc and Emile pulled the diver next to Rod down by his flippers as he tried to flee to the surface. The race was on, each starting at an ankle and attempting to out eat the other.

Unable to ward off Gisele's insatiable advances, Rod succumbed to death in the arms of the woman.

On the surface and in the boat, Lauren scanned the water from above with the searchlight. The water was boiling with more than the usual amount of air bubbles and it concerned her. A second later and the light reflected off the balding head of Jean-Luc bobbing in the water. She rushed to the side of the boat.

"Jean-Luc! Are you okay? What's happening down there? Is anyone hurt?" she called.

He paddled his way closer to the boat, keeping his face away from her light. Lauren reached down and grabbed his outstretched hand just as it got within range. Jean-Luc rose from the water, biting down hard on her left shoulder. Lauren jumped back, a chunk of flesh remaining in the zombie's mouth as he fell back into the sea.

"What the fuck, Jean-Luc! Have you gone crazy?"

The zombie smacked his prize with glee, his chewing no longer encumbered by the salt water.

"Oh my God..." Lauren dry heaved as she watched her boss' delight in eating her flesh.

Emile's head popped up next to Jean-Luc's, then Rod's and two other divers. All had the same dead look in their eyes, and gnashing teeth Lauren could almost feel as they clicked in anticipation of stripping her bones of its flesh.

She untied the boat from the buoy, ran up to the captain's chair, and started the engine. She didn't know what was going on, but she knew she wasn't staying any longer to find out.

A million thoughts raced through Lauren's mind as she sped back to shore. All her hopes and dreams of starting a new life when her contract with Club Caribe expired in six weeks were vanishing before her eyes.

She'd just abandoned the dive master, the captain and six guests, nearly a mile from shore. Would anyone believe her story? At the end of the week, she was to take the final test for her captain's license. There was no way that would be happening now.

Beads of sweat covered her brow. She smeared them across her forehead with the back of her hand, feeling grease and grime balling underneath.

Jean-Luc must have given me the bug he had, she thought.

Stopping the engine as she struggled to focus on the upcoming dock, her chest slammed against the steering wheel, knocking the wind out. The torpedo-shaped inflatable guard hanging from the side of the dock *whooshed* and deflated on impact.

Lauren wandered aimlessly on the upper deck, and fell down the ladder opening to the hull deck, no longer having the sense to climb, or much sense of anything at all. Though her legs took the brunt of the fall, she managed to upright herself, ambling towards the dock as the boat rubbed against a pylon, bumping against it by the force of the incoming tide.

Stepping onto the dock, she didn't see her roommate's kitten, Shark Bait, waiting to greet her. The kitten rubbed its face on her ankle, smelling blood, and licked a tiny cut with its sandpaper tongue.

Lauren shambled forward, bumping Shark Bait's nose hard enough to cause it to jump away. The small creature was nothing more than a nuisance, getting in the way of her burning desire to feed.

"I don't get it? It's June, we're in the Caribbean, and it's hot and humid, but you're wearing short-shorts, flip flops, and a leather jacket. What's up with the leather jacket?" Nancy asked Natalie, taking her drink from Lenny the bartender.

Natalie steadied her organic martini. "My arms get cold. Leather is natural anyway. You'd be surprised how well it breathes."

"Your arms couldn't get cold in this bar. This is the main bar; you'd think they'd crank the a/c up a little. That's my only real complaint with this club. It's almost impossible to find a place to cool off." She had to move out of the way of a determined Lenny, now sporting a Reception Team shirt and busy carrying a couples' luggage.

"This place is dead," Bo said, the umbrella from his drink scratching his nose while sipping through his straw.

"Well, it's been a long day. I guess everyone's tired. Look at the Goes sitting over there." Nancy pointed towards two sectional couches piled with slothful male and female Goes from various teams. "Look at them: young, virile. I bet I could tell you each one of their personal stories just by reading their faces."

"Fuck that, we're on vacation. I know how to get this party started!" Truett made a beeline for a floor lamp, removing the taper drum-style shade, and placed it on his head.

Lisa groaned.

"How do you have sex with that man?" Nancy asked.

"I use the most readily available aphrodisiac—champagne," Lisa said, turning to the nearest bartender, who was named Jedi. "Hey, Jedi, I'd like two glasses of champagne, please."

The ebony god gave her a wide smile, showing his perfect teeth, and lifted two full, tall crystal glasses of the sparkly goodness from behind the bar and placed them before her, as if anticipating her request.

"Oh, thank you," Lisa said, wondering if perhaps the 'force' *was* with him.

Truett sauntered over to the couches and addressed the Goes. "All aboard, ladies!" Then, pulling an imaginary lever in the air, he said, "Woo woo. Barrrr riiiide! Get on board this train. Ah-chug-chug-chug-chug-chug…"

Leaping from the couch with glee, Eve was the first to place her hands on Truett's hips, as he mechanically stepped forward, moving his elbows back and forth, emulating the side rods of a steam locomotive. Louden, Meaks, Joshy, Francois, Ashley, Mari-Annie, and Lenny quickly followed suit. Lenny had changed into Water Sports team attire.

"AMF's for my friends here!" Truett declared, reaching the bar.

A hail of cheers rose from the Goes as the bartenders snapped to. Jedi lifted two of the icy drinks from behind the bar, handing them to Eve. Who carefully poured one into a thirty-ounce squirt bottle.

Each member of the crew now happily held the delicious and potent concoction of vodka, rum, gin, tequila, blue curacao, and a splash of Sprite.

Truett lifted his glass. "Cheers to my friends. Why is this drink called AMF anyway?" With animation, he lifted his hand up to his ear.

"*Adios, mother fucker!*" the crew roared in unison, before tilting the glasses back.

Lauren entered through the side door without anyone other than Eve noticing. The once bronze glow of her tanned face was now ghastly white, with deep pits around her eyes circled in black. Blood was seeping from various cuts and scrapes from the fall she'd taken, as well as the bite from Jean-Luc, making a mess of her shirt and shorts.

"Hey, Lauren. I see you're in makeup for the zombie show. I know this'll be the first time for you to dance since your dental work, so I've got some liquid courage for you." Eve shoved the straw in Lauren's mouth just as Lauren was about to give her a *hug,* squeezing the bottle until the sides almost touched.

"Look at you, you must be thirsty. You haven't even cried *uncle* yet." Allowing air into the bottle, Eve squeezed the remaining contents down Lauren's mouth until it was empty.

Lauren stepped back, her arms spread open from her side, while tilting her head towards the ceiling. Mouth opened, her eyes rolled into the back of her head, she tried to walk. The impulses animating her legs fired in reverse order. As she intended to move a foot right, but it went left, causing her to perform a wicked dance in her attempt to maintain her balance.

"Oh, I get it, practicing your dance routine. I bet you're nervous. Jedi! Another drink for my friend here!" Eve yelled.

A fat, middle-aged, balding man with a bright red head from too much sun, approached the bar, pointing towards Lauren. "I'll have what that young lady over there is drinking."

"Here's an extra copy of your key, Mr. Adams. Don't worry about the other one. I'm sure someone will find and return it," Eric in Reception, said.

"Thanks, Eric. Anything you can do about the air conditioning in the dining room? It's hard to find a cool spot outside of my room. Hell, it's even hot inside this lobby," Mr. Adams said.

"Sorry, Mr. Adams, the a/c works hard twenty-four/seven. It's hard to cool down the moist, tropical air. Have you made it to one of our nightly shows in the theater?" Eric asked.

"No."

"We have one every night. My favorite is 'Cabaret.' I have a starring role. You should check it out, the cool breeze from the water blows across the theater, keeping it cool. Tonight's show is about zombies." Eric stopped as the outside doors opened with a thump, and five divers stumbled in. "Oh look. Here are some of the zombie dancers now. I don't know why they're wearing wet suits; must be a wardrobe change."

Stephanie, the other receptionist, called from behind the counter, "Jean-Luc! What are you doing in here? You're getting the floors all wet!"

Jean-Luc stopped. He pulled his lips back and exposed his teeth.

"That's not funny, guys. You need to get down to the theater, the show starts soon. Take it out of here. Go on, shoo," Eric said, miffed.

The other four walking dead broke away from behind their leader, heading straight for Mr. Adams and Eric.

A vicious snarl from Jean-Luc froze Stephanie in place, her mind whirling in disbelief. Lifting the false counter, Jean-Luc was on her before she could escape, pinning her against the wall.

Eric shrieked as Mr. Adams fell to an onslaught of ravenous zombies, each marking his territory, and dividing him into four sections. Rod and Emile started from the top, ripping away the tender cheek and neck meat. The other two satisfied their cravings by starting at the thighs, gouging out chunks of meat with each mouthful.

Mr. Adams' screams turned to gurgles while choking on his own blood. The zombies were eating him alive, the pain beyond anything he could have ever imagined. Nerves searing from sharp teeth enflamed his entire body, until he passed out from the pain, to then fall into an eternal sleep.

Eric pounded on the back of Jean-Luc's head with a complementary guest umbrella, but it did nothing to slow the ravenous zombie down. A pool of blood grew on the floor, dripping down from Stephanie's beautiful golden hair.

Jean-Luc never noticed Eric disappearing from his side as his undead brethren pulled Eric away, continuing the feast.

Savoring the body like none before, Jean-Luc laid Stephanie on the floor and began eating her entrails. Her large intestine tore at his second bite, bursting the depleted remains of dinner three days before. Corn stuck between his teeth from Mexican night. As Jean-Luc worked his way up, remnants of fish, rice, and beans squirted out, filling his mouth from Bahamian night. The small intestine secreted the goodness of Italian, leading to the final prize of escargot and fine cheeses from French night in her stomach, the meal she had eaten just two hours earlier.

Ironically, the song, *Your Body is a Wonderland*, played joyfully across the lobby speakers.

"Where should we sit?" Lisa asked, looking over the available seats in the theater.

"Let's sit somewhere close to the end. If it's really bad, we can make a quick exit," Truett said, waiting for his Irish coffee to cool enough to sip.

"Rod loves these shows," Nancy said. "This isn't our first trip to Club Caribe, you know. The Goes train really hard for this. They're not paid anything extra either. It's their gift to us. Rod told me to save him a seat. The dive trip should be heading back now." She took a sip of her colorful drink.

"Natalie and I are gonna go over to the food table in the back and talk to Ralphie. I've seen these shows before and…let's just say they're not for everyone," Bo said, making a quick exit and pulling Natalie by the hand, not wanting to hear any whining from the others.

White cloth draping over a rectangular table presented an array of handcrafted flowers made from fruits and vegetables, surrounding samplings of ripe cheeses, crackers, and dips. With a wide grin behind the table, Ralphie stood invitingly, always ready to aid and assist in his guests' dining pleasure. He was a large man, his face sharp as chiseled granite, his eyes cold as blue steel.

"Hey, Ralphie, you've outdone yourself again," Bo said, admiring the presentation of food.

Natalie snatched up a creation of triple-cream brie dotted in caviar and radish dust, and bit into it. "Mmm, mmm. This is better than sex."

"As always, ma'am, my reward is your pleasure," Ralphie said, taking a slight bow.

"This is wonderful food art. I'm amazed at the variety of dishes that you offer at each meal. How do you manage to outdo yourself each time?" Bo asked, before crunching down on a cracker dipped in a pâté of sea urchin and squirrel brains marinated in watermelon vodka.

"Years of training."

"Oh yeah, where'd you get your training from?" Bo asked, chasing his first bite down with another.

"US Army Rangers. Gulf War 1 and 2. I was deployed in Afghanistan for the last eight years before making Club Caribe my home. I thought it was time to explore the creative side of my personality."

"Wow, I never would have figured that. Excellent choice, my friend, you've found your true calling in life." The lights dimmed over the theater. Bo turned towards the stage, then turned back to Ralphie. "Oh, and thank you for your service."

"The honor and privilege is all mine," Ralphie said with a smile.

A large screen to the right of the stage came to life with scenes of zombies rising from the surf, attacking the busy Goes and startled guests relaxing in the sun. The next scene was a dining room flooded with the undead, making a mock meal of the host and cooks busily preparing food. The last scene ended in the lobby, where the attack of the undead continued, until the last of the living turned, and the mob of zombies walked menacingly towards the camera and the viewer.

"Man, that was a really bad movie," Bo said.

Natalie punched him in the shoulder. "Be nice. They're just doing this for fun. Try to get into the spirit of things."

The curtains parted, and music swelled from above, darkening the mood with a creepy song by Marilyn Mansion. Six of the male Goes fronted by the six foot seven Cedrick began the gyration of the angst of the dead. Each was adorned in tattered clothing of mock filth and skin plagued with imitation rot.

"Hey, this looks pretty good," Lisa said.

"I know. I hope Rod gets here soon," Nancy added, taking a quick look towards the back to see if Rod had arrived.

The song came to a frenzied conclusion and the lights dimmed. Scurrying in the cover of darkness, six female Goes in the garb of the undead replaced their male counterparts. The dance of the undead continued.

The men waited behind the curtain for the song to end. Next, they would join the women on stage in a routine simulating zombie courtship. From behind, Jean-Luc and his hungry crew arrived, attacking the unsuspecting dance members. What screams weren't drowned out by the loud music, blended in as part of the act.

The zombettes finished the last *lumber and shuffle* of the routine at the conclusion of the song. The curtains closed, the lights dimming once more.

"Okay, what's holding up the guys?" one of the Goes asked; it was Ashley.

"Goofing off behind the curtain is my guess. Let's go get them, the song's about to start," Meaks said.

Walking past the curtain, Meaks bumped into Joshy, her boyfriend, ready to greet her. "What the hell are you guys doing back here? Get your ass on stage!"

Joshy hungrily grabbed for her chest. She slapped his hands away just before contact.

"Not now, horn dog. We've got a show to perform. Great, you've got fake blood all over your hands and now it's on me. What's going on here?"

Wrapping his arms tightly around her, Joshy hugged her with a passion unlike ever before, cracking her ribs, and crushing the breath out of her. He began his first cuisine of the undead by eating the lips he used to love to kiss.

The other women similarly fell to the onslaught of walking corpses, their blood quickly spilling across the floor.

"Seems like the show should have started back by now," Truett said.

"Probably wardrobe malfunction. Some of the women were about to fall out of their shredded tops. I wish Rod would hurry up and get here," Nancy said.

"Me too, I don't want him to miss a free shot of French tits," Truett joked.

From either side, coming from behind the stage, two groups of cast members, joined by a diving team, mechanically walked towards the waiting guest.

"What's going on now?" Lisa asked.

"Oh, I get it. They're going to come out and pretend to attack the crowd as part of the act. Hey look, Cedrick's right there." Truett stood up from his chair. "Hey, Cedrick, hey buddy, over here! Come take a picture with my wife."

Lisa stood by her chair and waited. "Wow, he sure is tall. He's such a good actor, too. He's almost making me scared."

Lisa turned, posing as Truett focused the camera. Cedrick loomed from behind her, then bent down to bite her neck.

"That's it…that's it…got it. Wow, perfect shot!" Truett looked up from the image captured on his camera to see Cedrick chomp down on his lovely wife's neck. Blood rained down her chest like a crimson waterfall. With her scream weakening his knees, he stumbled forward to rescue her.

Chaos quickly ensued as the wave of undead cut through the crowd, taking down the weak and the slow at first. Blood was splattering in all directions, bathing the dead and undead in a christening of blood and gore.

"What's happening in there?" Natalie asked, quickly clinging to Bo's side.

"You two get back. I know how to handle this." Ralphie rolled out his knife collection and selected a twelve inch butcher knife and a cleaver, but before he could come from behind the table, he looked up to see a zombie almost upon them.

Bo leaped into action with a front kick, knocking the zombie's head so far back that the neck snapped.

Ralphie was at his side in a heartbeat. "Where'd you learn that?" he asked.

"Japan. I went to college in Tokyo. I didn't spend my free time playing Pokémon. Hey, he's still moving."

Ralphie dropped to one knee, bringing the cleaver down straight through the zombie's neck, severing the spine. "He's not moving now."

Another attacker came at Natalie. She raised her forearm to block the snake-like strike of the zombie's bite. The dead man bit down hard, but his teeth couldn't penetrate the leather jacket she wore.

Ralphie's twelve inch blade went in one ear of the zombie and poked out the other. Another one was down, but there was still a lot more to go.

"Hoo-ah!" Ralphie screamed from the top of his lungs, and charged towards the turbulent crowd in the theater.

"We've got to get out of here, now!" Bo yelled, pulling Natalie away from the horrific scene.

"What're we going to do?" she asked.

"I've got an idea. This way, hurry!" Bo led her down the narrow concrete walk, the serenity of the lush landscaping a forgotten blur. "Good! I see the boat's still at the dock. Pray we can make it there before any of them get us."

Their journey unimpeded, the two ran down the dock, the faint echo of their hollow steps mingling with the calm of the ocean waves below. Bo helped Natalie onto the boat first, then followed, making a quick check above for any surprises.

"It's clear. I'm taking us out." He started the engine, reversed course from the dock, and turned the boat to the open sea.

"Bo, can you come down here? I've got something for you to see," Natalie called.

Concerned as to just what was keeping Natalie on the bottom deck, he fast stepped down the ladder to join her.

"Look who's onboard with us. A cute little kitten," she said.

The kitten sat listless underneath a bench.

Bo retrieved a flashlight from the console, and shined the light down over the kitten.

"It might be sick. Its eyes looked glazed over."

Natalie bent over and scratched the kitten behind the ear. "Ouch! The little bugger bit me!"

Backing away, Bo examined the bite mark on her hand. "It's a small nip, you'll live."

Natalie nodded, then began to feel a strange pain in her head, her vision blurring slightly.

"You know, we didn't even get to eat dinner tonight. I hope it doesn't take so long to find help that I get hungry enough to eat you." She didn't laugh at her quip. In fact, the thought of eating Bo didn't seem unreasonable at all.

Natalie's eyes turned milky under the dim moonlight, her mouth watering with anticipation.

Outside the small airport a mere three football fields away from Club Caribe, one hundred and twenty Frenchmen, weary from a direct ten hour flight, sweltered in the noonday sun.

"Where are the vans to drive us to the club? This is an outrage!" an aging man said, his white shirt translucent from sweat. "This is my third trip to this resort. There are no Goes to greet us and no vans to drive us. I've paid many Euros for this vacation. I demand to see the captain of the resort."

A representative from the airport management, a young man of twenty-five, stood in silent attention, allowing the upset traveler to vent. In the background, an old man strummed two chords on a five-string guitar, singing, *"If you can afford this vacation to my island you can afford to put money in my hat."*

"Sir, we have tried calling but no one will answer. You said you have been to the club before. It is but a short walk to the reception area. It will not take more than fifteen minutes," the young man said.

The aging Frenchman threw his arms at the sky and cursed. "Come, I will lead the way," he said, grabbing his luggage, and leading the march forward. The others quickly fell behind him, eager to check in and find respite from the blazing sun.

Though the van ride to the resort took only a few minutes, the trek on foot made the experience entirely different. The group passed an empty guard shack, causing the Frenchman to fume even more from the lack of management.

Nearing the reception area, he could see the awaiting Goes through the trees and shrubs as they gathered for the guests' arrival, each dressed in bright colors of the day's theme.

Sweat rolling down his forehead stung his eyes, and the Frenchman's ire grew to the point he felt like his head would explode. As he rounded the topiaries, the expected entourage was waiting to greet him with open arms as well as open mouths.

Barke and Chocki, the captain and co-captain of the resort were there. The host of Goes, many of whom the Frenchman had met on his previous trip, were there also.

The Frenchman froze in his tracks, letting his luggage fall to the ground. Gasps and startled cries erupted from behind him, as others by his side laid eyes on the blood and gore-stained zombies of Club Caribe.

A tradition of an open buffet to greet new arrivals was suddenly established at Club Caribe. Every zombie ate all it wanted, but none finished their meal feeling full.

BERTHA

TERRY ALEXANDER

The goal was simple, triple the size of any given animal for little or no extra cost. The potential benefits to mankind were enormous. The profit line far out weighed any worldly benefits. The Val-Mont Corporation had secretly worked on the project for years. Their scientists had concocted a mixture of synthetic protein supplements added to livestock feed to stimulate growth.

Unfortunately, when the shit starts to roll downhill, it's like a snowball, growing larger and picking up speed. When it hits you, it'll bowl you over leaving you stained, smelly and dead.

Andy Parker raced to the culvert and crawled inside. Things were bad today. The walkers roamed the grounds of *Fountain Head Lodge*. Every time he tried to get to a vehicle, the nasty things cut him off. To make things worse, Bertha wandered the countryside, eating everything she could find, either human or zombie.

"Is she back?" a female voice asked.

Andy knew Regina's high-pitched whine. "Yeah, Bertha's still out there. I think she can smell me. I used to be one of her handlers before she changed. I think she recognizes my scent."

"Who in the hell had the bright idea to give growth hormones to a gorilla? I can see cows and sheep, things like that, but a damned ape." Regina moved deeper into the darkened culvert.

"It was Jenkins' idea. He thought it would make a big splash when we had the barbeque to sway the investors." Andy brushed dirt from his face. "Come on. We'll crawl out the other side and get back to the lodge."

"Hell of a way to make a splash." She crawled toward the dot of light thirty feet ahead. "You know they may be wandering around on the other side."

"You can bet on it. Jenkins and Malone, some of the others, they're still around." His hand brushed her ankle in the close confines. "There's more coming in every day."

"Jenkins hired me a week before the festivities. I was eye candy for the big executives he was trying to woo." Regina pulled a short barreled .22 revolver from her jacket. "All he really wanted to do was get in my pants."

"Bob always was a pussy hound. Be careful when you climb out. Remember, shoot for the head."

"How could I forget?" Regina glanced through the opening. She hesitated a moment. "Here I go." She crawled into the sunlight.

Andy followed close behind. The nearest zombie ambled near the forest fifty yards away, unaware of their presence. "I think that's Jenkins," he whispered. "This way. The lodge should be over the hill." He grabbed Regina's hand, pulling her along.

"I wish we could eat some of that barbequed brisket." She sucked air through her teeth.

"Bad idea. It's contaminated. We need to find some transportation and get out of here." His hand clamped down on her shoulder, forcing her to the ground. "Duck, Bertha's coming this way.

"Damn it, not so rough." Regina's shirt ripped under his grasp.

"Shhh. Be quiet." Andy covered her mouth. "Bertha may be a zombie, but she can hear a pin drop."

The colossal ape stood upright. Her milky eyes scanned the grounds. A shard of bone protruded through the side of her smashed, bulbous nose. It jiggled as she sniffed the foul air.

Bertha's eyes locked on Jenkins and a low growl rumbled deep in her chest. She moved quickly, crossing twenty feet from the cowering pair. Her large paw closed on Jenkins' chest, lifting the squirming zombie to her wide open mouth.

"Come on." Andy pulled Regina to her feet. "We've got to run for it. We need to move while she's eating."

Regina broke into a sprint. Her feet almost flew over the short grass of the manicured lawn.

"She's seen us!" Andy shouted. He glanced ahead. A hundred feet separated them from the safety of the lodge. "Faster." He caught her elbow but the material ripped under his grasp. "We've got to move faster!"

A loud, ominous growl sounded behind them. The heavy thump of Bertha's ponderous footsteps seemed to vibrate the ground beneath their feet.

"We can make it. Keep moving, we can make it," Andy urged, pulling Regina along. He risked a glance over his shoulder. Bertha was moving toward them, quickly closing the distance. Her gore-smeared face pulled back in a snarl, bits of Jenkins' shirt and his flesh caught between her teeth.

They passed under a roadside awning, the roof giving Andy a measure of comfort. His confidence soared. For a brief instant he knew they were going to get inside safely. They raced through the flower garden bordering the driveway. Then a piece of gravel rolled under Regina's foot and sent them sprawling when she reached out for him to support her.

Andy rolled to the pavement, both knees scraped and bleeding. He felt disconnected, like waking from a dream, taking a second to shake his head to clear away the cobwebs.

A loud snarl yanked him back to the present. Bertha was drawing closer, her split and tattered lips pulled away, exposing large incisors.

Oh hell, this is real, he thought and rolled away from Bertha's searching paw, catching Regina's belt and yanking her upright.

"What happened?" she mumbled as she ran a raw bloody hand over her forehead.

"Keep moving, we've got to get inside." He pulled her to the glass door. "Come on, Bertha's right behind us."

They bolted through the door a split second ahead of the monstrous ape. It stopped at the glass barrier. Andy pushed Regina to the far side of the room, near the check-in desk.

"Why did she stop? She could shatter the glass if she wanted." Regina panted, holding her aching side.

"Jenkins kept her in a thick glass cage. She tried but she couldn't break it. Now she's scared of the glass. It's a conditioned reflex. I wonder what he did to her?" He collapsed in a chair near the elevator, drawing deep breaths through his open mouth. "He went too far with the supplements, added something that caused the change. The animals got sick…" He stopped to clear his throat.

Regina ran a hand through her long red hair. "I know they have a first-aid kit around here somewhere. I need to clean and bandage this." She held her injured hand up for his inspection.

"I'll check behind the desk." He slowly got to his feet and rummaged behind the counter. "Here it is."

"I wish we could find some bigger guns." Her face wrinkled in pain as he cleaned the wound.

"The security guards all have side arms. There may be a shotgun or rifles in some of the vehicles, but you'll have a hard time getting close enough to get one without getting killed. Besides, we'd need a cannon to hurt Bertha." He patted the raw flesh with an iodine pad.

"It's already been a week. We haven't seen anyone else since this started. It could have spread all over the state by now. We'll run out of food and water soon. What'll we do then?" Her free hand clenched into a fist.

"We have to figure out a way to get to a car and get away from here." He wrapped a loose bandage around her palm, attaching it with two strips of tape.

"Grab a chair. I'll clean the grit from your knees." She tugged the metal box toward her.

"Forget it, I'll be okay," he said.

"Look, this disease, virus or whatever it is, can be transferred through open wounds. You won't be good to me or anyone else if you're a damn zombie." Her eyes pinched together. "Now sit down."

Andy grumbled under his breath but he limped back to the over-stuffed chair. Regina knelt before him and gently pulled the thin material from the deep, blood-clotted scrapes.

"You said the animals got sick. What happened?" she asked.

Andy nodded. "A couple of months before the barbeque, Jenkins doubled the doses for each animal. They got sick, wouldn't eat, then their fever spiked at 108, and thick mucus began draining from their nostrils. I checked on them one morning and they looked dead, but then they started moving. I knew something was wrong. They didn't act the same and Jenkins refused to have the vet check them out."

"I wish I'd never seen Jenkins. I knew this job was bad news the minute I took it," she said. "But I needed the money."

Andy winced as she applied the iodine. He noticed a glimmer of a smile play across her lips. "When he brought in the butchers to get Babe ready for the barbeque, they told him something was wrong with the steer. The meat didn't look right, but Jenkins didn't want to hear any of it. We served the guests roasted zombie. Damn, I'm glad I didn't eat any."

"I nearly did. I had a piece of brisket halfway to my mouth, when that damn ape broke free and started eating everyone." She rubbed her temple. "My head's pounding."

"Take a couple of aspirins." He fished a small tin from his pocket. "We need to get to a vehicle. Find one that we can break into and get the hell out of here."

"Every time we go out we only have time to check a couple of cars before Bertha and her zombies are on top of us. I'm beginning to think we need to hide and sit it out." She rose to her feet, "I've got to find some water."

"If we can get all the walkers on the far side of the lodge, away from the parking lot, maybe we'd have a chance to get something running." He stared through the shaded windows. "Wait a second. The Humvee, the one Jenkins hired to bring the big shots in from the helicopter pad. It should have the keys in it."

"Yeah, it's also got a big gut-eater trapped inside it. We'd have to deal with him." Regina tilted a bottle of water to her lips and washed the pills down.

"If we can get all the other ones on the far side of the building, we can blow its brains out and take the Humvee." Andy jumped to his feet. He gritted his teeth against the throbbing in his knee. "Let's take a look at the other side." He hobbled toward the stairs leading to the second floor.

"I don't like this." She followed him. "What if the zombies found a way inside?"

"Keep your pistol ready." He pulled a .32 revolver from his pocket. "Remember, we have twelve bullets. We can't waste any." He walked into the center of the stairway, drawing a deep breath, as he reached the second floor landing. He stared down the shadowy corridor for several seconds, before taking the first step.

Regina bumped his back as they crept toward the large window. She jumped to the wall, her eyes wide, the pistol shaking in her hand. A thumping sounded from the room on their right.

"There's one in there," she whispered.

"Don't panic. It can't hurt us if it's in there." He tip-toed to the window. "Look at Bertha. She's climbing that TV tower just like it was a tree." He nodded toward the steel structure in the distance. "We need to account for Bertha when we make our next try."

"I don't think I want to try again. We need to stick it out. The authorities will find us eventually." She leaned against the wall. "Those business men out there will be missed, and someone will come looking for them."

"You said it yourself. We don't know how far this has spread. It could be weeks before we get any help, maybe months." He scratched his head. "We don't have that much time."

The door crashed open and slammed into the wall behind them, and a snarling security guard stumbled into the hallway, the blue uniform torn and filthy. The zombie's dead eyes fastened on the pair highlighted against the window. The scabby, sore-dotted head tilted, sniffing the air. A low growl sounded deep in its throat. It charged toward Andy and Regina with hands outstretched.

"Oh hell, the shit's hit the fan." Andy shoved Regina to the far wall. "Take him down."

"You don't have to be so damned rough about things." She sighted her .22 on the zombie's head. "A girl likes a little tenderness, you know, a little kindness." Her finger found the trigger. "Die, you stinking bastard!" she shouted.

The bullet tore a line down the security guard's cheek, blasting away the bottom half of its ear.

"Nice shot, Annie Oakley." Andy lined the .32 on the pallid forehead. He thumb cocked the hammer. At four feet, he fired. The zombie jerked and stumbled, falling face down, sliding along the polished floors. "Guess what? We've gained a pistol." He stuffed the pistol into his waistband while kneeling by the body. Then, shaking fingers removed the 380 automatic and ammunition from the guard's belt. "They'll be looking for us now. We need to move."

"Let's go," she nodded.

Andy slowly led Regina down the hallway. He stopped midway. "You know, maybe we're going at this all wrong." He licked his lips. "I've got a wild idea. We've been trying to keep the zombies out. Why not bring them in? I don't know why I didn't think of this before."

"That fall hurt you worse than I thought." She massaged her forehead. "My headache's coming back." She locked eyes with him. "That's the stupidest idea I've ever heard, bringing the damn zombies in here with us. We need to lay low and ride this out."

"No, you're missing the point. We get them in here and then we go out there."

"You're crazy. What about Bertha? What are we going to do about her?" she demanded.

"I've been to car shows in this place. There's a big door they use to bring the cars through. We need to get to the auditorium and find that door. If we can get them all inside, we can limit their movements, keep them in one spot." A large smile brightened his face. "If this works, we can get out of here."

"There's a lot of 'ifs' in that idea."

"Well, it's a good idea and it's the only one I have. Unless you have a better one? If so let's hear it."

She frowned and crossed her arms over her chest. She had no better idea.

He flashed her a wink. "That's what I thought. Look, think positive. This might work out."

He limped down the stairway. "Move careful. We don't want to attract any more attention right now." They followed the posted directions. Finding a massive ground level stage, the empty seats began at floor level and stretched up to the entryway. "There it is." Andy pointed at the huge overhead door.

"Okay, *Mr. Wizard,* how's your plan work exactly?" Regina folded her arms across her chest again. "How do we get the zombies in here?"

"Noise for one and scent for the other," Andy smiled. "First thing we need is a pair of rubber gloves."

"Why?" Regina frowned.

"We're bringing stinky here." Andy winked.

Moving the rotting corpse proved problematic. "My God, this thing stinks." Regina wrapped a pillowcase over the lower portion of her face to help block the odor. The security guard's soft flesh oozed through her hands. "I can't do this." Color drained from her face, and tears filled her eyes as she gagged.

"Come on. We can do this," he said.

Together they rolled the cadaver onto a sheet and carried the unwieldy burden downstairs. "We'll need a lot of stuff, anything we can pile around the outer area to make it hard for the zombies to get up the stairs." They packed mattresses and chairs, tables and lamps along the front row of seats, leaving a narrow passageway to allow an escape.

"I'm beat. I need to rest." Regina flopped into a plush seat. "Do you really think this will work?"

Andy sat cross-legged on the floor. "It's the best chance we've got. When it's time, I'll make as much noise as possible. That should lure the zombies inside, and if we're lucky, maybe Bertha, too. You'll be near the upper doors covering my back. I need to find a way to close that overhead door when the time comes. If we can get them all inside and slam it shut, we can get away while Bertha's enjoying breakfast."

"You're quite a salesman." Regina shook her head. "You never get tired of talking. Besides, I'm not going to stay here alone."

"I am a pretty good salesman." He nodded. "Jenkins used to say I could sell ice to Eskimos."

She stifled a laugh. "I'd love a bath and some clean clothes. I've been too scared to think about cleaning up."

"There's some clothes in the office that might fit you, and you could wash up in the pool." Andy rubbed the week old stubble along his jaw. "I'll keep a lookout while you bathe."

"You could join me in the pool." A twinkle gleamed in her eyes, a mischievous smile playing along her lips. Her hand found his. "Come on. We deserve this."

He peered through the glass doors. The pool area appeared to be deserted. They crept inside, pistols held at the ready. Regina inched to the edge of the pool and stared into the water. Satisfied that no zombies lurked under the surface, she laid her bundle of clothes near the handrail.

"Looks clean," he mumbled, watching in awe as Regina kicked off her shoes and quickly disrobed. She stood for a moment, allowing Andy a good look at her body, then dove beneath the calm surface.

"Oh, my God." Andy tugged at his clothes.

"Come on in. What are you waiting for?" Regina teased. "The water's perfect."

Andy tripped on his underwear. He flopped into the pool, creating a huge splash. Regina's arms circled his neck as he surfaced. Her lips found his in a powerful embrace, one filled with an intense desire for the touch of another. Andy felt his manhood stiffening, as her hard nipples pressed against his chest.

"I really need this." Tears pooled in the corner of her eyes. "I've got to have a man's touch once more before…" The words trailed away.

"You don't have to explain. I understand." He pushed her to the shallow end of the pool. Her legs circled around his waist. She closed her eyes, then drew in a sharp breath when he penetrated her. Their fierce, animalistic love-making ended quickly with deep guttural moans.

Regina palmed water and poured it over her face. "Are you up for another? This time we'll make it last."

"Anything for you." Andy's lips settled at the nape of her neck, nuzzling lightly. "Anything for you."

They watched the dawn break over the tree tops, shadows falling before the light. In the forest below, Bertha smashed through the small trees, uprooting bushes as she searched for breakfast. The human zombies fled from her approach.

"It's nearly time." Andy released Regina's hand. "We need to get ready."

She nodded, climbing to her feet. "I hope this works," she said. Her lips lightly brushed his. "For luck."

"We'll need some." Hand in hand, they walked to the auditorium. "I hope that rope we rigged to the door works out."

She nodded. "Me too. How's the leg? Can you run?"

"I'll manage." They reached the doors. "Good. The doors are secure. When I come out we'll lock this one." He slipped inside. The darkness seemed to cling to his body like a physical thing. The battery operated emergency lights glowed along the walls, providing him a sense of direction. He slowly descended the stairs and found the chain in the semi-darkness. A quick jerk set the door moving.

Oh God, I hope this works, he thought.

The hard lump in his stomach swelled to gigantic proportions. Flies buzzed around the security guard's body, the stench nearly gagging him. He rigged the rope to the chain, silently offering a prayer that his cobbled together double pulley system would work and shut the overhead door, thus trapping the zombies inside.

The darkness thinned to light. Andy blinked several times, his eyes adjusting to the sudden influx of light. *It's now or never.* His hands closed on the metal trash can and short length of pipe. "All right, you bastards." He banged on the trash can. The harsh metallic sound echoed in the cavern-like showroom and set his ears to ringing. "Come on, I'm waiting!"

The first zombie raced inside within seconds. "You must have been close." Andy dropped the trash can, braining the zombie with the pipe. A stream of yellowish blood flowed from the creature's ears. It slumped to the floor like a rag doll.

"Are you all right?" Regina called.

"I'm good. Get ready. They're coming." Andy retreated to the barrier around the stage. He banged the steel pipe on the floor. "Come on, damn it. I can't wait all day!"

Thirty zombies raced through the giant doorway. The thick stench of bloated, decaying flesh overwhelmed the undead's senses, sending them into a feeding frenzy. Grunts of rage and hunger filled the chamber. The dead things streaked to the bodies. Dirty, grimy, blood-caked hands pulled the loose flesh from the bones, stuffing their mouths with the rotten meat.

Andy eased through the gap in the barrier, ready to make a mad dash to the door. *Come on, Bertha. Where are you? I'm serving up a five course meal for you over here.*

Then Bertha's huge shape blotted out the sunlight. Her nostrils widened, drawing in the smell of rotting flesh. The metal frame of the doorway scraped hair and flesh from her arms and legs as she forced her way inside. Her paw closed on the nearest walking cadaver, and lifted it to her gaping mouth.

"Pull the rope!" Andy bolted up the stairs. "Pull the damn rope!" His feet pounded on the steps. "Hurry, pull the rope!"

With a tremendous crash, the door slammed to the floor, bathing the interior of the auditorium in darkness, broken only by the emergency lights and the single entry where Regina waited. Andy ran to the sliver of light while chaos reined below him. The sound of rapid footsteps and flesh striking on metal reached his ears.

"Run, Andy. Damn it, run!" Regina shouted.

Don't think about it, keep running. Don't think about it. Andy drew a deep breath through his open mouth. Pain erupted in his knees, spreading to his thighs and down to his ankles. He pushed it from his mind and kept running. A loud banging on the metal door sent shivers up his spine. *The darkness, Bertha hates the darkness.*

A tiny sliver of light fell on the stairs in front of his feet.

She's tearing the door down. I should have thought of that.

Fear pumped energy to his tired legs. Regina's hand found his, as he bolted through the door. "We've got to get to the Humvee!"

The heavy thumps of their running feet echoed off the walls. They burst through the glass doors into the bright sunlight and raced to the Humvee. Metal shrieked behind them. Bertha would be free in seconds.

A gray, bloodless face with torn skin pressed against the driver's side window of the Humvee. Andy's hand closed on the door handle, the security guard's pistol gripped tightly in his hand. The door wouldn't budge.

"Damn thing's locked." He lifted the gun and fired a round into the window. The zombie's skull exploded in a putrid yellow mass, along with the glass shards spraying in all directions. Andy reached inside and unlocked the door, pulling the rancid body roughly to the ground. He checked the ignition and found the key still in it. "Get in quick." He hit the button on the armrest, unlocking the passenger door.

"It stinks in here." Regina found the power button and lowered the window, hanging her head outside.

Andy slid behind the wheel and turned the key. The engine caught easily. He pulled the gear lever into D. Smoke boiled from the tires, as he pressed the gas pedal to the floor. The stench burned his tear-filled eyes. He coughed violently. "That's the smell of death."

"Andy!" Regina yelled. "She's loose! The bitch is loose!"

He slowed to take the curve going to the highway, dodging through the maze of parked cars. The thick leafy trees along the roadside blurred together as the Humvee passed beneath them. He floored the gas pedal again on the straight road. "Where's she at?"

"She's cutting through the woods. Faster, she's gonna try to cut us off from the highway!"

The vehicle sped toward the interstate. Bertha jumped to the onramp a split second ahead of the Humvee. She stood on the ramp, arms held loosely at her sides, waiting for the vehicle's approach. Her mouth stretched open and she let out a wild, savage roar.

Andy hit the brakes. Smoke fogged from the squealing tires. He turned the wheel and jumped the curb, driving on the grass. "We've got to get on the interstate." The Humvee plowed through a barbed-wire fence, large chunks of grass and dirt flying from the tires.

"She's moving; coming this way!" Regina screamed.

The heavy vehicle spun on the shoulder. The back tires caught on the asphalt and sped down the highway. "We're gonna make it. We're gonna make it," he said.

A small blue Volkswagen flew through the air like a bomb and landed on the roadway in front of the Humvee, broken glass and crumpled metal showering the vehicle.

"Damn it, she's bombing us!" Andy glanced in the rearview mirror. The massive ape plucked a large red and white Ford pickup truck off the ground, lifted it over her head like a toy, and threw it at the Humvee.

The Ford arched through the air but crashed to the pavement harmlessly behind them. A pent-up breath hissed through Andy's teeth as more distance was put between the Humvee and Bertha. "We made it."

The gorilla faded from view in the rearview mirror.

Regina leaned over and kissed him on the cheek. She sat silently for a moment, staring at the abandoned cars parked along the highway. Several zombies milled around the vehicles. Sensing a meal, they stumbled after the Humvee but soon gave up. "Damn it, they're everywhere. How much gas do we have?"

"The tank's full. We're good for a while. I want to put as much distance between us and Bertha as possible. We'll worry about tomorrow later." He weaved the Humvee between the cars clogging the highway, silently praying they'd find a safe haven by nightfall.

ABOUT THE WRITERS

Aaron Rayner is an amateur writer from the South of England where he lives with his very supportive wife. So far he's appeared in Pill Hill Press's Daily bites Anthology and has several more to be featured in various Anthologies over the coming year, including one from Wicked East Press. He's expecting his first child in February, and is trying to write as much as he can before the sleepless nights kick in.

Terry Alexander lives on a small farm near Porum, Oklahoma with his wife Phyllis. They have three children and nine grandchildren. His work has been published in anthologies by Living Dead Press, Static Movement, Moonstone Books, Paper Cut Publishing, Cyberwizard productions, Knightwatch Press, Mini Komix and at frontiertales.com. He is a member of the Oklahoma Writers Federation, Ozark Writers League, The Arkansas Ridge Writers and The Fictioneers

Vincenzo Bilof is an educator living in the Detroit area, with publishing credits that include five stories with SNM Magazine, and an appearance in Book of the Dead 6 by Living Dead Press. Poetry credits include SNM Magazine, Miller's Pond, Nuvein Magazine, and The Detroiter. Currently finishing the zombie-apocalypse novel Under a Red Sun.

Max Booth III: When not trying to take over the world, Max serves as a story/copy editor for Dark Moon Digest and writes a monthly column titled "The Cellar Door" for the e-magazine, Dark Eclipse. And he does it all while wearing the fanciest of hats.
Contact him at madd_maxxx3@yahoo.com.

Chantal Boudreau is an accountant by day and an author/illustrator during evenings and weekends, who lives by the ocean in beautiful Nova Scotia, Canada with her husband and two children. In addition to being a CMA-MBA, she has a BA with a major in English from Dalhousie University. A member of the Horror Writers Association, she has several stories published in a variety of horror anthologies, in online journals, magazines and as stand-alone digital shorts. "Fervor," her debut novel, a dystopian science fantasy tale, was released in March of 2011 by May December Publications. Other releases contracted for this year include her novel,

"Magic University," the first in her fantasy series, "Masters & Renegades," to be released in the fall of 2011.

Anthony Giangregorio is the author of 37 novels, almost all of them about zombies, and has edited over 30 anthologies.

His work has appeared in Dead Science by Coscomentertainment, Dead Worlds: Undead Stories Volumes 1-7, and Wolves of War by Library of the Living Dead Press. He also has stories in End of Days: An Apocalyptic Anthology Vol. 1-5, the Book of the Dead series Vol. 1-6 by LDP, Zombie Zoology by Severed Press, and two anthologies with Pill Hill Press.

He's also the creator of the popular action/zombie series titled Deadwater and his action/ horror novel Dead Rage is being optioned for a movie. Check out his website at www.undeadpress.com.

Tim J. Finn is a member of the New England Horror Writers and a graduate of Grinnell College, where he earned a BA in English. He currently has a story in Rymfire's eBooks anthology "State of Horror: Massachusetts," and is working on a novel about a vampire hunting an ex-Boston cop.

Scott T. Goudsward lives and writes in New England. Writing seriously since 1992, he is a founding member of the Essex Writer's and Artists Guild and is also in NEHW (New England Horror Writers.) His published works include Shadows Over New England and Shadows Over Florida. Both books have made the HWA Stoker prelim ballot and been nominated for The Rondo Award. His first novel "Trailer Trash" was published in 2007 and he has edited the anthology "Traps."

Dane T. Hatchell lives in Baton Rouge, LA. He has stories appearing in over fifteen different anthologies from Living Dead Press. You can contact Dane at Enadious@gmail.com.

Bennie L. Newsome was born and raised in Birmingham, Alabama where he currently resides. He considers himself to be a unique person full of humor, two qualities he strives to instill into his work. In addition to his short story, Justice is Served, Bennie has four short stories published to date (one of which is contained within Open Casket Press' first anthology: Headshots Only) and several others scheduled to debut in the 2011 calendar year. Check out his website at www.bnewsome.yolasite.com.

Suzanne Robb's debut novel "Z-Boat" will be released by Twisted Library Press. She has several stories in current and upcoming anthologies. In her free time she reads, watches movies, plays with her dog, and enjoys chocolate and Lego's. For more check out Ramblings of an Anxiety Ridden Mind at http://suzannerobb.blogspot.com

Rebecca Snow lives in Virginia with her husband and a mass of wayward cats. Her fiction has been published in a number of small press anthologies. She can be found lurking online on twitter @cemeteryflower, facebook (look for the bloody hand), and at cemeteryflower.blog.com. As far as she knows, she's never run over a hitchhiker or eaten bad beans.

Alan Spencer is a horror author from Kansas City. His novels include "The Body Cartel," "Ashes in Her Eyes," "Inside the Perimeter: Scavengers of the Dead," and "Zombies and Power Tools"—The last two published by Living Dead Press. Keep an eye out for his forthcoming book "Cider Mill Vampires." Seek him on Facebook or e-mail him at: alanspencer26@hotmail.com

Richard Salter is a British born writer and editor now living near Toronto, Canada. He has a dozen short stories published and in 2008 he edited the anthology Short Trips: Transmissions for Big Finish Productions. Later in 2011, he has new stories appearing in Phobias from Dark Continents Publishing, Iris in Purple from Obverse Books, and Solaris Rising: The New Solaris Book of Science-Fiction from Solaris Books. Visit his website: http://www.richardsalter.com

Dustin Stevens is the author of the novels "Number Four" and the soon-to-be released "Just a Game." He holds a B.A. in government from Harvard University and a JD/MPH from the University of Montana. He currently serves as Senior Policy Analyst for the Hawaii Primary Care Association.

CLAN OF THE BIGFOOT

ANTHONY GIANGREGORIO